"Buckle in! Book three of the Minnesota Marshalls, *Ned* is a thrilling twist of romance and suspense. Classic Susan May Warren through and through."

KATE G., GOODREADS

"Wow. This heart-stopping, thrilling adventure had me enthralled! And once again, Susan May Warren also delivered on the faith journey."

BETH, GOODREADS

"Goodness but this book is so good! *Ned* starts off fast and really doesn't slow down much at all. Even the ending doesn't seem like a true ending since.....well, you are going to have to read the book to find out!"

AMY, GOODREADS

"Susan May Warren is one of my favorite authors to read and whenever I hear there's a new book out, I'll run to buy it! I highly recommend you pick up *Ned*. You just might end up like me, waiting on pins and needles for the next book!"

MARYLIN, GOODREADS

NED

THE MINNESOTA MARSHALLS
BOOK THREE

SUSAN MAY WARREN

NED

THE MINNESOTA MARSHALLS

ONE

How Ned hated walking into a country naked.

And sure, he had clothing on—a pair of 5.11 tactical pants, a job shirt over a long-sleeve pullover, a pair of waterproof tactical boots, and tucked into his pack, a wool hat, and even tac gloves.

But he'd left his Navy-issued Glock-19 at home, along with his side holster, and his KA-BAR, and even his dive knife because, well, that just might get flagged, and if he carried permits it would most definitely slow him down with Helsinki customs.

And Shae's kidnapper already had a sixteen-day, twelve-hour-and-twenty-minute lead on him.

So, naked he went as he pulled down his backpack and slung it over his shoulder along with the rest of the passengers on the Airbus A220-300 flight out of Charles de Gaulle Airport to Helsinki, Finland. Outside, rain hit the glassless windows, the sky black.

They'd flown over a night-covered but lit Helsinki, the lights of the city doused by the rain, the Gulf of Finland dark and unforgiving, holding the city in its clasp. They'd landed about ten kilometers north, in a city called Vantaa that sounded like some primordial Viking beast.

"Hey, watch out." Behind him, Fraser had ducked out of the way, then caught Ned's pack before he beaned a petite blonde woman on the other side of the skinny aisle. "That thing is lethal."

"Sorry." Ned glanced at her, and for a second, she reminded him of—well, maybe everyone reminded him of Shae right now. In her late twenties, maybe, the woman wore a fleece and jeans, her hair pulled back, not unlike the attire he'd last seen Shae wearing.

But of course, she didn't have Shae's cute nose or beautiful expressive lips, or that sense of challenge and even courage in her sky-blue eyes.

The woman not Shae responded in what Ned thought might be Finnish, holding up her hand. Gave him a brief smile.

He stepped back to let her out in front of him.

Fraser clamped a hand on his shoulder, then pushed him forward. "No harm, no foul, but let's get you off this plane before you take someone out." His brother wore a cast on one hand, still in recovery from surgery a few weeks ago. But it hadn't dampened Fraser's *let's do this* attitude, and frankly, Ned needed him. Cast and all.

Now, Fraser might be kidding, but Ned heard the warning in his brother's tone.

Okay, so maybe he'd been a little crabby with the flight attendant when she'd asked him to sit down for landing instead of prowling the cabin like a lion. He'd just been trying to stretch his legs.

Maybe settle the antsy that boiled inside him.

Twenty-three hours of travel, not to mention a five-hour, forty-minute layover in a crowded airport, trying not to fall asleep in a vinyl gate-seat turned his muscles into knots.

A little something to go with the state of his stomach, maybe.

"Any new messages from Ian?" Fraser asked as they moved forward.

"Since the last thirty-three he left in Amsterdam?"

"He'd be here if he didn't have a newborn," Fraser said.

"And will hop on a plane if I don't keep him updated. He's like her father. He'd move the ends of the earth to find her." He'd reached the front of the plane.

"Thank you. I hope you enjoyed your flight," said the KLM flight attendant, the one who'd not-so-politely directed him back to his seat. She gave him a fake smile as he exited onto the jet bridge.

Aw, he wasn't usually a jerk.

Only when his fiancée—or rather, in-a-blink-of-a-bad-fight-when-things-went-terribly-wrong *former* fiancée—was taken.

Yes, *kidnapped.* Because there was no mistaking the way one tall blond Finnish man with the name Dana Munson—an alias for Hansi Nikula, aka, Scandinavian human trafficker and all-around bad guy—had shoved her into a car off the streets of Lausanne, Switzerland.

Hansi's list of crimes had turned Ned a little cold. Of course, he'd already been spinning out, ever since Fraser had tracked down the street video from the hotel of Shae being nabbed.

The time stamp couldn't have been worse—a mere ten minutes after Ned had told Shae that she was too independent. That he couldn't do his job constantly worried about her.

At the time, it'd felt dramatic. But hello, now never mind not doing his job—he could barely *breathe*, the thoughts spiraling out to—

Nope. She had to be alive.

Please, God.

The passengers shuffled out, and Ned followed the Shae look-alike down the air-bridge and then into the customs area where she headed to the line for Fins.

"We're over here," Fraser said and lined up with the other foreigners. Dogs on patrol roamed around the passengers, sniffing.

"Did you rent a car?" Ned said, turning to Fraser.

"Uber. I didn't want to have to wait in line." Fraser turned over his wrist, glanced at his Casio watch.

"Please tell me you didn't bring any contraband with you."

"Of course. My Sig Sauer is packed with my socks."

Ned looked at him.

"Sheesh, calm down, bro." Fraser pushed him forward.

Calm had long ago left the building.

In fact, calm had packed up while Ned stood in a hospital in Montana, having flown out to Mercy Falls, where Shae's uncle Ian lived, because he thought she might not be talking to him. Thanks to their fight.

Thanks to his fears of, well, exactly this.

But back then, exactly two days ago, he'd simply been worried he wouldn't be able to put the ring back on her finger. He'd rehearsed his apology a hundred times by the time the plane landed in Kalispell. *Please, forgive me. I'm sorry I'm so controlling. Of course I trust you.*

The words had sort of died when Fraser had texted him the footage of Hansi grabbing Shae.

He'd gotten the first flight back to his home in Chester, Minnesota, and arrived less than eight hours later. And by then, Fraser had contacted his boss, former Navy SEAL Chief Hamilton Jones, who had contacted one of his former teammates, a man who ran a think tank slash black ops organization called the Caleb Group.

Logan Thorne had appeared on the Marshalls' doorstep with a dossier on Hansi as well as alias IDs for Ned and Fraser, who had insisted on going with Ned despite his role safeguarding a princess who just happened to be staying with the Marshalls—but that was a different story. And it was then that Ned realized he actually *knew* Logan, from a bygone time when Logan had been a MIA-declared-dead soldier from Chester.

And then all of that didn't matter because, six hours later, Ned was on a plane for Helsinki, a last-known address for Hansi in his grip, Fraser on his six, a lunch from his mother for the plane in his pack, and prayers in his heart.

The man in front of Ned had cleared passport control, and Ned stepped up and slid his worn passport, the one with a few stamps and frayed edges, through the small window. Looked at the officer, hoping he resembled a Bruce Danielson.

From Cincinnati.

Traveling here for the convention on therapeutic heat.

He even swiped off his Bengals baseball cap and smiled.

The man stamped his passport, and Ned didn't look at Fraser, aka Vinnie Danielson, as he passed through the swinging gate.

Instead, he plunked his backpack onto the Helsinki Airport custom's baggage scan belt and stepped into the scanner, arms up, legs spread, as if he might be a criminal.

Maybe. Because Ned had entered the country with something akin to murder in his heart.

The officer on the other side motioned him through, then held up a hand for him to stop. He wanded him, slowing at the spot where Ned had recently been wounded, and maybe just a little irradiated with some rogue caesium-137.

But he was fine, just fine and—

"You're good to go."

Ned picked up his bag, shouldered it, then turned to wait for Fraser.

And that's when the dog barked. He looked down to see one of the patrol shepherds barking at his bag, alerting.

What?

The dog came with a two-man team—his handler and a rather young but earnest security officer holstering two sidearms, who now gestured to Ned's bag.

Fraser stepped out of the scanner. No extra wanding for him. He picked up his backpack and raised an eyebrow at his brother.

Ned walked over to the counter, set his pack on it. Reached to unzip it before getting barked at by the security officer.

He held up his hands as the man rooted through his bag.

"What did you bring?" Fraser said, leaning over to him as he walked by him.

Ned said nothing, his brain rooting through the contents. He'd packed his gear so often as an operator, who knew what he automatically added to his pack. While the security officer pulled out some base layers as well as another T-shirt, he glanced at the clock.

Nearly midnight.

Perfect for an unexpected sneak and peek at Hansi's flat.

Or more. Please, let Shae be there and not already vanished into the world of human slavery—

The dog barked as the officer pulled out a baggie of—

Apples. Aka foreign fruit. Oh, Mom.

Fraser didn't bother to hide a smile as the security officer dropped them in the trash.

Then they scanned everything else in Ned's pack, including his skivvies, wanded him thoroughly, and by the time he joined Fraser, twenty minutes later, he felt strip-searched.

"Not a word," Ned said as they headed out to the curb for their Uber pickup. The chill in the late-October air cut through his job shirt, and he took off the Bengals cap, dropped it in a nearby trash can, and grabbed out his wool hat from a side pocket in his pack.

"Arrested for carrying contraband fruit," Fraser said. "Your team will love that."

Ned gave him a look, but Fraser was grinning so wide he finally exhaled.

Okay, maybe it was a little funny. And yes, Trini and Ford and the rest of Team Five might get a good laugh out of it, wherever they were. He'd been granted medical leave for six weeks after the incident in Slovenia, so he'd been out of touch with the team.

Hopefully they were about chasing down that last canister of caesium-137 that'd vanished from the stash they'd captured.

Even better, they might be chasing down the key players from the Russian mafia group who'd stolen it from a Swiss nuclear plant.

"That's our Uber," said Fraser and pointed to an orange Saab headed their direction, its lights shiny against the wet pavement.

"You put in Hansi's address?"

"It's a twenty-minute drive. Center of the city."

Ned knew that—he'd spent a good part of the first leg studying the neighborhood, the ochre-colored apartment building, the courtyard outside the house, and a layout of the building. He knew which apartment was Hansi's, how to infil, and even what stairs to use for his emergency exfil out of the two-bedroom apartment.

Logan had even sent in one of his overseas operatives to watch the place for the last twenty-four hours.

Apparently there was no movement, but that didn't mean Shae wasn't tied up inside...and that was as far as Ned let his brain travel.

They climbed in, Fraser and him both squeezing into the tiny back seat, their packs on their laps. Their driver was an older man, balding, in a leather jacket and glasses.

"Americans?" he asked. "Tourists?"

"Work," Fraser said.

Ned looked out the window. The city rose ahead, bright lights sparking into the night, his last conversation with Shae in his head.

"What if Dana and his people weren't...weren't good people? What if they found out you were alone and...I don't know, tried to kidnap you? Or rob you or...or rape you?"

He wanted to shake away his words, as if by speaking them, he'd manifested his very fears.

"Don't you trust my judgment?"

His chest burned with the memory of his next words...

"You're just so..."

"Naïve? Stupid?"

"Independent!"

He closed his eyes.

"You okay, bro?" Fraser said beside him.

He sighed. Opened them. "I will be, if we find Shae."

"You'll find her," Fraser said. "You two always find a way."

Maybe he was referring to their last great, terrifying

adventure—a race through the Bob Wilderness in Montana four years ago when a murderer had tried to track down Shae.

They'd survived, but just barely.

"I should have proposed then." His jaw ground. "Instead, I focused on my Navy career, becoming a SEAL, and I left her to wait in limbo."

"She's hardly waited around, Ned. She's built her own career. Didn't she recently have a gig somewhere in Europe taking photos for an ad campaign?"

"Yeah. I think she was in Brighton, or maybe Lauchtenland."

Fraser glanced at him. "Lauchtenland? That's where Pippa is from."

Pippa, as in the bodyguard for Princess Imani, the royal currently holed up at the Marshall family home. The same Pippa that Fraser seemed to have something going with, given the way she'd kissed him goodbye last night.

"Huh. Small world," Ned said.

They'd entered the city now, the suburban neighborhoods with their quaint red roofs giving over to office buildings and apartment houses, all sandwiched next to each other. It reminded him a lot of Amsterdam, or maybe Berlin, or any number of the historical cities of Europe.

"I think they're having some big sporting event there. International. Shae said something about taking pictures of a stadium along with local tourist attractions."

The car had pulled up to the curb next to a five-story building —no balconies, closed shops on the first floor. From his surveillance, he knew a small drive led to a courtyard in back.

They got out and headed toward the building as if they belonged there.

The Uber drove away, and Fraser stopped in the arched tunnel that led to the back. Put a hand on Ned's shoulder. "Take a breath."

"Are you telling me to brace myself?" Ned shrugged off Fraser's grip.

"Maybe."

"Fear not, that's all I've been doing since..." He swallowed. "She has to be alive, Fraser. She—" Yeah, maybe *breathe* was exactly the right command.

"Let's go." Fraser turned and headed toward the courtyard.

Here, all the apartments hosted balconies, and a thick drainpipe from the roof snaked down at the corners of the building.

Hansi's apartment was fourth story up, two balconies in from the corner.

Fraser pulled out his gloves, a hat, and then worked on his pack and cinched it down. Ned did the same.

"I'll go first." He didn't love the climb up, but the pipe looked solid, and he'd climbed many a drainpipe.

Now he grabbed it and used it as leverage as he climbed up, wedging his feet into the brackets that held it in place. Fraser waited at the bottom, not wanting to strain the pipe with his weight. Ned reached the fourth floor, then leaped for the balcony, just out of his reach. He grabbed the rail, then swung himself onto the small space, narrowly missing a planter of dead geraniums, then climbed up on the far edge and leaped over to the next balcony.

He landed hard but caught himself on the edge and righted just as Fraser landed on the balcony behind him. "One-handed," Ned said. "Good job."

"The cast helped, but I'd prefer the stairs next time."

"Let's say no on a next time." He turned to the door.

It latched at the top, inside, and again Ned wished he weren't naked. Okay, not completely naked, because he pulled his Leatherman PS out of a zippered pocket. It came TSA approved, without the blade, but the pliers were strong enough to wedge into the top of the frame. Then, with a kick, it separated the lock from its bolts.

The door shuttered open.

Twinkle-toes, aka Fraser, landed on the rail beside him, then dropped down.

"Me first." He put a hand on Ned's chest.

Maybe, okay. Because the sight of a dead Shae just might buckle Ned's knees, and someone would need to be upright just in case Hansi heard them coming.

Was waiting in the room with a hunting rifle.

Ned stepped back.

Fraser pulled out his own Leatherman, the TSA version, and this time opened the nail file.

Better than nothing, maybe. He motioned inside and Ned nodded, put his hand on Fraser's shoulder.

Fraser nudged into the apartment, armed with his silly nail file. But really, he could go barehanded and Ned would trust him with his life.

They'd entered a bedroom, the double bed unmade, clothing on the floor, a smell emanating from somewhere that had Ned's hand over his face.

His gut dropping.

"Just stay calm," Fraser said, his hand over his face as well.

Because yes, it smelled very much like—

"There's a body in the family room," Fraser whispered, having walked through the bedroom. "Stay here."

Right.

But Ned waited a half beat as Fraser edged out into the darkened family room. Sparse, with just a table and a lone sofa, a massive flat-screen on the wall. Streetlight gleamed through the galley kitchen out onto the wooden floor.

And in the middle of the room, a body, sticky blood shiny against the light.

Ned nearly collapsed at the sight of a *male* body.

"Is it Hansi?"

Fraser knelt next the man, pulled out a Bushnell light and scanned it over the mess.

"Blond guy, reddish beard?"

"That's him."

Fraser's light flashed over the body. "Throat was cut."

Yeah, Ned saw the gaping wound, Hansi's wide eyes as if in shock.

"Maybe Shae's still here." He headed back into the bedroom and opened the standing wardrobe, but just hanging clothes. He searched the bathroom—empty. Fraser came out of the kitchen shaking his head.

Ned headed to the second bedroom and found an office.

With a computer.

He unplugged it and was shoving it, along with the power cord, into his backpack when he heard it—

"Siren," Fraser said, popping his head into the room. "We gotta go."

Ned found his feet, shining his own Bushnell around the room. The beam landed on a wallet, passport, and keys.

And then—his breath caught.

A puddle of gold, what looked like a necklace. He bent and picked it up, the dolphin charm on it dangling between his fingers.

"Ned?"

"It's Shae's." He turned to Fraser, still holding it. "She was here."

"And she's not anymore. We gotta go." Fraser grabbed the wallet, keys, and passport. "Now."

But Ned couldn't move. "She was here. What if she left something for me?"

"What, like a secret message?"

"Maybe. I mean—"

"This isn't a Brad Thor novel. Consider the necklace the message and *let's go*." He grabbed Ned's backpack strap.

Ned jerked away. "Hansi is dead—our leads, gone. We need *something*."

"You got his computer."

Ned looked up. "I want his phone." He flashed the light

around the room, then strode back out to the body. Knelt, digging through Hansi's shirt, then pants pockets. Nothing.

Steps, outside, banging, and then—

"Now, Ned!" Fraser grabbed him up and propelled him into the bedroom.

Then out onto the balcony as police—probably police—banged on the door to Hansi's flat.

Lights had flickered on from apartments around them. Namely, their escape route. Ned glanced over the edge.

"I'm not interested in breaking a leg." But Fraser put his leg over the edge anyway. "C'mon. I'll lower you down."

Right. Fraser would dangle over the edge and let Ned climb down him to the next balcony. Then Ned would pull Fraser in, and they'd repeat all the way down.

Hopefully.

Ned flung himself over the edge as the door to the flat broke in. Used Fraser's legs to give him leverage and swung into the lower balcony, its light still off.

Then he held up his hand for Fraser to grab it and pulled him into the balcony, nearly on top of himself.

"Haven't done that in a while," Fraser said, picking himself off Ned. "Let's go."

They repeated the move to the second balcony, then the first, and finally landed on the street below, hugging the building as shouts came from above. Lights scanned the courtyard.

Ned's breath tightened in his chest. Beside him, in the shadows, Fraser didn't move.

The lights finally vanished, the voices back inside the building, and Fraser hammered Ned's shoulder, the "move out" signal.

Ned sprinted for the corridor out to the street.

Free—with the computer, but shoot, he hadn't gotten the cell—

"Stop!"

The voice lifted from the opening of the tunnel, and a man

stepped out, outlined by the light of the sidewalk. He lifted his hand. A weapon? Ned couldn't tell.

"Stop running."

Not on his life. He didn't spare Fraser a look as he lowered his shoulder and headed toward the man.

OH, SHAE AND HER BIG IDEAS WERE GOING TO GET herself—and maybe the man she loved—killed.

Stick around in Switzerland, go hiking, make friends—yep, great ideas, Shae. Brilliant.

Shae sat on the big king-sized bed, her knees drawn up, her arms around them, staring at the dawn as it swept through the thick forest surrounding her prison, listening to the last fight she'd had with Ned.

"You're just so..."

"Naïve? Stupid?"

"Independent!"

All of it, probably, and that was the problem.

And now she had no one to rescue her but herself. Because there was no way Ned would track her down in Nowheresville, Russia—she thought maybe it might be northern Russia. They'd driven her over the border from what she thought was Finland, given the close proximity to Russia. And she'd only figured that out from the speech of the border guards who'd apparently thought nothing of a couple thugs toting a clearly distressed foreign girl in the back seat.

Welcome to the Motherland.

Never in her wildest dreams...*Oh, Ned, I'm sorry!* It was her only thought as they drove another two hours along bumpy roads until they reached the remote estate.

She'd gotten a good look at the place when they removed her hood right before they pulled her from the car. Not like she had a clue how to find civilization from here. But maybe the hood was just to keep her brain churning over the memory of some Russian thug—she'd named him Vlad—running his knife across the throat of her, well, former friend turned kidnapper, Dana Munson.

Yeah, that had turned her cold—and that was saying something, because her bones had sort of frozen over, and she'd really stopped feeling anything when said friend had come up behind her in Lausanne, Switzerland, and forced her into a car.

And when she'd yelled—fought, really—he'd held her down while a female—Shae remembered her as Janna, a girl she'd met while hiking—had jabbed her with some sort of knockout drug.

She'd woken locked in a bedroom—four stories up and in another country, given the big blue ocean she'd spotted through the buildings. Over the past two weeks, Dana had turned downright unfriendly, especially after she'd kicked him while he delivered oatmeal early on. And once, she'd attempted a run for the door, but he'd grabbed her and not-so-nicely threatened her with damage should she try it again.

She'd tried it again.

Her jaw still hurt. So she hadn't been that sad when, one day, the scuffle outside the room made her break free of her room just in time to see Dana hit the floor.

Not fast enough to get away from Vlad, though.

Yet. Because she *was* going to escape. She just hadn't quite worked out how.

The place reminded her of old stories of the Czar and his family, the house old and ornate, with a parquet floor inlaid with different types of wood, and soaring ceilings with ornaments from which hung grand, dusty chandeliers.

Her room came with a creamy pink-and-brown Turkish carpet, a king-sized bed in a tall frame, thick brocade curtains, and a television on the wall, turned perpetually to a Russian music channel. She'd finally figured out how to mute it with a button on the bottom.

Attached to the room, a bathroom tiled in pink with a deep soaking tub suggested the room had been designed for a daughter, or maybe a wife, although she found it creepy that the window had been nailed shut—and not recently, given the paint covering the bent nails.

Said window looked out onto the back of the house— nothing but snow between herself and the bramble of spooky forest. In fact, bushy evergreen and tall birch cordoned the entire perimeter, blocking off any escape path away from the estate.

She'd been lost in the wilderness before and had lived. If she had to, she could do it again.

Probably.

But in truth, even if she did get away, where would she go?

So, as she'd sat here for the past two days, she'd come up with a plan.

One that just might work.

A knock at the door, like it might be room service, and it opened without her responding to one of her young guards, dressed in a pair of wool pants, boots, and a wool sweater.

Ah, young Slava. She didn't know Russian, but he'd talked to her a bit in broken English when she first arrived. As if sensing her fear. Sweet, in a captor sort of way.

She smiled back, in a cowering kidnappee sort of way.

They had a fake relationship, her acting grateful when he brought her kasha or raw bacon or some kind of beet soup. What little English he spoke had netted her his name and the sense that he was in some militia group, given the badge on his arm—not unlike something the Hitler Youth might have worn.

So, yeah, that was comforting.

He always arrived armed, with a hip holster and his simple flip cell phone in his shirt pocket.

Now, he entered as she slid off the bed. Over two weeks in the same clothing had her smelling pretty ripe, but at least she was warm, still dressed in her fleece and jeans, her wool socks, and boots.

Maybe not warm enough for subzero temperatures, but it hadn't snowed since she arrived, and the snow on her windowsill in the bathroom had melted, so that boded well.

"Good morning, Slava," she said as he brought in a bowl of corn kasha, a dab of butter on top, and a bowl of sugar on the tray along with a cup of tea.

She eyed the open door, and as he set down the tray he said, "No try run."

"No try run," she said, and wrapped her arms around herself.

He stood up and she picked up the tea.

Here went nothing.

She sipped it, gasped and jerked it away. "Hot, hot!"

And then the tea just happened to spill on Slava.

He cursed, stepped back—

"Sorry! I'm sorry—" She picked up the napkin on the tray—thoughtful of them to think of it—and stepped toward him, wiping his shirt.

He held up his hands, then grabbed her wrist. "Nyet—nyet!"

She jerked the towel away with her other hand. "Sorry."

He glared at her, then gave her a shove.

She landed in the nearby straight chair, the towel on her lap, her hands raised. Quivered her lip.

His glare softened. "Ladna," he said. Then pointed to her food. "Eat."

She nodded and pulled the tray toward her.

He watched as she layered sugar—there wasn't enough to choke it down, but she made a show of it. Took a bite, nodded. "Thank you."

"Nasdarovia," he said and headed out of the door. She heard the lock turn. Footsteps.

Then she lifted the napkin and retrieved his cell phone.

Please, *please*—

She headed to the pink bathroom and shut the door. Turned the lock.

No try run. But maybe try call.

She sat on the deep shelf of the window, leaning in, and flipped open the cell. Grimy, with one button missing, the phone had seen better years.

But it sported two bars.

That should do.

Please, please. She dialed Ned's number. Please have an international plan—

Ringing. She closed her eyes. More ringing.

Please.

The phone went to voice mail.

Ned! She pressed redial.

Ringing.

Outside, she heard the door open to her room with a slam.

Please.

More voicemail.

Ned! C'mon.

She hung up and pressed send again.

Again, dialing, and then ringing. Banging on the door outside the bathroom.

"Zhenshina! Otkroi dver!"

Ned, please—

"What!"

The sound of his voice jerked her for a moment—

"I don't want what you're selling."

"It's me! Ned, it's me!"

A beat, and now Slava was kicking the bathroom door. It shuddered.

"Shae? Oh my—Shae!"

"Listen, Ned. I don't have time—I'm in Russia."

"What—"

"I think it's northern Russia, maybe near the Finnish border—I was driven here. It's a big estate—"

The doorframe cracked. More shouts, this time added voices.

"Are you hurt?"

"No—I'm okay, but Dana—"

"I know about Dana." His voice had turned dark, low, and she half expected an *I told you*. Instead, "I love you, Shae. I will find you. Just stay alive. Stay alive!" She heard snapping from his side of the phone— "It's Shae, can we track this?"

And then the bathroom door came in.

Slava charged toward her, fury in his eyes. Behind him, two more guards, both young, both angry.

"I love you, Ned—"

Slava ripped the phone from her hand as she let out a scream. He put the phone to his mouth. "Da svedaniya." Then he hung up.

Stared at her. Shook his head.

She got up, put her hands up. "No run away."

He slapped her.

She spun, hit the wall, and fell to her knees, her head spinning.

Blood filled her mouth.

Hands on her arms dragged her up, but she spun and kicked out and caught Slava in the shin.

He pulled back his fist, but one of the other guards grabbed it. "Nyet."

The other guard grabbed a towel from the sink and flung it at her. She pressed it against her mouth.

Then the first guard grabbed her arm and dragged her from the room.

And maybe, for a second there, she'd thought they were protecting her. Thought that there was some decency in them, keeping Slava from hitting her again.

But no. They dragged her out of the room, down the hall— and now she got a good look at the expansiveness of the place. A garden out back with a greenhouse, and another wing of the house. Yes, it had to be some sort of royal palace, especially with the patterned parquet flooring, the gold-painted molding, and now the view from the balcony that overlooked a massive living room with shiny travertine floors.

The guards dragged her into an office at the end of the hall, with a dark mahogany desk and bookcases, blood red wallpaper and a man standing over a table.

Her backpack lay on the table, the contents spread out. Her extra socks, phone—now dead—a charger cord, water bottle, a bag of almonds, a notebook, pen, and most of all, her Canon EOS R5, with 45 megapixels, full frame CMOS, 5940 autofocus zone, 2.1 mil dot 3.15 inch tilting touchscreen, 20fps of continuous shooting, and the ability to shoot movies at 8K.

The best stills camera she'd ever owned, coming in at a price tag of five thousand dollars.

It lay on the table, sort of a centerpiece to all her other debris. Certainly, however, they didn't kidnap her for her camera?

Hello, they could have it.

A man stood with his hands clasped behind him at the window, his back to her, a Caesar ring of hair around his balding head. Not quite six foot, he was wide-bodied, wore a suit, and stood legs apart, as if surveying the troops.

Now he turned. Gray eyes, thickened face, he studied her, and while he had a sort of soft, grandfatherly shape, the look in his eyes sent a shiver through her.

Father Lenin in the flesh.

He sighed then and walked toward her. "How unfortunate, your behavior, because we had other plans for you."

She raised an eyebrow. "Plans to what? What do you want from me?"

He sighed. "We already got what we wanted. But now..." He lifted a shoulder. "Who were you calling?"

"My mother. She misses me."

His eyes narrowed and he glanced at the guard next to her. Oh goodie, now she might get hit again. She braced herself.

Instead, he motioned for the guard to drag her over to a chair. Forced her into it. The man walked up. "We will find out."

She lifted a shoulder and ran her tongue around her cut

mouth. Mostly a tear on her lip, but oh, it throbbed. Threatened to send tears into her eyes.

But she'd been through worse. Watched her first boyfriend get beaten to death before her eyes. Then was kidnapped and shot and nearly suffocated by the same murderer. So a little slap by some Russian thug wasn't going to crush her.

"I see," he said. "Well, if your friend happens to come looking for you, we'll have to make sure he doesn't find you, huh?"

She stilled.

"American girl, blonde hair, still pretty. You're worth something." He looked across the room, and she followed his gaze to a man she hadn't seen before, sitting on an overstuffed chair. "What do you think, Lukka?"

He had a full head of dark hair, matching gray eyes, and was built as if he worked out, his jacket tight around his arms. "I can sell her."

Sell. Her?

And she sort of lost herself then, the simple, dark, cruel way he said it just landing in her bones, her soul.

Her voice trembled. "Listen. I'm...my uncle has money. Lots of money. He's a billionaire." Okay, not quite that anymore, but he'd recovered well from his loss a few years ago. "He can...let him ransom me."

The older man's eyes narrowed, and he took a breath, folded his arms over his chest. "I don't believe you." He motioned to the guards.

Hands grasped her arms and lifted her.

"Believe me. His name is Ian Shaw. He lives in Montana."

"We could send her to Sevvostlag," said Lukka.

She stilled. He probably said it in English to strike her blood cold, because the rest he delivered in Russian.

The older man nodded. Smiled.

"What—where's that! That sounds like a gulag!"

Now Lukka smiled.

"Is it Siberia? Are you sending me to Siberia?" She twisted, looking back at Lukka. He'd folded his arms, watching her.

"My fiancé is going to find me! And when he does—" She shut her mouth as they dragged her through the door.

What? What was he going to do?

Get himself killed? Start a war with Russia?

Oh, good job, Shae. Give him away. Now they could lie in wait for the man she loved to find her.

Somewhere in Siberia.

Two

Ned had died, more than a little, his entire body caving in when Shae's call cut off on her scream.

He nearly threw his own phone against the wall.

But not before he had the presence of mind to hit the callback number.

It rang and rang, and was then cut off.

His next call died immediately, and he imagined whoever owned the phone was now removing the sim card and crushing it beneath his jackboot.

What. An. Idiot.

Now he stood at the window of the tiny one-bedroom flat overlooking the south harbor of Helsinki, where a massive cruise ship had docked, surrounded by smaller ships, a few sailboats, their hulls gilded against the rising sun. He wanted to put his fist through it, but that wouldn't help anyone. Instead, he leaned his head against the pane. "I can't believe I didn't answer her call—twice!"

"Bro, you're lucky you saw it. Don't you have all your unknown calls set to spam?" Behind him, Fraser sat at a small table, nursing his thirty-fifth cup of coffee, the smell of the instant brew biting in the tiny flat.

"Given the current MO of Shae calling me from unknown numbers, that's a practice I'm going to stop. Hello, car warranty people and vacation rental spammers, have at me."

A chuckle, and Ned rounded and looked at the man sitting on the blue foldout futon—a man who still bore the mark of Ned's charge in the scrape across his chin.

Yeah, well, he should have identified himself better than just *Roy*. Should have elaborated that he was one of Logan Thorne's men, the one who'd been watching Hansi's house. Because a mere "Stop!" wasn't exactly going to slow Ned down.

He'd tackled Roy going full speed, and yes, Roy was a big man and had managed to stay on his feet, but not before being slammed against a building, his face scrubbing against the brick.

Ned had to give him props. Roy had bounced back fast, spun and tackled Ned before he did something stupid like run out into the street where the Helsinki police were parked.

Apparently, a neighbor had seen the American duo sneak in—probably some kid up late gaming—and alerted the cops. And now Helsinki's finest had questions about a dead body that Ned and Fraser couldn't answer.

So they'd instead opted to hole up in one of the Caleb Group's safe houses, or maybe just an Airbnb that Roy had rented. Whatever. It got them off the streets and gave them a second to breathe and figure out who might have killed Hansi.

And maybe get some shut-eye—an attempt he'd made and failed in the one bedroom, with Fraser taking up more than his portion of the tiny bed.

So he'd been prowling when her call came in. Swiped it away. Then again. And the third time...

Russia? She was in Russia? What was she doing *there*?

"Can't you track the call or something?" he said now to Roy.

"We're trying, Ned. We have Coco trying to get the information on the call. From there, she might be able to track it, but the likelihood of getting an exact location, especially from Russia..." Roy shook his head. "But I've got an idea."

Ned turned, glanced at the man. Tall, solid, the man had gone from Navy SEAL to rogue undercover Caleb Group agent after an op that went wrong in Afghanistan—or at least, that had been Fraser's abbreviated explanation on their way to the safe house.

"I have a friend who has connections to Russia—I'll see if he can root around and get some information." Roy was texting as he spoke.

"That's going to take days," Ned said. "We don't have that kind of time." He looked at Fraser. "She *screamed*. Shae is not a screamer."

Fraser just lifted a shoulder, then he leaned his chair back on two legs and scrubbed his hands down his face. "Ned. What I know—and remember—about your girlfriend—"

"Fiancée—"

He held up a hand. "—fiancée, is that she's smart. Really smart. Didn't she run from some killer and hide for five years?"

"Yes, but..." He took a breath. "Why Russia?"

Roy had pinched his mouth tight. Looked away.

"What?"

"According to our research, Hansi was involved with a number of human trafficking groups—one of them the Petrov Bratva."

Ned stilled. "Wait. Those were the same guys we picked up in Slovenia, deploying a dirty bomb."

Roy considered him. "I was briefed just a couple days ago on that. You met Ziggy, one of our contacts."

Ned nodded. "She helped us track down the bomb, and Jonas, my brother, was weirdly involved—anyway, do you think that...I mean, there's no connection to *me*, is there?"

This had Fraser leaning his chair forward. "You mean, she was taken because you were on the team that grabbed the radioactive waste?"

Ned lifted a shoulder.

"I don't think so. How would they know you're on Team Five? It's not like that information is public."

Right. He ran his thumbs into his eyes. This whole thing had him in knots, leaping to impossible what-ifs.

He looked up, then, "She was taken before we tracked the caesium, before our assault on the Petrov group. Before we secured the radioactive waste."

"So then it wasn't revenge," Roy said. "Which, unfortunately, brings us back to plain old human trafficking."

"You're not helping," Ned said.

"I know. But if that's the motive, maybe we have a place to start. We have a list of known players in the industry and can reach out to other groups that might have ideas. Interpol, the Global Alliance Against Trafficking in Women, International Justice Mission, Operation Underground Railroad to name a few." He picked up his phone. "And I'll ask York if he can reach out to his Petrov contact."

"York?"

"One of our guys," Roy said. "He used to be a spy in Russia, among other things. Still has contacts with the Bratva." He looked at Ned, then Fraser. "You might know him. He's married to your cousin, RJ."

"I heard about him from Ford," Ned said. "But I didn't know they were married."

"We don't hang out as much as we'd like with the Montana boys," Fraser said. "Although Ford runs with Ned on the teams."

"Does Ford know she got married?" Ned said.

Roy looked at him. "How should I know? I know Tate does—he helped us find York when he vanished a couple months ago."

"York vanished?"

"We thought he was dead, actually." Roy looked up from his phone. "He had some business to take care of. Tate joined the Caleb Group."

"Tate is a spook?" He looked at Fraser. "Did you know this?"

"I've been watching wine ferment."

Hardly, but Fraser had been largely off the grid after he'd been captured, then freed, in Nigeria last summer.

"By the way, you and Tate could be brothers. You two look like twins."

"Never. I'm better looking."

Roy laughed. "Where did you and Shae meet?"

"Minnesota. During a tornado."

"Oh?" Roy raised an eyebrow.

"We were at the same country music concert. The tornado came through and we took cover together."

"That was when Creed went missing," Fraser said. "Right?"

Fraser had been deployed somewhere.

"Yeah. And then a few months later, I drove out to Montana to attend a wedding, and Shae and I and her friend Jess got, well, kidnapped, by a murderer who wanted to kill Shae."

"You sure you should be with this girl?" Roy got up and walked to the small fridge. Opened it. The light skimmed over his lean face, his thin beard. He retrieved a malt drink and opened it.

Ned looked at Fraser, who helped him not at all by raising a shoulder.

"Let me tell you about Shae. She is the toughest girl I know. I know you think she grew up the niece of billionaire, but she grew up with a drug-addicted mom who lived with so many different men it's a miracle Shae wasn't abused. When she was ten, she escaped with her mom after a guy beat her mom up. She stole the man's car and drove her and her mom out of Houston to somewhere in Dallas, where they ran out of gas. She lived in that car for a month, stealing and digging out of dumpsters to keep them alive. Her mom eventually got so sick, Shae—whose name was Esme at the time—had to choose between taking her mom into the hospital and being taken away by CPS, or letting her mother die—so no choice there, but she knew she'd lose the only family she had. The terrible thing was that CPS didn't step in, didn't find her, and a few weeks later, when her mother got out of the hospital, she found Shae and went right back to their crazy life. It wasn't until after that, when her mom got arrested, that her uncle Ian stepped in and took her home and suddenly her whole life changed. Except it didn't, not in her head, and she fell for a guy named Dante—good guy, but they were teenagers, and despite the world Uncle Ian gave her, she didn't believe in a future that was any different than her mother's. And maybe Dante would have been different, because they were out hiking, and she saw a man kill his girlfriend and then come after them, and Dante died trying to protect her."

Roy was holding his drink, just staring at him. Fraser wore a frown.

And it could be that he was a little more earnest than he needed to be, but maybe he was trying to convince himself too, just a little, that yes, Shae was tough.

"So she ran and hid, and yeah, she was scared, because this guy who murdered her boyfriend was known in town and had power, so she hopped on a bus and traveled two states away and reinvented herself and started a new life as Shae Johnson. Went to college, got a degree in design, and then, because she's also the bravest person I know, she returned home, and when the murderer tracked her down and tried to kill her—again—this time she fought him and won and—"

His voice broke a little, so much hope and maybe a little fear in it. "—and for the past four years she's been patiently waiting for me to propose, building her career, traveling. She's independent and smart, and I don't know how she got into this mess or ended up in Russia, but yeah, if anyone has the courage and willpower and even brains to survive this, it's Shae."

Roy took a breath. Nodded. Finished his drink.

Fraser leaned back, his arms laced behind his head. "Feel better?"

Ned took a breath. "Maybe a little." But actually, no. "Hearing myself talk, I'm starting to wonder if..." He ran a hand behind his neck. "It's never bothered me that she was so willing to wait for me to propose until now. As if...maybe she didn't actually need me. Or didn't want to."

"Well, she needs you now, Ned." This from Roy, who was crushing his can. "She called you."

"Of course she needs me now, but...aw, it doesn't matter. We'll find her, and we'll get married, and maybe then I'll stop worrying about her so much."

Silence to his words, and Fraser raised an eyebrow.

But that was the answer, right? Marry her. Keep her safe. "I just would like to deploy knowing that she's not going to find herself running from a murderer, or kidnapped, or even in some car accident and hiking through the wilderness on her own."

Roy had picked up his phone as a text came in. "From Logan. The Finnish police picked up your photos from passport control, and there's a BOLO out for Bruce and Vinnie Danielson." He pocketed it. "We need to get you guys out of Finland and hook you up with new identities. Pronto, before you land in Interpol."

"And then what?" Fraser said, getting up.

Roy grabbed his jacket. "I think the answer is obvious." He pulled on the jacket as Ned grabbed his backpack. "How's your Russian?"

SHAE JUST HAD TO KEEP HER WITS ABOUT HER. STAY alert. Find landmarks.

Listen for clues.

Anything to help Ned find her. Because he *would* find her. He was smart. And no one stood in Ned's way when he wanted something. He was the most tenacious person she'd ever met.

He'd have to be if he hoped to track Shae across Russia to whatever gulag they'd decided to take her to.

At least she traveled in style. Probably, no prisoner had ever been transferred to Siberia in a private Gulfstream jet with leather seats, long sofa and entertainment area, bar, and most of all, a back bedroom where she'd been shoved to endure the long trip.

They hadn't even bothered to hood her when they drove her to a nearby airstrip shortly after her call and what seemed like hours ago. And they hadn't tied her up either. But it wasn't like she was going anywhere, right? The flight attendant, a pretty woman who acted oblivious to the fact that Shae was confined to the room, had brought her some potato and beet soup and bread, and this morning, as they'd crossed over the Urals and jetted toward the wasteland of Siberia, had offered her cold noodles and tea.

Could be worse. Could be moldy bread and rank water.

No, could be *a lot* worse. She could be raped or beaten or sold into slavery.

Although, Lukka's behavior—the sense that he didn't want her hurt, just confined—didn't bode well for her future.

Untouched goods. Nice. She didn't want to let on that *virgin* was also among her list of qualities. Yikes. So yeah, maybe give her gulag. She was from Montana...well, part of her was from Montana, at least. She knew how to survive cold.

And the rest of her just knew how to survive.

Please, Ned, find me.

They'd stopped twice for fuel, and she'd looked out the window both times to see trucks or buildings at the airfield with names on them written in Russian.

So, not a big help, since she couldn't read Cyrillic. But they were headed east—way, way east, given the setting of the sun and then the chasing of the dawn. She'd gotten some sleep—well, not exactly sleep, but she'd closed her eyes and tried to listen to the conversation outside the door.

Useless, given the thrum of the engine and, again, the Russian.

Now she sat on the edge of the bed, staring out the window as they soared through clouds, the terrain below dark and ribbed with gray rivers, splotches of snow. So, maybe they were already in

Siberia. The earlier mountains had given way to flatlands, and now, again, she spotted mountains to the north.

Not so different from the beautiful Rocky Mountains of Glacier National Park, maybe. Growing up on Ian's ranch—at least, the wonderful years she'd spent there—the mountains had been both foreboding and majestic, awe-inspiring yet gritty.

An intoxicating mix, and maybe a little why she loved Ned. He'd always been unbreakable, really, and now that he'd become a SEAL, it seemed he'd added an edge of danger to his aura. She'd been in love with him since the moment they'd been trapped together during a tornado, when he'd helped her treat some of the victims. And then, months later, she'd become a victim when his car was forced off the road. She'd broken her ankle and he'd carried her on his back—even when shot—to safety.

And then he'd attacked a man who was trying to kill her, saving her life.

So yeah, she was more than a little crazy about Ned.

But he also scared her.

And maybe *scare* wasn't the right word, but he had an intensity, a passion, a drivenness about him that left her undone. He always knew what he wanted.

And she...she followed her heart.

Clearly, right into trouble.

But it was more than that. She used to fear that he'd die being a SEAL. But now she thought he'd die a little not being one. He never did anything small, and when he went after it—well, it was a little like holding onto a wild mustang, the wind in her hair, but dangerous too.

So she had tried not to. Tried to give him room. Tried not to get in his way.

And she wasn't so stupid as to not know that with a proposal came expectations—she wasn't unaware of his hope of a family, a home. And...

Sheesh, she hadn't the first clue what that looked like— thanks, Mom. And Uncle Ian had been a bachelor, so their home life had been late night takeout, or his housekeeper feeding her at his big granite island.

Aw, it didn't matter. She'd marry Ned in a blinding second.

And wow, she was good at the what-ifs, because it was very, very likely that she'd never see Ned again.

What was the survival rate of gulag? She'd read it somewhere, and it wasn't good.

Behind her, the door opened, and the flight attendant came in. She wore a pair of black pants, a gray blouse, and maybe she was less of a flight attendant and simply a female bodyguard, because she also wore a short black jacket with a shoulder holster. Long dark hair piled up behind her head, elegant and lethal.

"Come vith me."

Right. Shae followed her into the cabin where Lukka sat with two of his bodyguards in the plush leather seats. The woman gestured to a seat in front of Lukka, and Shae lowered herself onto it.

"We're getting ready to land," Lukka said, his dark eyes studying her.

Oh. Indeed, she felt the engines shift and the plane begin to descend.

"I'm not going to sell you," he said quietly, his hands folded in his lap.

She looked at him. "What?"

"I think you are more useful than that. I will contact your uncle. Give me his information and, should he comply, then..." He lifted a shoulder. "We will be done with you."

Oh.

Lukka leaned forward. "Until then, I don't want trouble from you."

Her eyes widened, and she nodded. If anyone could get her home, it was Uncle Ian.

The plane banked and she looked out the window. They'd left land and were now out over the sea. She struggled to place it—had they already crossed the entire country?

Maybe. The sea was dark blue, angry, frothy, and wild, even as the plane neared a massive peninsula. Oh, why hadn't she paid more attention in geography?

She did, however, know a little about the far east. About Alaska, and the Bering Strait, and Japan, and it seemed to her that there was something out east between all that.

Aw, it was probably still Siberia—

Except, no, they crossed over the land, and below, she spotted more mountains and what looked like smoke rising from craters to the north.

Volcanoes? Snow capped the mountains that rose as if pushpins across a lush green forest, and carved out of it, a city lay, quiet and expansive, edging a massive bay.

And beyond that, more water.

Wait. That was the Bering Sea.

Which meant—

"Kamchatka. It is beautiful, is it not?"

She looked at Lukka. Nodded.

"And there she is. Sevvostlag. After the great Kolyma camp. Now, she is a floating fortress."

What?

They'd descended more, and she made out—what, that rusty cargo ship? It floated in the middle of a harbor, two smaller ships attached, one that looked like a passenger tug.

"Wait—are you talking about the ship?"

"Our beautiful floating hotel, for the workers of the Petrov Oil and Gas Company." He said it in English, with a smile.

"The gulag is on a ship?"

"Not a gulag. We are the new Russia. This is work camp."

Aka, prison. She stared at the ship. It was an old woman with runny makeup, rusty lines dripping down her sides, the thirteen-story superstructure yellowing, with broken windows and steel rigging hanging rusty and fraying. It looked like it could barely stay afloat, let alone sail the high seas. Containers were lined up on the deck, and a massive ladder led along the side of the boat from the smaller ship beside it.

A massive crane, probably once used to transport containers onto the deck, had been cut off at the top.

She looked broken, despairing, and exactly what Shae might have imagined for a prison ship.

The plane flew over the ship, then banked, straightened out, and landed, the mountains rising to the north, the sea to the south.

And the ship waiting in the harbor.

She couldn't breathe. Lukka reached forward and unbuckled her. "There's nowhere to run. So don't try."

Right. Yeah, well, don't hold your breath, Lukka.

Because if anyone could get her off a ship, it was her Navy SEAL.

IRIS NEVER MISSED A CALL. IT WAS SORT OF HER hallmark claim to fame as a back judge. No missed calls.

Her career, her reputation, her future as an official in the European League of Football, or even her ticket to the NFL, depended on it. So no, she wasn't going to let a mouthy American wide receiver with the Vienna Vikings, Hudson Bly, get up in her face.

Even if was a game-changing call.

"Are you blind? That was clear passing interference! The cornerback tripped me—I didn't even have a *chance* to catch the ball."

And yes, he might stand a foot taller than her, but she'd been here, done that with arrogant former arena ball players, and hello, the over-sized wideout, with his Montana-Australian accent, wasn't going to make her sit down. Or cower.

Or change her call.

"The catch was successful; the Prague Lions have the ball." She motioned the catch to the referee behind the quarterback, who blew the whistle for the play clock to start.

Overhead, the sky had turned bleak and gray, a hint of rain in the air and haunting the massive, now defunct, Great Strahov Stadium in the Strahov district of Prague. They used it mostly for training now, but it still held the greatness of the second-largest sports stadium ever built. It seated over fifty-thousand people, and she'd been here once when it hosted the Sparta Prague soccer team.

Or rather, futbol.

She glanced at the play clock. Three minutes left in the fourth quarter—she'd be out of here in an hour.

Plenty of time to meet her contact near Old Town, Prague.

Not that her mind was on that—she had a game to call. But she hated being late.

Especially for the CIA.

Bly threw her a word and sprinted off the field while his defensive line came on. She ignored him—okay, maybe she saw as he whipped off his helmet and grabbed water from some innocent and too helpful trainer and squirted the liquid over his short, dark hair. As he pointed to the field—ahem, her—and lit out a barrage of words to the coach that came over to calm him down.

Jerk. Just because he was an American didn't mean he got special treatment here in Europe. And yes, he might be a bit of a superstar here, but back in the states, he'd had a dismal run. She'd even heard he'd been sidelined with a concussion injury back in college—just talk among her crew of officials.

She made it a point not to get personal with the players, not to be biased or even assign common penalties to them. Last thing she wanted was to see something that wasn't there.

The Prague Lions' coach requested a time-out, and crew chief, referee Yannick Mayer, granted it, then walked over.

"Don't let him into your head." The German was an

impressive former wide receiver turned referee who stood easily six foot four. Probably, Hudson Bly wouldn't yell at *him*.

"No worries." Although yes, that was exactly what she was doing.

"It's just a scrimmage."

"I know, but a few of these guys are on the all-star team, and they're playing some team from the US in a few weeks, so I need to pay attention. The US refs won't miss anything."

"You're just hard on this team because they remind you of your Vikings back home."

"No, they're better than the Minnesota Vikings—they can hold onto a third-quarter lead."

He laughed but shook his head. "Still, these guys don't have a chance against even the third-string powerhouses of the Minnesota defensive line," he said. "Even with the American recruits."

"But they give it a good show, and the league is growing, and it gives a chance to players—and officials—to hone their skills while waiting for their open door to the show."

"Is that where you're headed?"

She lifted a shoulder. "I like my croissants and café au lait."

He pointed to a player coming onto the field. "Keep your eye on the Lions' new wideout. They're going to be formidable this year, and that American receiver from the University of California is a key hope for landing in the top of their division."

"They're giving him a lot of time this game. He has more catches than Bly. Poor guy clearly tripped over his own feet."

Yannick laughed, then blew the whistle and headed up to the line of scrimmage.

Iris hunkered down and focused on her job—settling in twenty yards into the backfield, on the wideout side. She counted eleven defenders—good—then counted the eligible receivers.

She kept an eye on their new wide receiver as the ball snapped, and she backed up, watching the play develop. An option, the quarterback for the Prague Lions faked, then tucked the ball and ran.

He was demolished at the line of scrimmage by the Vienna Vikings.

The Vikings shut down the Lions, three and out, and Bly came back in for the Vikings. He managed to pull in a couple of long lobs, and the Vikings finished the training game one touchdown up.

The sky started to drizzle as she packed up her gear and headed into the officials' locker room.

"Want to review the tapes?" Yannick asked as they entered the co-ed room.

"Sure. But not now—I have a meeting." She stripped off her zebra shirt—wore an athletic shirt under it—and reached for her oversized pullover. Thankfully, they had private showers, but the ELF was about as ready for a female official as the NFL. Still, she'd learned some tricks. Like an oversized pullover that she used to dress under.

"A date?" The question came from Zach Warton, another American who had come over years ago, in the early days when the idea of American football in Europe was the stuff of wishes and John Grisham books. A German by descent, he spoke Swiss and German and looked more like a professor than a ref, with the exception of his massive arms, evidence of his off-field bodybuilding activities.

"Not a date. Coffee." She headed to the shower.

"Sounds like a date to me!"

She glanced at Abe Bartmann from Georgia, who'd played for Georgia Tech before throwing in his cleats and turning to officiating. He became one of the best umpires in the NFL, but his daughter wanted to go to school in Paris, so he'd moved to Europe after his divorce and started over.

She sort of felt safe with Abe on the field—something about him spoke authority, even more than Yannick. Abe didn't let anyone run him over, was keeper of the offensive holds, and stood between teams at the coin toss.

"Not a date!" In fact, if it were in that category, it would be a breakup. She wasn't sure how she'd gotten herself embroiled with the CIA, but she wanted O-U-T.

She stepped into the shower and pulled the door shut. In her kit she carried a shower cap, so she tucked her hair in it, then washed off and emerged ten minutes later smelling less like a football field and wearing a pair of jeans, Converse, a padded jacket, and a scarf.

Prague could get cold in the fall.

The guys were showering in their areas, so she packed up and headed out into the night.

Prague glittered under the fall of twilight. She loved the Old City, with the Gothic churches and cobblestone squares. She'd already pulled up her GPS, and it wasn't a terribly long walk, but she hopped on a train and two stops later got off at St. Thomas' Church.

The walk to the Augustine Hotel took just five minutes, but in that time, the sky had opened up, and she took off running, glad she'd worn her Converse.

Still, she was almost soaked by the time she entered the lobby of the four-story hotel through the arched courtyard off the street.

He'd said to meet him in the restaurant, so she headed there, past red sofas and a giant teardrop chandelier dripping from a center skylight.

She stopped by the maître d' and offered his name.

"Alfonzo Martinique?"

The female attendant showed her to the back, where she found the man sitting on a bench, drinking a cup of coffee.

Alfonzo was in his early forties, maybe, with dark hair, cut in an almost seventies style, sideburns, and a dark five-o'clock shadow. Reminded her a little, strangely, of Jon Hamm, the actor, but then again, he was a spy and of course he'd be handsome.

Except for that scar on his forehead.

And he had a sort of dark, evil aura, so no, thanks.

"Iris," he said and pushed to his feet. "Please sit. I ordered you a café au lait. I hope that is acceptable?"

"Fine." She sat on the chair opposite him. Took a breath. "I won't—"

"Are you hungry?"

Not the way her stomach was churning. "No. And really, maybe no on the coffee too. I know that I helped out once—and I'm still a patriot, but once was enough. I don't want—"

"We need you, Iris."

"Listen, I know I'm an ex-pat, and I do love my country." She took a breath. "But I'm not interested in being a spy, or even whatever this is. I have a job. A life—"

"Don't you want to be a hero, like your brothers?"

She cocked her head. "I don't have to be a SEAL to be a hero."

"No, but you helped us out once before."

"And that was enough." Just three weeks ago, Alfonzo had intercepted her in Milan after a game and asked her to drop a package in Berlin. Fine. "Besides, I was on my way to Berlin. But I'm not going to leave packages in random train lockers all over Europe." And, oh, she still had the key, maybe— "Do you want—"

"I need you to follow someone." He'd cut his voice down.

"Are you not hearing me? I have a life, and like it, and am not interested in becoming—"

"He's an American, here in Europe, and he's delivering information to people who want to destroy our government."

A beat. She sighed. "I don't—"

"It's the Russians." Alfonzo put a finger to his lips.

She looked away as the waiter brought her the coffee.

"It can only be you. And yes, this one last time. To save your country."

Oh brother. She looked at him.

He did look earnest. Fine. She picked up her coffee. Took a

sip. Met his eyes, her jaw tight.

"I need you to be at the Charles Bridge tonight at nine p.m., and watch who he talks to and if he gives him anything."

"Who's he? And what is he passing off?"

"I don't know what the package is...just the location and time of the drop. And you don't have to get it. Just take pictures." He slid her a cell phone.

She looked at it. "Is this like a gadget from Q? Or is it M—"

"It's a cell phone. The code is your birthday."

He knew her *birthday?*

A sort of shiver rippled through her, finding her bones.

What else did he know about her?

"When you're finished, drop the phone in the mail." He pulled out a small manila envelope. "Easy. And then I never contact you again."

"Never?"

He crossed his heart. Weird.

"I just have to take pictures. I don't have to talk to anyone, don't have to get involved..."

"Just take pictures. Can you do that?"

She sighed. "And then this is it. No more ambushes outside stadiums, no more secret messages under the door of my hotel. Just pictures, and we're done."

"Make sure you get the person he meets with. And, if you can, a shot of the drop. We believe there's a leak in our department, and we just need to connect the dots."

A leak. *In the CIA.*

"Okay. I'll do it."

He leaned back. Picked up his drink. "I knew I could count on you, Iris." And then he smiled.

It offered no reassurance. Still. Just this once. For her country. She took another sip and managed not to choke on it. "Okay, so who is my target?"

He looked her in the eye and said softly, "A traitor named Hudson Bly."

THREE

D*on't die.*
    And maybe Hudson was being a smidgen dramatic, but as he stood on the alcove of the bell tower at one end of the infamous Charles Bridge in Old Town, Prague, the rain hard upon the cobblestones, all he saw in his brain was an old clip from an ancient movie where Tom Cruise, the spy of *Mission: Impossible,* nearly died on this bridge.

Or maybe it was someone else. Hudson just didn't want it to be him.

He clutched an encrypted jump drive in his grip, his fist warm in his pocket.

The only thing warm, really, thanks to the extended practice and the fact he'd come straight from the locker room.

His three-thousand-dollar Gucci Jordaan crocodile loafers had clearly taken one for the country.

And he was hungry. In his other hand, he held his phone, and now he glanced at the recently texted picture of his contact. Light brown hair, medium build—although he looked tough enough—a scattering of whiskers.

He'd be wearing a red slicker, according to the latest text update.

He peered out into the rain.

No American spy, Tom Cruise or otherwise, in a red slicker, standing in the rain in front of one of the Gothic statues.

Legend had it that once upon a time, in the seventeenth century, heads of slain rebels were arranged on the bridge, red running through the cobblestones.

Now, just rain slicked the bridge, the lamps bleeding out wan light.

The kind of light people died in.

Yeah, this was a stupid idea. He should just go—

He turned, was nearly clobbered by a fast-walking man. Tall and dressed in a raincoat, hiking boots, and a baseball hat, he carried an umbrella, pulling it close as he hustled out into the torrent.

"Excuse me."

He mumbled something he didn't recognize because, of course, he didn't speak Czech.

Just leave.

His phone buzzed in his hand, and he nearly jumped out of his sodden clothing.

Harry.

Maybe it was an emergency with Mom— "Yeah?"

"Bro! I just caught the replay of your last game. Well done on the TD catch!"

He imagined his brother hanging out in the HQ for the PEAK Rescue team back in Montana where he worked. His Australian accent bled through the line, and frankly, felt oddly like home.

"How was practice today?"

"Not great. Hey, I gotta—"

"Where are you? Are you in the *shower*?"

"What? *No.* I'm standing on the Charles Bridge, in Prague. In the rain."

And of course, Harry asked the obvious. "Why?"

"Super great question, because actually, I don't know." And

maybe he shouldn't have said that much—after all, national security was on the line, but...aw, who was he kidding? He wasn't Tom Cruise, or anyone important, and maybe he was just really, really... "I did a stupid thing."

"What now?"

A sip, so his brother was drinking something, probably coffee, and it just made Hudson's gut tighten.

He should be in a restaurant, eating.

"What do you mean by *now*?"

"Sorry."

Hudson dodged another couple headed toward him, holding hands. They didn't even look at him, but he cut his voice low. "I'm exploring other job opportunities." Silence.

"What job opportunities? Uber driver?"

"Oh, you're hilarious." But yes, that could be an option if the doctor meant his words *One more concussion and it could kill you.*

C'mon, Doc, calm down. Guys like him had so many concussions their brains practically rattled around loose in their heads.

Besides, he hadn't had a concussion in...at least one season.

"So, what are you into?"

"Just...you know, doing a little...thing. For my country."

Silence. "What, are you a *spy*?"

"No." Yes. Sort of. "Not really. I just...you know—"

"Hud, don't do anything stupid." His brother had taken on that, well, Harrington-the-Big-Brother tone, and shoot, he should have kept his mouth shut.

"I'm only a courier. Nothing big. Just meeting someone, helping out our country. Being a patriot."

"Are you kidding me?"

"It's nothing. About a year ago I met this guy named Roy who wanted me, sometimes, to help courier information around Europe. Not all the time, but whenever they needed to deliver sensitive material that, you know—"

"Could get people killed? Hud!"

"Is *sensitive*. He called it old-school."

"*Dad* is old-school. He works in the mud every day, herding and roping cattle, fixing fences, and keeping away pests. You, brother, are not old-school. You're fancy cars and European selfies and—"

"I've got one year left at best!" Oh, he didn't mean to shout, although in the rain, no one could hear him anyway. Still, he schooled his voice despite the clench of his chest. "I'm just trying to do something right here, Harry. I'm not you. I didn't spend a year in Australia saving lives. All I have is football. So yeah, I'm standing out in the rain, freezing my backside off, waiting for a guy—"

Of course, that's when the wind whistled against the bridge, nudged the bell near the tower, and it emitted a long, low moan.

And with it, like an eerie movie, a body came walking out of the fog at the other end of the bridge. Head down, wearing his hood up, and a red jacket.

Bam.

"Gotta roll, bro."

"Oh, for—"

Hudson hung up and watched as the man walked by the couple, dodging them as they did some sort of dance move. Then he passed the man with the umbrella, moving out of his way too—nearly hitting him, his head still down.

Hudson took a breath, ready to edge out when, suddenly, the man stumbled. Pitched forward.

What?

The couple ran up to him, grabbed him by the shoulders. Then the woman screamed and took off, the man hesitating, then running also.

"Hey!"

The man in the red slicker gripped the railing and got up, and that's when the man with the umbrella ran back. Leaned down, trying to help him.

Red Slicker Man hit him. It barely fazed Umbrella Man, who slammed his umbrella, point first, into Red Slicker.

He grunted, hit his knees—

And then Umbrella Man wrapped his arm under Red Slicker's chin and held on.

Hudson had watched enough movies to recognize a sleeper hold.

No. Not on his watch.

"Stop!"

His word was eaten by the wind and rain, but he didn't need it. He took off running, full speed, putting his entire body behind the tackle, and took out the man at a full run.

They landed on the pavement, and he rolled off, back to his feet.

Umbrella Man had rolled over, was scrambling away on all fours.

Not so fast. Hudson grabbed him up, spun him, and slammed his knee into the man's gut. He grunted, then pushed Hudson away.

Stood up.

Hudson rebounded fast and sent his fist into the man's—

Oh no. Umbrella's hood had fallen off and—so, *not* a man.

He pulled back, but not before the woman turned, then just like that went over the edge.

"No!" Hudson ran to the railing just in time to see her splash. Then the river ate her, the wind and rain and current dragging her away.

Wait. Had he just *killed a woman?*

Maybe she'd jumped?

He ran to the other side, hoping to spot her, but nothing.

A grunt, and he turned to see Red Slicker Man had pushed himself to a sitting position, his hands pressed to his gut. Blood poured out between his fingers. Another wound—this time across his chest, also ran with blood. It pooled out onto the bridge, washed by the rain.

"Okay, okay, just—don't move." Hudson ran over to him. "Just stay put. I'll get help—"

"No help."

Right. Because help would raise questions.

"It's not deep," Slicker said. "I stopped it before it could puncture anything major. I think. I hope. And the other is a flesh wound."

Hudson didn't know why the sound of the American voice surprised him. It held a hint of a twang though, as if the guy might be part cowboy, or maybe a little country.

Now he knelt in front of him, and the man looked up. His hood fell back.

Blue eyes. Light brown hair, from what he could tell, and yes, a thin beard. "Have you visited the Prague Castle?" Slicker asked, mostly a grunt.

"Yes. Don't forget to climb the tower." Hudson took a breath. "I have the package, but I can't leave you out here."

The man nodded. Coughed, then winced, but held out his hand, the one not holding onto his wound. Hudson helped him up. Then Slicker pulled his hood back up.

"I need something to stop the bleeding. Or at least slow it. The rain will wash the blood trail away."

Right. Hudson had nothing except— "How about my sock?"

"Gross, but yes."

He pulled off his shoes—they were soaked anyway—and peeled off his socks. Black with white stripes. Slicker opened his coat, made a ball of one of the socks, and shoved it with a grunt into his wound. The other sock he shoved into the gash across his chest. Then he closed his coat. "Let's go."

"Where?"

A tremulous breath. "How far is your hotel?"

"Not far. It's near the stadium. Two train stops."

Slicker ventured out, and Hudson wasn't sure if he was supposed to help the guy, or maybe that seemed too conspicuous.

But when he nearly tripped, Hudson grabbed his upper arm. "You okay?"

"I will be." More grunts. Hudson couldn't tell if he was still bleeding.

"What happened?"

"When I walked by the woman with the umbrella, she cut me."

So, it *was* a woman.

"I was still reeling, trying to identify the pain, when I fell. Just dizzy, but I was still trying to dissect what I saw when she came back at me."

"Stabbed you with her umbrella. I saw it all. Did you know it was a woman before you hit her?"

"No. But I got a good look at her then."

Hudson tried to think if he'd gotten a good look. Probably not. "Black hair?"

"Maybe brown. Brown eyes, lean face and nose. She was, what—maybe five-nine?"

Hudson did remember her as being tall. "You think you can take the train?"

"Probably not a great idea."

But the man was still grunting, shuffling along now, slower, as they reached the end of the bridge.

"Let me see the wound."

The man opened the coat, and Hudson inspected the socks. The chest wound had slowed, and so had the puncture wound. And the man was right about the rain washing everything away.

"It's a short ride. I think you can make it."

Hudson pulled him away from the bridge, down to the street where he'd gotten off the train car. Waited at the stop.

The train pulled up, a long one with three cars. He got on the front. A couple more people got on the middle, another in the back, but he kept his eyes on his contact. The man slid into a seat and sat very still.

"How far is the hotel?"

"Two stops."

The man drew in a breath. Here in the light, he seemed in his mid to late thirties, and when he closed his eyes, he wore lines on his face.

"You think you're burned?"

The man opened one eye. "I'd say so. Otherwise, how did they know to wait on the bridge?"

"Who's they?"

The man closed his mouth, gave a small shake of his head.

Right.

They got off in front of the stadium, and Hudson guided him another block to the long, two-story Lindner Hotel with its outside doors and balconies.

That was providential.

He led the spy to the second floor, nearly putting his arm around the guy to help him up the stairs, but just his luck one of his teammates would see him and, well, he wasn't going there.

Instead, he stood behind him in case he fell. Then he rushed ahead and opened his door.

The man came inside. It wasn't a big room—a king-sized bed, a bathroom, a small sitting area. The Vienna Vikings didn't have a massive budget for travel.

He eased the man down on the bed.

"You'd better get towels if you don't want me to bleed on your sheets."

Hudson headed to the bathroom, grabbed a few towels, and set him down on them, then helped him ease off his coat.

"You probably need stitches for that puncture wound."

"Maybe. It's the tear across my chest that hurts more, though." He wore a fleece, so the fact the knife had torn through his fleece and the Under Armour beneath it said the woman—assassin?—had meant business.

"Was she trying to kill you?"

"Maybe send a message. Shoot, I really liked this shirt. My wife gave it to me." He pulled one arm out of his shirt, then

Hudson helped him ease the other off and the shirt over his head.

This wasn't his first scar. Slicker's torso had a few nicks and cuts on it, but probably something that Hudson might expect from a spy.

Interesting that he was married. Or maybe that was a cover.

He was right about the chest wound. It wasn't deep but had parted his skin above his chest, leaving a six-inch slice.

He sat up, trying to look at it.

"Glue should take care of that," Hudson said. "I have a few nicks that deep they patched up on the sidelines."

"Right. Good. As for the puncture wound, I'll pack it and get one of my guys to look at it. Take the sock out and let's take a look."

Hudson knelt and removed the sock, easing it slowly out of the wound. Blood spilled out of it, and he pressed it back in. "It looks deeper than you think."

"Do you see any white or yellow goo?"

Hudson made a face at him.

"I'm just asking because if you do, it's pierced the inner layers of skin, and yes, I'll need not only stitches but antibiotics."

"I don't know—"

"Sheesh. Just take the sock out and look again." The man lay back, his eyes closed, and talked through clenched teeth.

Fine. "This will hurt."

"No duh. Just check."

Slicker made just the slightest noise as Hudson inspected the wound. "No white stuff."

"Okay. Then I'll pack it and...shoot."

"What?"

"I might be going into shock."

"What?" Hudson stood up.

"I'll be fine. Just...I'm starting to sweat, and my heart rate is going up."

He was also breathing faster.

"If I pass out, then...well, call for help."

"Are you going to pass out?" And then what? Hudson stood up.

"Put my feet up. And get me a cold cloth."

Hudson dragged the man's feet onto the bed. "Don't die."

"Still alive."

He headed into the bathroom and got a wet cloth. Came back. "What's this for?"

"My forehead." He reached out and took the cloth. Opened his eyes. "Listen, calm down. I've just lost a lot of blood and overexerted myself. But we stopped the bleeding, and I'm going to be fine."

"And if you're not?"

The man pulled a pillow under his head, took a long slow breath. "Then I guess you'll have a dead man in your bed."

Hudson just stared at him. "Perfect." He strode away and set the jump drive on the small desk. Stood, staring at the man through the big wall mirror. "Who are you?"

Slicker closed his eyes. "Just a guy from Montana."

Just a guy...

Banging jerked his attention to the door. "Hudson Bly, let me in!"

Who knew his name? And it sounded female. And...familiar.

He glanced at the man who had opened one eye. Then the other. "Who is it? Do you know them?"

He went to the door and looked through the lock.

What did she want? "It's...one of the officials from today's game. A woman."

He looked again. Really, what was Iris Marshall doing at his door?

"Go away, ma'am."

"No." She stepped closer to the door and seemed to put her mouth near the crack. "I saw you."

He stiffened. She saw him? When? Where? "I was just out for a walk."

"On the bridge. I saw you—"

He opened the door. Stood there. She stood a good foot shorter than him but possessed all the fierceness of a giant. At least, on the field.

Now she looked worried. And shaken. Oh, maybe she had seen—

She pushed the door open and shoved past him.

Then she stood at the end of the bed, her hands on her hips. Took a breath, her voice low. "I knew it. I can't believe it, but I knew it."

Hudson closed the door. Turned. "There's an easy explanation—"

She rounded on him. "Really? There's an easy explanation for how my hotshot, trouble-making cousin Tate ended up bleeding in your hotel room?"

SHE REFUSED TO CRY.

No matter what they dished out...no crying.

Shae gritted her teeth as she clung to the wall of the shower, her eyes closed as the spray hit her, brutally cold, designed, probably, to shake her to her bones.

It did. And it wasn't just her nakedness—she simply disembodied herself from the fact that a couple of Russian women had barked at her, practically ripping her clothes from her.

It was the bleakness of it all. The ping of the water against the hull of the ship, the bare metal floor, the rusty drain, the darkness that pervaded this lower level of the cargo ship.

The entire place bespoke despair, and this pelleting of her body with icy water only drove it through her skin to her soul.

She hung her head and tried not to shake.

The water stopped suddenly, and someone barked at her. She

looked up, and the female guard—stout, with colorless eyes and short brown hair cut in a bowl, wearing a pair of black pants, jackboots, and a white shirt—circled her finger.

Turn around.

Shae folded her arms and turned, kept her head down and held her breath as the spray hit her.

Don't cry.

In a moment, the woman with the hose—a sharp looking blonde who wore her hair so short it looked like a buzz cut and who had also stuffed her body into a pair of black pants and a white shirt—shut off the spray and threw Shae a towel about the size of a napkin. But she used it to dry off as best she could and then ran it over her hair. It was probably depositing things into her scalp, but who knew with the dim light and the smells that emanated from the room. Not a big room—three showers with showerheads, and why they couldn't have let her take a normal shower...well, again, it was probably a psychological tool.

Meant to destroy her.

Not. Gonna. Happen.

She tossed the towel back at the short-haired, plump guard and walked over to the table where sat a gray jumpsuit. No underclothes, but whatever. She picked it up and noted that a number was painted in red on the back. Twenty-three. It seemed a little big for her, but she shook so hard from the cold that she didn't care, unzipped it and pulled it on. The material rubbed against her skin like canvas, or maybe burlap, but at least it was clean. The number twenty-three was also painted on the upper breast. So, that's who she was. Bloody number twenty-three.

No. She was Shae Johnson, formerly Esme Shaw, and she wasn't lost. Ned would find her. Or Uncle Ian would ransom her.

Don't cry.

They tossed her some fabric shoes—boots, really, formed out of thick wool—and she slipped her feet in, the warmth immediately finding her iceberg toes.

"Udi tooda," the brunette said. "Go there." Shae dubbed her Natasha and followed her, still shaking.

She'd gotten a good look at the ship as Lukka and his ilk had led her from his private car to a tugboat moored at one of the long deep-water docks in the shipyard and given her a ride out to the massive rusty container ship.

For a long moment, she considered just losing herself over the side of the boat. But the air spoke of chill, and the few splashes of water seemed frigid, so until she came up with a plan...

Don't cry.

She held herself together as they hauled her off the tugboat onto a massive staircase that climbed the side of the ship. Then she was on deck and surrounded by cables and old machinery and a line of shipping containers lined up next to each other, windows cut into the doors, covered by bars. A massive, thirteen-story superstructure rose from the aft of the ship, and she spotted a couple guards standing at the rails armed with AK-47s.

Not that she knew what kind of gun it was, but suddenly she was in a Bond movie, so she fully expected some rogue general to appear with plans to take over the world.

Instead, she was handed off to Natasha and Ivanka and brought downstairs through a massive stairway that led from the main deck to the enormous belly of the ship. Here, containers were stacked side by side in four rows, two aisles between them.

The containers were empty, the doors open—massive sliding doors connected by one bar at the top. Inside sat simple cots, all the beds made, no other belongings.

Cells?

The place reeked of sweat and rust and human waste, so a real home away from home.

One star, do not recommend.

The showers and bathroom were located at the far end of the ship through a giant metal door. The smell could buckle her knees. Maybe forty showerheads in all, and open holes in the floor for waste.

She wasn't sure why they bothered to douse her down.

Except, of course, that now, as she walked back out into the corridor lit only by dark and dirty fluorescent lights, her woolen feet silent on the floor, small amidst the massive yaw of brutal, raw metal, it seemed as though the shower had stripped her of, well, herself.

Replaced her with number twenty-three. Small. Unknown. Lost.

Not lost. Not. *Lost!*

Natasha stopped in front of a container, the door open. Maybe six feet deep, the container held only a narrow cot, a striped barren mattress, a blanket and bare pillow folded on the bed.

Nothing else. No bathroom, no sink.

No light.

The woman motioned her inside, and only then did she notice that on the door was written the number twenty-three.

Right.

She stepped into the container. The floor was plywood and recently swept. But it had clearly been inhabited before, because etchings on the walls revealed Cyrillic words, and even a number.

2304.

She lowered herself onto the bed. Looked at Natasha, who said something to her.

Then, as she sat, the massive door was slid closed. It seemed all the doors were on one unit, because the entire place shuddered with the click of the doors sliding into place.

And then, darkness.

Not total darkness, but enough to throw the container into despair. A smaller door cut into the massive sliding panel contained a twelve-by-twelve barred window through which the wan light from the ship bled. But Shae could barely make out her hand in front of her face.

She got up, looked out of the bars.

The guards had continued walking down the hall, away from her, the sound of their footsteps eaten by the expanse.

Alone. Shae pressed her hand to her chest, stumbled back, and hit the back of her legs on the cot. Fell on it.

Her breathing quickened.

Stay calm.

This couldn't be the rest of her life. Lukka would call Uncle Ian. He would ransom her.

Or Ned would find her.

Or...

Don't. Cry.

She closed her eyes. Concentrated on her breathing. *God knows where we are, right?*

She didn't know how, but Ned had tiptoed into her brain. And suddenly she was back in Montana, under a starry sky, huddled with him against the cold, hurting from her car crash, but safe, oh so safe, with Ned, who'd rescued her.

Again.

Her chest hurt at the memory of their conversation. *You don't get it, Ned. I cause trouble, even if I don't mean to.*

That had never felt truer than right now. Oh, her stubbornness. Why did she always have to do things her way?

We are not alone, Shae.

Not then, but now she couldn't be more alone, really.

Don't...

Aw, it didn't matter. Because there was no one here to see her sobs.

So Shae rolled over, put her hands over her face, and let herself cry.

HOW SHE HOPED SHE'D MADE THE RIGHT CALL—THAT all-American wide receiver Hudson Bly wasn't a traitor to his country. And maybe so, because when Iris had seen Hudson Bly standing under the bell tower arch of the Charles Bridge, something had just felt...off.

Maybe it was the way he'd run out and taken out the person who'd stabbed his contact—that was at least how the math she'd done had identified the man who'd crumpled on the bridge.

Fact was that she'd had to stand in the distance, using her camera, really, to zoom in and record the event.

Only when the victim's hood had come down had she realized—no, it couldn't be.

And then, her gut had kicked in.

This didn't feel right. None of it, from the too-easy setup with Alfonzo to the fact that Hudson, all-American Montana football player, had turned traitor. Nope. No way.

Although, he had gone overseas to play football, so she'd given it a moment's pause.

And then she'd spotted Tate.

Tate Marshall, the cousin she'd always had a little crush on the few times their families had gotten together. Tate Marshall, who'd gone into the military and then become the bodyguard and finally husband of Gloria Jackson, the ex-VP-elect's daughter.

She'd read all about the terrible betrayal of "Glo's" mother against her nation in a recent issue of *People*. The woman sat in a federal prison, her sentence commuted by President White from execution to life in prison.

But Glo was pregnant, and Tate and she made such a cute couple that Iris was rooting for them.

So what was he doing on a bridge on a rainy night in Prague? With Hudson Bly?

The question had made her follow them both back to the Lindner Hotel, where she was also staying, thanks to an ELF contract.

She'd watched Hudson help Tate to his room, debated about thirty seconds, and decided to make the call.

Banged on Hudson's door.

And now stood at the foot of Hudson's bed, staring at her handsome cousin as he bled all over Hudson's fluffy towels.

"He needs a hospital," she said on the tail of her question to Hudson.

Especially since she didn't need an answer, really. Somehow, Hudson had gotten caught up in a clandestine kerfuffle. And at first, she thought maybe he'd been tricked, but now...

She pressed her hand to her stomach. Tate wouldn't be into anything treasonous, right?

And if not, then she was the one who'd been had.

Maybe.

"Iris?" Tate had opened his eyes, a grimace on his face. "Seriously?"

"Hey, couz." She walked over to where he pressed a— "Is this a sock?"

"My sock," said Hudson, and she glanced at him. He stood away from Tate but close enough to step between them, and she had the sudden sense that he just might do it, too.

So, a patriot, maybe.

The sock dripped blood as she removed it to look at the wound. "From the umbrella."

"How much did you see?" Hudson held over the garbage can for her to drop the sock into.

"All of it. Get me a hand towel."

He disappeared into the bathroom.

Tate swallowed. "I'm a little afraid to ask how you're here."

"Right back at you."

He looked good, despite the blood and gore. Still handsome, still the guy who her heart had sort of swooned over. He was about five years older than her, so had been the perfect age for her seventh-grade heart to pitter-patter after.

Now, he looked like the warrior she'd always imagined him to be.

"Are you..." She blew out a breath and took the towel Hudson offered her. He had a nicer room than she did—a king-sized bed, a rarity in Europe, and a sitting area. She'd gotten a single room—single bed, single dresser, barely enough room to get dressed in. But that's what happened when you were a fancy football star, regardless of which side of the ocean.

She turned back to Tate, rolled up the towel, and pressed it gently into his wound. He sucked in a breath. "A spy?"

She met his eyes.

"No. Not really. I mean—I work for a...never mind. I was supposed to meet your pal here, pick up some information." He looked at Hudson now. "You still have it?"

Hudson nodded.

"What information?" She said it quietly, but her heart had sort of jumped.

Hudson's mouth tightened, like he might be the holder of the secrets of JFK. Please.

"I was sent by the CIA to watch you," she said, probably breaking all protocol, but something wasn't right in Denmark. "They said you were a traitor." She looked at Hudson, then at Tate. "Please tell me that I didn't just land in some treasonous plot."

"We're the good guys, Iris," Tate said, trying to work himself into a sitting position. She helped him. "But I'm curious. Who told you that?"

"My CIA contact. Calls himself Alfonzo. He asked me to take pictures and send them back to him." She pulled out the phone. Glanced at Hudson. Sighed. "Tell me what is going on, and if I believe you, this goes in the trash."

"Believe me, couz," Tate said, but Hudson shook his head.

"How do we know we can trust her?"

She just stared at him. "Hello? It's me."

"I know it's you. Miss I-can't-even-see-a-targeting-penalty—"

"You tripped. And it would have been pass interference, not targeting—"

"Whatever. Why should I—we—trust you?"

She gaped at him. "Because...I..." She drew in a breath.

"Because my brothers are SEALs, and I'm...I wouldn't betray my country!"

"Neither would I," Hudson said. He drew in a breath, his jaw tight.

He'd shed his wet jacket and stood there in a T-shirt and jeans. She'd never really seen him up close without his helmet. He stood about six foot three or four and was built like a Viking, so apropos to his team's name. Dark-blond hair cut short, a square jaw, deep gray-blue eyes, and every inch of him hard muscle. While Tate was military built, Hudson was all honed, athletic muscle, sinewed arms, powerful triceps, and long, lean legs. No wonder he needed a larger room. He sort of took up all the space.

Now his quiet voice seemed almost out of place, but his eyes settled on hers, and that was enough to radiate his sincerity.

Okay then. "How did you end up on that bridge?"

"You first."

"Fine. I was contacted a couple months ago by Alfonzo, who asked me to carry a package to a train station in Berlin. Said it was of national importance. I met him today to tell him I'm out when he asked me to watch you."

"What did this guy look like?" Tate said.

She shrugged. "Black hair, tall. Had a scar over his forehead." She drew a line over her eye to emphasize. "He said he was CIA."

"He was, if it's the man I think you're talking about. He matches the description of a man named Alan Martin. He's a rogue spy, disavowed by the CIA, but also one of VP Jackson's masterminds. He helped her conjure up the entire plot to assassinate White, and most recently, we think was involved in another Russian plot to deploy a biological weapon in our country. Not to mention another attack on the president. Not a good guy."

Tate was sweating, and it had her leaning forward to press her fingers to his neck.

"What are you doing?"

"I'm worried about you. Your heartbeat is a little fast."

"Bleeding here."

"Like I said—you need a hospital."

He closed his eyes. "What I need is for someone to call Roy. Or Ziggy. They'll know what to do."

"I know Ziggy," said Hudson. "She's my contact and the one who passed off the jump drive." His gaze flickered to Iris. "Oops."

"So, you were passing off a jump drive. To Tate." She looked at Tate. "And then what?"

Tate sighed.

"C'mon. You're clearly in no position to go anywhere. Hudson and I will..." She glanced at Hudson. "Make the delivery."

Hudson raised an eyebrow.

"It's important information, Iris. My boss didn't tell me what it is, but it's life or death—"

"Calm down, Tate. We got this. Where were you supposed to drop this off?"

He sighed. "Paris. At Napoleon's grave, in the Hôtel des Invalides. Tomorrow at noon."

"We can do that." She looked again at Hudson. "Right?"

His mouth was tight, but he nodded.

"But first, we have to make sure you stay alive. Does Glo know you're over in Europe getting stabbed?" She had taken the washcloth from his hand and now went to the bathroom to re-wet it.

When she returned, he had his eyes closed.

She turned to Hudson. "Can you get ahold of this Ziggy person?"

"Yes. I have a texting app I can use."

"Use it. I'm not sure how much time Tate has before he hits full-on shock."

Hudson stepped away to text, and she pulled out her phone. Then the envelope. The return address was a PO Box in Luxembourg. She folded it and was about to drop it in the trash when Tate reached out, grabbed her wrist.

"Don't."

"He's...a traitor."

"But maybe, too, we can use it to find him." His grip loosened.

Her gut said that was probably a bad idea, but she put the envelope back into her pocket, along with the phone.

"I texted Ziggy, and she told me to leave Tate here and go. That she'd get him."

Iris stood up. "What? No. I'm not leaving my cousin here to die—what if she doesn't get here in time?"

Hudson drew in a breath. "There's a train that leaves just before midnight for Paris. She wants us on it."

She stared at Tate, then back at Hudson. "Then tell her to hurry, because I'm not leaving Tate to die in a hotel room, alone in Prague."

FOUR

Thirty-six hours. Thirty-six excruciating, informationless, thumb-twiddling hours during which Ned wanted to do anything but get on a flight to Berlin, get a change of identities, then hop on a train to Paris, sleeping on a narrow bunk and listening to Fraser snore all night.

Roy had rolled over, the pillow over his head, and hadn't moved until they'd pulled into the Paris station early this morning.

Ned, however, had sat up, watching the countryside rumble by, trying not to dream up nightmares of what might be happening to Shae.

They'd already survived so much. *God knows where we are, right?*

He'd said those words to Shae while running from a murderer, his shoulder dislocated, his ribs deeply bruised. But he'd been trying hard to keep her alive, to keep himself from despair, and now the words tumbled back to him.

You know where she is, right?

No answer, but maybe, deep inside, something reached out and held him. *We are not alone, Shae. And we are still safe.*

Yes. He'd said it then, but he still meant it now. At least, he was trying to.

Please, God, watch over her. Give her a protector. Keep her safe. Help me get to her.

Yes, thirty-six hours was too long.

He was up and packed and ready to disembark long before the train hit the Nord station. He got off and found a map.

"Take the B line down to Châtelet, then switch to the fourteen train over to Madeleine Station, then get on the eight down to École Militaire. We can walk from there." Roy ran a line over their route.

Ned had never been to Paris, so he didn't argue. Even when Roy got off the B line and climbed the stairs to the street level and found a bistro.

He bought them breakfast, a ham sandwich slathered in salty butter and creamy cheese on flaky French bread.

Shae would have loved it.

He also downed two strong shots of espresso, and the coffee went right to his veins. He'd gotten up, picking up his pack, was staring out at the foot traffic in front of the under-construction Notre-Dame.

He'd seen the fire on television. So much destruction of such a beautiful piece of history. "C'mon, guys, let's get going."

Roy was looking at his phone. Now he set it down. "Change of plans. Well, not on our end, but our courier got made last night in Prague. We're meeting someone else."

"Same place?" Ned said.

"Yes, but I don't like it. Ned's right. Let's get going. I'd like you two to stay back on overwatch, just in case the meet goes south."

"Who are we meeting?" Fraser grabbed his pack also.

"Someone one of our contacts works with. He's an American and does work for us in Europe now and again."

They crossed the street and headed toward the subway. "About a month ago, our offices were hacked, and although Coco shut it down, they might have siphoned out some information—like our NOC list and even some of our encryption software. Thus, we're hand-carrying the intel we need from Russia."

He swiped his day pass and the turnstile released. Roy passed through, then Ned and Fraser did the same.

They headed down to the fourteen train.

The Paris underground was a labyrinth of tunnels and passageways accessed via stairs and escalators that connected every corner of the city via the métro system. He passed a couple buskers playing violins as they turned the corridor for their train. The place smelled of oil and dust, the scent of history embedded in the brick and cement walls.

Sometimes, being in ancient cities like Paris, or even Berlin, hearkened to stories of battles and world wars and the sense that history never really changed. It simply cycled around, evil trying its hand again at destroying the world.

Good eventually winning.

Please, let them win.

The fourteen train whooshed into the station, and Ned got on, found a space near the front of the car, his pack to the wall, away from thieving hands. Folded his arms over his chest. Fraser had taken a similar stance near the door.

Roy had gotten on and walked away from them, as if not with them. Maybe it was a tactic, but Roy was quiet, pensive, and serious. A little dark, maybe, but most guys in this profession had a place inside where they camped out sometimes, dealing with things that they didn't want to drag into the daylight.

Ned had a place like that. Shae had walked into it a couple times and dragged him out without asking questions. He put a hand to his chest, to the acid there.

Please. God. Let this work. Let them find her.

Two stops and they go off at Madeleine, then got on the eight.

Four stops and the train let them off at a park. The trees had lost their leaves, now curly and brown and snagged in the shrubbery that lined the park. The grass, too, had gone to slumber, turning crunchy and hard. They took the sidewalk toward the Cathédrale Saint-Louis des Invalides, walking in the shade of the day between tall, ornate buildings.

All of Paris seemed grand, old, with dark, black mansard roofs and soaring columns fronting every building.

Two blocks later, they came to a massive garden, with its dying flowers and a stone courtyard leading up to a towering gold-capped cathedral that housed Napoleon's tomb as well as other soldiers of note.

The entire complex was impressive, given the map on the plaque on the front, the cathedral, and sparkling front fountain. Massive steps spilled out from the entrance, and a couple tour buses had pulled up outside to offload groups from Japan and China, now strolling the area. School children ran up and down the steps, their backpacks slipping off as they played.

"We're meeting inside," Roy said and handed them each a ticket. "It's a Paris Pass. You can get into all the museums for a day."

"Goody, goody," said Ned and took the ticket.

"We still have a half hour. I say we get inside and you two find a place to keep an eye on me."

Done.

Ned headed up the steps and showed his ticket, then entered the quiet sanctuary.

He'd never been impressed with churches, but this knocked him quiet for a moment. Creamy white stone and travertine flooring, soaring ceilings, and in the middle, a vast circle with a marble railing. Ned walked over to it.

On the story below, an elevated polished-wood—or maybe it was some sort of dark stone—coffin sat on a raised dais.

Napoleon Bonaparte. Huh. He'd read about the conqueror in school. A hero of Paris who had finally become king and was then exiled. Ned stayed for a moment, then wandered off and found himself in a room with one of Napoleon's brothers—another coffin made of marble.

He camped out there with a view of the center ring.

Spotted Fraser as he wandered in also, then headed to the opposite side, admiring some art against the far wall.

Then came Roy. He, too, stopped to peer into the grave, then walked around and stood in front of the massive nave with its ornate gold cross and stained-glass windows.

To Ned's surprise, Roy knelt, then crossed himself, then got back up and headed over to read a plaque.

Tourists moved in and out of the area, mostly the tour groups and children, but a few Americans. A woman with a day pack holding onto her husband's hand. Another man—a big guy with dark-blond hair and a chiseled face. He came in wearing a black parka, his hands in his pockets.

Felt a little out of place, maybe, and Ned kept his gaze on him as the big guy moved around the circle, heading for the plaque at the front.

Bingo.

He stepped out from behind the coffin, moving to the next room, closer to Roy.

Roy moved away from the plaque, heading into the adjoining room—another coffin, probably one of Napoleon's generals.

But the man didn't follow him. Instead, he went to stand before the altar, not unlike Roy.

But a woman stepped up behind him. She wore a raincoat, her hood up, dark glasses, and also held her hands in her pockets.

And she followed Roy.

And then, as Ned watched, she came right up to Roy and spoke to him.

They were a little hidden behind the coffin, so Ned hoped Fraser had a good look at them, but it was the man who had Ned's hackles up. He couldn't be sure the duo had come in together or if...yes, he was definitely watching them.

And then he turned, his gaze directly on the hand-off.

Maybe it wouldn't have gone south had the man not taken his hands out of his pockets. Had he not moved forward.

Had the guy not seen Ned and decided that maybe Ned was a threat, because in two big strides, the man had crossed the room and slammed into him.

"Excuse me," he said.

Ned had sort of been knocked into the wall, but he bounced back, aware that the guy stood five inches taller, but unfazed.

And then it all went down, because Fraser grabbed the man in a tackle, bringing him down onto the travertine. People screamed, and Ned jumped back and suddenly—

"Fraser, what are you *doing*?"

Ned froze. Fraser too, which allowed the big guy to get an elbow in his ribs that caused Fraser to send out a grunt, and then Big Guy rolled and pushed Fraser right off him, as if he might be a child.

Fraser scrambled to his feet and rounded, his eyes on—

Well, Iris.

Iris?

What was his sister doing here?—and click, click, the Red Slicker, the hand-off—*wait.*

"Iris?" Ned said, then cut his voice low. "Are you—"

"Let's get out of here," Roy said, and gestured to the sudden camera action they had from the tourists.

Oops.

Roy held up a hand and headed out of the building in a half run, Iris behind him. Ned caught up fast, especially when Fraser tapped his shoulder, and in a moment, they were out in the sunlight, quick-walking out of the building and around toward the military section of the compound.

Big and Angry came up behind them, looking as confused as Ned felt.

They stopped in an alcove around the side of the building, and Roy pulled them into a room that housed military armor in a glass case. A bronze horse stood, a monument in the center of the room.

Roy put a hand on the horse's flank and just stood there,

breathing. Then he rounded, staring at Ned, then Fraser, then Iris and her bodyguard. "Seriously?"

Oh.

"And—who is this?" He pointed to Iris. "And how do you two know her?"

"She's our sister," Fraser said. Then he looked at the big guy. "And you are?"

"He plays for the Vienna Vikings," Iris said, looking not super pleased at Fraser. "And he was Tate's contact."

A beat.

"Tate?" Ned said. "Tate, our cousin Tate?"

"The very one. Who got stabbed last night on the Charles Bridge meeting Hudson here with this information, so it better be important."

Ned just blinked at her.

"Is he okay?" Fraser asked, catching up to the important part.

"Yes," Roy said. "Ziggy texted this morning."

"She got to him in time and took him into the hospital. Or wherever you spooks go to for medical help."

"I'm not a spook," said Ned.

"Me either," Fraser said. "Are you?"

Iris's eyes widened. "No. I'm..." Then she sighed. "Maybe I was sort of involved in something clandestine, but I'm not...this was clearly a huge mistake."

"No doubt," Hudson said. "Sheesh, Iris, how many people in your family are going to get blood on me?"

He wiped a trickle of blood from his nose.

Fraser's mouth tightened around the edges.

"Just the two," she said, but looked at Ned.

He held up his hands.

"This family," Roy said, and shook his head. "Okay, we got the jump drive, let's get going."

"I want to know what's on it. Why did Tate nearly die for this information?"

Roy looked at her. "That's not your role. You don't get to know—"

"Shae's been kidnapped."

Roy looked at him, something lethal in his eyes.

"She's her sister-in-law! Or going to be. And—"

"What do you mean, kidnapped?"

"Two weeks ago, from Geneva. She was taken outside Ned's hotel," Fraser said. "We tracked her down to a guy in Finland who turned up dead. But she called Ned on the happenchance and told him she was in Russia."

"And Roy activated his contacts to see if he could get any information from Russia. Actually—RJ's husband. Did you know she was married?"

"Of course. We text sometimes. York. He's a good guy. She met him on a trip, I think. They eloped."

Roy made a sound, deep in his chest. "Okay, we need a computer."

"Maybe I can help," Iris said. "I want to know what's on the jump drive."

"No." Fraser's voice was quiet, but firm. Iris looked at him.

Growing up, Ned had always had a healthy respect for Fraser and Jonas, and more than once they'd jumped in to protect him. But Iris, as the only daughter, had had her scrapes with the two, and now Ned spotted the old spark, the one that had made her and Fraser go round and round in the living room of their home, even as kids.

He even had a memory of her winning a few times, Fraser backing down.

Not today.

"No, Iris. I love you, and I'm not sure how you got involved, and—" Fraser held up a hand to stop her argument—"we're super grateful for your help. But no. Ned and I and Roy will take it from here. Shae's in big trouble with some pretty bad people—at least, that's what we think—and the last thing we want is you getting hurt in any way."

"Fraser—"

"Nope." He shook his head, and Ned saw the big brother kick in, a sort of velvet over steel demeanor. "Please, take her home," he said to Hudson.

"I don't...we're not together."

"Take her home," Fraser said. "Keep her safe."

Hudson's eyes narrowed, but he took a breath and nodded.

"I don't need his protection, Fraser. I can get home on my own."

"Where do you live, Iris?" Hudson said.

"Lake Como, but—"

"We'll grab the first flight." He pulled out his phone. "I'm getting us an Uber."

"Seriously."

Ned stepped forward and pulled her into a hug.

And she stopped fighting. Put her arms around him. Took a breath. "She'll be okay, little brother. I'll be praying." She pulled herself away and met his eyes. "That, I can do."

"Yes. And thank you." He managed a smile.

"C'mere," Fraser said and also gave her a hug. "I love you, sis. Even when you're ornery."

"Ornery is one word for it," Hudson said, and Ned looked at him. Interesting.

"Our Uber is pulling up in front," Hudson said.

Iris nodded, then looked at Roy. "Get Shae back."

"I'll do my best, ma'am."

She followed Hudson out.

Silence fell between the three men.

"Can't you Marshalls stay out of anything?"

Ned frowned at him. "I'm not sure I know what you mean."

Roy sighed. "I know. I know." Then he shook his head and walked away.

Fraser lifted a shoulder, then followed him.

They crossed the street, and Roy seemed to know where he was going when he led them back to the métro. They got on the eight, rode it back one stop to the C line, got on, and then rode that to the Eiffel Tower station.

The monument rose, tall and imposing, as they crossed the bridge and headed down the sidewalk.

Suddenly, Roy stopped in front of a door next to a patisserie, entered a code, and the door opened.

They passed through a lobby, another secure door, then up a flight of stairs, and Roy used a key to open the door to an apartment.

He dropped his bag on a chair near the door, then held it open as they entered. Closed it. Entered a code by the door.

"Is this your home?" Ned said, taking in the small but tidy kitchen, the main room with the black leather furniture, the flatscreen, the four-person table. He couldn't see beyond that, but it looked like a couple bedrooms, a bathroom.

"Nope," Roy said.

No photographs, nothing personal, so it might be yet another safe house. Roy pulled a laptop out of his backpack and set it on the table.

Opened it, put in his code, then the laptop lit up.

He put in the jump drive and entered more passwords.

The drive opened to a file with photographs, maps, and a note.

Fraser had gone to the kitchen to raid the fridge and came back with a malt drink.

Ned sank down into a chair. "What is it?" he said, reading Roy's grim look.

"She's alive." He clicked on something and turned the computer.

Shae. She sat in a car, looking out the window at some airport tarmac, her eyes wide, so much fear in them it made him ache. He shook his head and looked away.

"At least, she was when this was taken, shortly after your phone call. According to our source, she was put on a plane and flown...here." He clicked on another picture, this time a map.

Ned stared at it as Fraser leaned over his shoulder.

"Is that Kamchatka?" Fraser said.

"Yeah." Roy scrolled in on the picture and pointed to what looked like a ship. "The source says she's here. It's a gulag ship owned and operated by the Petrov Bratva."

"A private mafia gulag?"

"Yes. They use the labor to repair and replace their gas pipeline that runs through Siberia. The gulag travels."

"And, it's virtually inescapable," Fraser said, "floating out there in the icy water."

"Yes," Roy said.

Fraser sat down and pulled up his phone.

"What are you doing?"

"Getting ahold of Coco. Ben and Jeremy Smith need flights to Russia, pronto."

Yes, they did.

Please, God, keep her alive.

If Shae hadn't been so hungry, she might have not fought for a slice of stale brown bread, a piece of raw bacon, and cold noodles.

But she couldn't remember the last time she ate, really—maybe on the plane—and this morning, when the guard had walked down the containers, running some stick along the edges to rattle everyone awake, Shae had woken, and her stomach had come alive with a vengeance.

Call it denial, maybe, but somehow she'd slept right through the arrival of the other prisoners, and even all night, in the chilly container. As she'd gotten up, nausea had swept over her, and she'd swayed, grabbing the wall of the container just as the massive metal door slid open.

She stuck her head out into the opening and spotted

outside her cell a wool jacket and a fur hat. Thoughtful. Other prisoners—both men and women—emerged from their containers. Maybe fifty in total, all of them wearing the same faded coveralls, many holding their jackets and hats, all with numbers on their chests, unwashed jumpsuits, grimy hair, weary eyes.

Despair.

And maybe anger.

Or perhaps that was simply the look of survival.

She glanced up at the woman across from her. Rail thin, with stringy black hair, tattoos up her neck and on her hands, the woman stared at Shae without an expression.

The man next to her was also staring at Shae when she looked over at him. Big man, bald head, black eyes, still muscled despite a disheveled beard. He, too, wore tats, including one on the center of his forehead.

She had wrapped her arms around herself, following as a male Russian guard gestured them up the stairs.

The frigid wind off the ocean nearly knocked her over, but the sunlight from a cloudless day poured into her bones. She followed the crowd to a large building on the deck attached to the soaring superstructure and discovered a cafeteria. Metal tables were bolted to the floor, and at a stainless serving line, fellow prisoners served up the bacon, raw noodles, and bread.

She took her bowl, and someone dropped the bacon inside. Another plunked the bread right into the noodles.

Her stomach roared. She picked up a glass cup of tea and found it scorched her fingers, so she carried it by the rim and looked to sit down.

Felt like first grade, but she didn't want trouble, so she found a seat alone.

And that's when nasty Twenty-Eight sat down beside her.

The dark-haired woman from across the corridor. She looked at Shae, then simply reached over, grabbed her bacon, and held it above her mouth, letting it dribble in.

Shae had nothing. Not that she wanted the bacon—hello, trichinosis—but—

The woman reached for her bread.

"Hey," Shae said and grabbed for it.

Twenty-Eight pulled it away, grinned. Said something in Russian. Maybe it was nasty, maybe not, but it got a snort from a guy who'd sat down across from them. Lean face, the bones protruding, dark-brown eyes, he shoveled the noodles into his mouth with Olympic speed.

"Give that back," she said to Twenty-Eight and leaned for the bread.

Twenty-Eight jabbed her in the ribs, and she jerked back, gasping.

Then Twenty-Eight turned and handed off the bread to a guy behind her. Oh, big Twenty-Seven.

Shae picked up her bowl.

"D'vai," said Twenty-Eight.

Nope. Shae shook her head.

"D'vai!" Not a shout, but a growl, something of menace in her voice, and a tremor went through Shae.

She didn't want to die in a Siberian gulag ship.

Her breath cut short, and she was about to push the bowl toward Twenty-Eight when a hand pressed on her shoulder.

And then, as if cowed, or shaken, Twenty-Eight simply shut her mouth, got up, and moved away from Shae.

What?

She looked up, and behind her stood a man. Dusky skin, golden-brown eyes and dark-brown hair that fell out of his wool cap, down to his shoulders. He wore a grim smile under a thick dark-brown beard and now gestured to the seat next to her, vacated by Twenty-Eight. "May I?"

English. Oh—she managed to nod, and the man sat down. "Don't let Vikka scare you. She's all bark."

"She jabbed me in the ribs."

"Oh, maybe a little bite." He smiled. "You okay?"

And just like that, her eyes filled. She swallowed and looked away.

"Right. Yes, I get that feeling."

Get. Ahold of. *Yourself!*

She blinked, took a breath, and turned.

A piece of bread sat on her bowl. She looked at the man, who gave her a grim smile. "You must be starving."

That's when she noted his number. Twenty-Four. "You're in the cell beside me."

"Mm-hmm. I saw your door closed when I came in from work." He dug into his noodles. She noticed he also had bread, so where he'd gotten the extra piece, she didn't know.

She picked up her fork and stared at the noodles. Her stomach roiled. Around her, only the barest conversation pinged off the metal walls, the grimy windows, most people eating in silence. Even the man next to her kept his voice low.

"My name is Shae. Johnson."

"They call you by your number here," he said. "Do you speak Russian?"

"No."

"Okay, then, your number is dvatset-tree." He rolled his R's. "Mine is dvatset-chiteree."

"Twenty-four."

"But you can call me Judah. Judah Lion." He held out a hand, chipped and gnarled, lean and strong as he gripped her hand.

The warmth seemed to go right to her bones, the nausea dissipated. She looked at her noodles. *Stay alive.* Okay, she could do this. She picked up her fork.

"Attagirl," Judah said.

She wanted to smile, but suddenly, with the first bite, she'd turned ravenous again.

"Drink the tea. It's watery but it helps get the noodles down." He picked up his own cup. "Besides, you need the liquid. Despite being surrounded by water, it's easy to get dehydrated."

She took a sip of the tea, and it did make the cold noodles go down better. "What happens after this?"

"We go to work." He took a sip of his tea. "We're replacing an old gas line that stretches from Yakutia to Kamchatka. It's a privately owned line by the Petrov Bratva—the Russian mob. And they own this prison ship, too, so we're their private slave labor."

"What does that mean?"

"It means we dig holes and lay pipe and travel with the line as we work. Which is why we're on the ship. Before this, as we traveled through Siberia, we were in train cars, so this is like paradise."

She stared at him. "How long have you been here?"

"Three years. Nearly." He glanced at her tea. "Finish that. We can have as much tea as we want, but we'll leave soon, so you need to finish up. I'll get you more."

She picked up the tea cup and drank it down, despite the burn.

He got up and headed over to the counter.

Outside, a few clouds had moved in to clutter the blue sky, and beyond the rail, the ocean was deep blue and a little frothy. She spotted a couple men at the rail. They'd hooked a black bag onto a crane and were now positioning it over the water. Weights hung at the bottom of the bag.

Judah sat down beside her and set more hot tea in front of her.

"What are they doing?"

"That's a burial at sea. Probably the former twenty-three."

She turned, stared at him, even as he took a sip of his tea. "Good man. His name was Vasily. He got cut by a rusty shovel a few weeks ago."

She turned back just in time to see the body drop into the sea. "But we're at shore. The corpse will just rise to the surface."

"No. It's weighted. And this is a deep-water port. And we're sitting on top of the shelf. On the port side, the sea wall drops off past six hundred feet. And the current is strong and takes everything right out into the Bering Sea. The corpse is gone, forever." He took a breath, glanced at her. "I suppose it's one way to escape."

She stared at him, wide-eyed.

He smiled. "Not that anyone does. There's not been one successful escape attempt in all the time I've been here."

"Why are you here?"

He sighed, set down his tea. He had kind eyes, a few wrinkles around them. "I made the wrong people angry."

Her thoughts went to Lukka's father, probably some mafia lord.

"And why are you here?" He raised an eyebrow. "Try and smuggle a little weed in with you on your epic vacation to Moscow?"

Her mouth open. "No. I was kidnapped in Geneva. And I have no idea why. And then they were going to sell me into some human trafficking ring, but instead they sent me here while they try and tap my uncle for a ransom." Her voice had begun to shake, and he pressed a hand to her arm.

"Breathe. It's okay. You keep your head down, do your job, eat your food, drink your tea, and stay away from Vikka and her ilk, and you'll survive."

She again pressed her hand to her mouth. But, okay. "Probably, it won't be long. Uncle Ian will ransom me." Or Ned would find her. *Please.*

But she had to be done with crying. For now. Because it got her nowhere but despair.

Judah's mouth tightened. A few of the prisoners were getting up, returning their trays, getting more tea.

"What?"

He sighed. "It's just that, right after I was taken, a ransom was offered to my family. They came up with the money, and it was delivered, but..." He raised a shoulder. "The Bratva isn't going to give up something that is valuable, and as long as my family wanted me, I was money for them."

"But they paid for you."

"They did." He finished his tea. "Unfortunately, it takes more than that to get out of here. Finish your noodles. The guard will be here soon."

She dove into her noodles, gulping down her tea, and tried not to let his words strangle her.

A horn sounded, and around her, the prisoners got up.

"What's happening?"

Judah picked up his tray. "Stay with me, and you'll be okay. But be sure to put on your coat and your hat—and don't lose that hat."

She put on her coat and clutched her hat as she followed him. He stood just over six foot and led her out as they returned their trays and went to stand outside.

"Line up according to number," Judah said to her now, and she got in line in front of him, weirdly calm knowing he was right behind her. Two lines formed—their fifty occupants, and another fifty from the other side of the ship.

She hazarded a glance and spotted maybe thirty women, total.

The wind buzzed in her ears, and she pulled on her wool cap, found it instantly warm. Her hands she balled at her sides.

Ivanka and Natasha from yesterday walked up and down the lines, armed, and she looked away from them. Another man stood at the front. A bear of a man, he had black hair, a matching beard, thick gray army jacket, boots, and an AK-47 strung over his shoulder. A few younger men walked around, similarly armed.

"That's Captain Boris at the front. At least, that's what I named him. He's in charge and controls access to the ship. Security for the entire place is on a master key card. It unlocks the panel for all the door locks for the containers, the main lock to below deck, and the elevator between decks as well as the upper floors. He wears it in his inside pocket."

She glanced over her shoulder. "That's very detailed."

He laughed. "Too many years observing people for a living."

Whatever that meant. The line started moving, and she followed the man in front of her, lucky Twenty-Two, down a massive set of stairs off the side of the boat down to a smaller boat, a transport ship.

Guards shouted at them, but she hadn't a clue what they were saying. She simply lined up between Twenty-Two and Judah, her head down against a surprisingly sharp wind.

"It won't be as bad when we get to the job site. It's outside the city and surrounded by forest."

It felt like most of the city was surrounded by forest as they disembarked, got on waiting trucks, and headed off to the site, just north of the city. A massive volcano loomed in the distance, rugged and beautiful, coughing smoke into the sky and covered with bushy green pine.

The city itself wasn't large, mostly nine-story apartment buildings painted ochre orange or grimy white, the scent of coal in the air. She didn't get a great view out of the back of the truck, but she did spot a gold-topped Russian orthodox church, a few buses, and along the street, warmly dressed people walking to work or school.

Just another day in Siberia. Transporting prisoners from gulag.

How could this be her life?

Judah sat next to her, his head down, eyes closed, as if he might be trying to sleep.

The trucks turned off the highway and onto a dirt road, and she knocked against Judah, then Twenty-Two, then tried to hold herself still and her noodles in her stomach as they traveled to the work site.

The trucks finally stopped, all ten of them, and she climbed out into the sunshine.

Shovels leaned against a rack, and on the back of a truck, steel helmets for welding.

A massive ditch exposed a black snake of unfinished new pipe in the ground next to a rusty line of piping.

"Get a shovel. Follow the diggers," Judah said into her ear.

"Where are you going?"

"I weld." He looked at her. "You'll be okay. I'll be nearby. Just...dig."

She watched him go, a hollowness rushing through her.

He seemed to sense her, maybe, and turned around. "Twenty-Three. You're okay." Then he smiled.

She wasn't sure what it was. The smile, maybe the calm in his voice. But she picked up a shovel and followed the rest to the pipeline hole.

And then, because she'd promised Ned she'd stay alive, she dug.

FIVE

"This is not Russia." Ned stood at the window of the Air One Rescue office in Anchorage, his entire body wrung out.

Four flights—from Charles de Gaulle, to Dublin, Newark, to Seattle, to Alaska. Thirty-three hours and forty-five minutes. And six hours before that waiting to get on the flight, not to mention the nine-hour layover in Seattle, where Fraser had insisted they depart the terminal and get a hotel.

An hourly hotel. Ned had wanted to disinfect the sheets before he climbed onto the bed, but he lay on the bed fully clothed, and in his exhaustion, managed to drop into a dead sleep.

Fraser had to flip on the bright lights and practically douse him with cold water for his body to start functioning again, but yeah, a quick shower and he was back in the game for the three-hour flight to Anchorage.

Not Russia.

As he'd pointed out when Roy had purchased the tickets, they needed a visa to get into Russia proper.

Which, of course, wasn't actually in the game plan.

And neither, apparently, was Roy accompanying them to the

other side of the world. He'd bugged out right after dropping them off at the airport with a "Don't die."

Right. But he'd called ahead, and in Anchorage, a guy named Dodge had picked them up at the airport, along with his brother Ranger, and driven them to the offices of Air One Rescue, located at a small airport right off the sound.

The lights of the city flickered against the pane. Already, snow covered the ground, grimy piles lining the city lots.

Dodge and Ranger Kingston, a couple of former military guys, leaned over the table with Fraser, who knew them both. Dodge was tall and wore a wool cap over his dark hair that curled out at the bottom, as well as a thermal shirt and a pair of jeans, boots. A pilot himself, he was talking flight strategies with a guy named Moose Mulligan who owned the rescue operation with a chopper on the pad in front, along with at least one fixed wing.

The other man, Ranger, had greeted Fraser with a handshake and a man hug—and from their conversation, Ned realized that Ranger had been on the team to snatch his brother from the Boko Haram in Nigeria last summer.

Ranger had a similar make and build as Dodge, with dark-brown hair and blue eyes. Ned put him around six-two, and he wore a flannel shirt, a pair of jeans, boots.

"How's Noemi?" Fraser said as Ranger walked over to the coffee pot. The liquid he poured out resembled tar, but Ned nursed his own brew, and beggars couldn't be choosers.

"Feeling large," Ranger said. "And she still has four months to go at least. And then we'll make the move to Minnesota to join Ham's team."

"You're joining Jones, Inc.?" Ned asked, and looked at Fraser. "That's your outfit."

"Yep." Fraser took a sip of the coffee, made a face. "Yeah, that's bracing." He set it down. "Ranger is a former SEAL—funny you two didn't cross paths, being in San Diego."

Ned considered him. The man had a few years on him. "Danger?"

Ranger smiled. Lifted his coffee.

Yeah, he'd heard about Danger Ranger, just tidbits. "You were the team sniper."

His mouth created a grim line, and he nodded. "Now I put together ops for Ham."

"Here's hoping you can figure out how to get us on a cargo ship just off the coast of Kamchatka," Fraser said.

"I'm already working on it," Ranger said. "Here's our problem. We can get you there. We can rent a Gulfstream and you do a HAHO drop over Kamchatka at night, drop in and connect with our contact there. It's your exfil that is the problem. Moose just got his hands on a beautiful Firehawk chopper, but its range with no reserve tops off at around 450 nautical miles. The closest US soil is Attu Island, about 600 miles off the coast of Kamchatka. It's a part of the Aleutian Islands, and the Japanese tried to take it in World War II. There's a coast guard station there with a landing strip. Dodge has a Bell 429 that he can use to ferry fuel, but even if we land there and fuel up, it's a one-way trip, and even then, it doesn't get all the way to Russia."

"We need a boat," Moose said. "I have a buddy who just bought a fishing boat down in Iliuliuk Harbor. It's a crab boat, but if they cleared the decks, they might be able to accommodate the Firehawk. I could see if Carpie is back in port and if he'd help us out."

Ned walked over to the map. "How close to the Russian border can you get without getting torpedoed?" He found the tiny island of Attu, then ran his finger over. Almost a straight shot to Kamchatka. "I'll steal a boat if I have to."

Fraser looked at him. "Going in without a solid exfil isn't a great plan."

"Better than waiting, letting something terrible happen to her." He looked at his brother, then Dodge, Moose, and Ranger. "Shae is tough. But we're talking Russian gulag here. Russian gulag controlled by the Petrov Bratva. Think about that one second. Are you horrified?"

Fraser clamped a hand on his shoulder. "Yes. But we can't do this sloppy—"

"I never said sloppy. But..." Ned braced himself on the table, leaned over it. Then he slammed his fist into it and headed toward the door.

"Ned—"

He ignored Moose and stepped outside, no jacket, just needing the cold, some air, anything to stop the roil of heat inside.

He stalked out into the middle of the lot. Stared at the sky.

Glorious, starlit, and vast.

Too vast. So many stars the sky was lousy with them. And the moon, bright, bold. He drew in a breath, the air brisk in his lungs, and the cold seeped into his shirt, his skin, and he shivered.

He closed his eyes.

Hey, sailor, what are you doing out here?

Outlet Beach, near the Coronado base. He remembered the day well. Surfing the punchy shore break, he'd wasted himself getting his groove on the board until twilight fell.

Yeah, he'd liked that night. Remembered how the mist from the night had still layered his skin, his entire body chilled, but he'd felt alive, had shaken off the near misses and sounds in his brain from his last op.

And then she was there, walking across the beach, wearing a light pink sundress, her skin kissed, her blonde hair down, smiling at him.

"I saw you surfing. You're getting pretty good."

He had unzipped his wetsuit, pulled it down to his waist, then grabbed a T-shirt and yanked it on. The sun had dipped into the far horizon, turning the sea to fire, and he wasn't far behind.

Oh, he didn't deserve her, and he knew it. She never asked where he'd been, when he'd return. Just kissed him goodbye and hello again. Walked with him along the shoreline as the sea chased them, washed away their footsteps.

"I made dinner. Fish tacos. I think I got the slaw right." She picked up his towel, held it out to him. "Come home."

He grabbed the towel and rubbed his hair, leaving it in spikes as he wrapped the towel around his neck.

Home. Not his home—he lived in bachelor barracks at the base, little more than a tiny room with a shared kitchen. But he was there so rarely.

Shae, on the other hand, rented a garage apartment two blocks off the ocean—a two-room addon to a larger house, so it wasn't fancy, but it had a massive glass garage door that opened to the outside, to a deck outfitted with a swing and a fire table and deck chairs and a hammock that he'd fallen asleep in more often than he should.

Yeah, home.

He barely remembered the tacos, but he did remember climbing into the hammock with her tucked next to him, watching the sunset and thinking *perfect*.

Right now, right here, everything he needed in his reach... yeah, *perfect*.

And then he'd kissed her, slow and long, with the ocean breezes finding their way to them, the night singing. She'd tasted of pineapple, and it wasn't the first time he'd wished they were married.

But he'd made it home still a gentleman, and probably got deployed a few days later, and of course, the night had faded into the next op.

His eyes burned. *I'm sorry, Shae.*

Footsteps, and he glanced over to see Fraser headed toward him.

Ned turned back, hating that his cheeks were wet.

Fraser came up beside him, his hands in his pockets. Said nothing for a long time.

"In Nigeria, the sky was just this bright. Stars were a little different, but still, black as night, and yet breathtaking. I remember looking up and feeling so small."

"And yet you had your buddy Colt with you."

"He was pretty roughed up most of the time, and I was in a lot of pain—but yeah, I wasn't alone."

Ned nodded. "I—"

"If you're going to shoulda-woulda, don't. It won't do you any good. Regrets like this get us nowhere."

"I just want to hit something, all the time. All. The time."

"I'll remember that," Fraser said and glanced at him.

Ned drew in a breath. "I should have married her years ago."

"Wouldn't have changed a thing, bro." Fraser looked at him. "You'd still be standing out here, wondering how the world turned upside down so fast. Might not be this—might be something else. Life isn't in our control, as much as we wish it were."

A beat, then, "I have this crazy memory of us going camping—tubing really, one summer. You remember that?"

Ned frowned. "On the St. Croix? Yeah. I was about ten, maybe. We tied all our tubes together and went down the river."

"Mm-hmm. That night we had a campfire, and I remember Dad talking about the river, and how alone, we would just get tossed by the current, but together, we could fight it."

"I was only worried about having to sleep in the same tent as Iris."

Fraser laughed. "Yeah, well, Dad told me that we were never meant to be self-sufficient. That we were supposed to be dependent. On each other. And most importantly, on God."

"Oh, wait, this is the God-is-my-teammate talk, right?"

Fraser smiled. "You remember that?"

"I was face down in an ER, the doctor sewing up my backside after I got shot, trapped by you and your big brother wisdom, so yeah, I remember."

"Good. Maybe you missed the part, though, where the biggest way we depend on God, our team leader, is to pray."

"I've been praying. Or trying to. It's hard when you can't breathe."

"I'm sure you have." His mouth tightened. "Pray some

more." Then he made a fist and pressed it against Ned's chest "You gotta keep praying until this knot goes away."

Ned wasn't sure that was possible.

Fraser again looked at the stars. "I heard once that peace isn't the absence of worry or fear; it's the presence of the one who is bigger than that."

Then he glanced again at Ned, gave a nod, and headed back inside.

Ned stood there, wordless.

Then he looked back at the heavens. Took a breath.

And prayed some more.

"GET YOUR HEAD IN THE GAME, HUDSON!"

Hudson ignored the shout from Head Coach Clay, pacing the sidelines as he picked up the football egg-rolling across the turf, then tossed to it to Coach Max, his wide-receiver coach. Coach Max caught it, rolling it between his hands, then motioned for Hudson to come over.

"'Sup, Coach?" He'd barely worked up a sweat today, the temps in the mid-forties, the sky a slate gray. Reminded him a little of playing in Montana, the scent of a storm in the air despite the high blue sky. He didn't mind a little snow on the field, especially back then, with his parents and Harry in the stands. And playing Griz football had opened up doors beyond the life of a hired cowboy, something his mother desperately wanted for both her sons.

"Are you going to play like that in the game tomorrow?"

He liked Coach Max. The guy might be Austrian, but he knew football, having played in the US for college, then coached in the ELF for the last seven years. He'd sent two of his ELF players into the NFL just last year.

Hudson hoped to be the third.

"Sorry, Coach."

"I've got the same question for you, Bly. You're not here. That's the third pass you've missed today, passes that are easily catchable."

Max wore a purple Vienna Vikings baseball cap, a pair of Ray-Bans, and a black jacket with the Vikings emblem on the breast. He tucked the football under his arm, put a hand on Hud's shoulder. "Your head okay?"

Oh. The last thing he wanted was for Max to start to think that his concussions were catching up with him, causing him brain fog, even confusion in the backfield.

"I'm good, Coach. I'll do better—"

"I know. You're a great clutch player, and we'll need you in the game against the Milano Seamen. But you looked tired out there, and again, like your mind is somewhere else."

His mind *was* somewhere else, frankly. Many somewhere elses. Like the Charles Bridge in Prague in the rain, and in his hotel room, staunching the bleeding of a stranger, with Iris Marshall as they rode the train in Paris to Napoleon's grave, and then, in slow-mo, the moments that led up to the attack by her brothers.

Her brothers.

But frankly, he'd seen the guy watching her—watching them, really, because the man's eyes had followed Hudson the moment he walked up to the plaque. Stayed on him when he moved over to the nave.

Then Iris had walked in, and Hudson had noticed him turn said attention to her. So yes, when he'd made a move toward her, maybe Hudson's instincts just kicked him. Call him crazy, but they'd just seen someone stabbed, right there in the open.

And he wasn't going to let the same thing happen to Iris. Yes, he didn't like her, and her know-it-all attitude drove him a little crazy—more than she knew, probably—but they were partners, at least in that moment.

So yeah, when the guy in the black jacket had made a move, so had Hudson.

Hadn't expected for a second to be ambushed by brother number two and land on his face on the travertine floor.

"Let's run the play one more time." Coach Max turned and tossed the ball to Jack Ernst, their QB, and Hud ran up to the huddle.

"You need me to walk the ball to you, Bly?" Jack said.

"Just throw me a pass I don't have to hurt myself to catch." He knew what Coach Max had said, but frankly, Jack's passes were often just above his fingertips, and he was already six-three. More than once, after jumping to catch a high ball, the cornerback had taken Hud out at his knees, the fall to earth nearly jolting out his breath.

Or maybe he was just getting old. Although, he wasn't quite ready to throw in his career at twenty-eight.

All of the offensive team spoke English: native for the three Americans and two Brits, and the rest—Ezzio, the Spanish tight end, a Swede at guard, and three Austrians—had learned it as a second language, so Jack called off the play in English.

They broke, and Hudson took his position on the outside, just a step back from the line of scrimmage. Jack sounded off and Hudson took off, in motion to the other side. Ran up to the line of scrimmage, set.

Jack snapped the ball.

The defensive player was still catching up when Hud took off. He crossed the line of scrimmage, juked to the right, then cut inside, running hard. Turned at midfield and the ball was right there, arrowing in, just over his head.

He leaped and pulled it in with one arm, clutching it to his chest, landed and turned.

The safety hit him from behind, but he took two steps before he fell, curling up to protect the ball.

The cold ground jarred his bones, but he held on, despite the two-hundred-plus weight pinning him. Because that's how it was done.

Bam.

They made 'em big in Germany, and the safety, a Luis Spiegel, took his time getting off Hud. But he extended his hand to his teammate and helped Hud to his feet.

"Schöner Fang," Luis said and banged on his shoulder pad as Hud tossed the ball to Coach Max.

"Danke," Hud said, then gathered in as Coach Clay blew the whistle.

Jack met his fist, and they huddled up, listening to the instructions for tomorrow's away exhibition.

But again, his mind seemed to unlatch, to travel back to Paris and the moments after Iris's brother Fraser had told him to bring her home.

I don't need his protection, Fraser. I can get home on my own.

Iris. Fraser had called her ornery. Hudson probably hadn't needed to add the snarky comment, but he couldn't help it. Her brother had nailed it.

He'd called an Uber, and while driving to Charles de Gaulle Airport, had pulled up flights.

"There's an EasyJet flight at six p.m. that gets you into Milan by seven-thirty. I'll have you home by nine and then..."

"What? You'll sleep on my couch?"

Maybe.

"Listen, don't be ridiculous. I've lived on my own in Europe for three years. I own my own apartment in Italy. I travel every single week, to countries all over Europe. I know Barcelona, Cologne, Frankfurt, Warsaw, most of Germany and Austria, especially Italy, and even Paris like I was born there. I speak three languages well, and two passingly, I have an international driver's license, and most of all, I can get on a flight all by myself. Even buckle in. And stay seated even if the seat belt sign is off. I know it's risky—I mean, I could end up in Greece—but I think I can get home by myself."

Then she'd looked at him, her eyebrow raised.

Shoot, he didn't want to like her, not really. She was bossy and a know-it-all, and most of all, had nearly cost him everything once upon a time and never, not once, acknowledged it or apologized, so, yeah, he really didn't want to like her.

But she was so...well, pretty. And he hated that he noticed that, but yeah, up close, and without her hair in a severe ponytail and under a hat, and out of her zebra clothes...Iris Marshall had looks.

She stood maybe five-five, a hundred thirty pounds sopping wet, had curves and muscle and pretty blonde hair that shone in the sun and blue eyes that seemed to miss nothing.

Except, of course, pivotal, game-deciding penalties, the kind that could get a guy injured.

So yeah, he should probably remember that.

Still, he'd made a promise. *"I'll get you home."*

"Oh, for the love!"

So, he'd booked them flights to Milan, although he'd found an Air France flight at 3:30 p.m., gotten in at 5:00 p.m., and then found an 8:30 p.m. flight on Austrian Airlines that got him back to Vienna by 10:00 p.m.

Because no, he didn't want to spend the night on her sofa, thank you very much.

"Hudson, did you hear me?"

He looked over at Coach Clay.

"The flight leaves at six a.m. Sharp. Six. A.M. That's the *morning.*"

"Right. Got it, Coach."

"Good. Okay, guys, get some rest. See you in the morning."

They broke and Hudson headed for the locker room. He liked the Viking's set up. They'd inherited much of the space from the Austria Wien futbol club, which was a boon, because the Austrians loved their soccer. Which meant each player had more than a locker—they practically had their own suite, with a hanging closet, a towel and toiletries shelving, a towel rack, although his gear and towels were laundered every day by the trainers, a place for his shoes, also cleaned daily, and private showers. He especially loved the massive players' lounge, with the big-screen televisions and lounge chairs.

He'd heard of some pretty impressive locker rooms in the NFL, but he still felt like a champion every time he saw his picture and name emblazoned above his area.

Reminded him sometimes how close he'd come to being a for-hire cowboy, living paycheck to paycheck.

One bad hit. One disastrous slam to his head.

But that wasn't today.

He hit the showers, took his time, shaved, and emerged an hour later in a pair of jeans, a dress shirt, and leather jacket, carrying in his duffel his dirty clothes as he walked outside into the chill. He bleeped open his Maserati MC20, a splurge for sure—it'd used up his entire signing bonus—but he just felt, well, safe maybe, when he slid into the creamy Italian leather seats. Listened to the engine purr.

Not his father's 1972 Ford pickup with the rusted wheel beds and torn seats. And he never started the car with the fear of sputtering or maybe ending up on the side of the road, waiting for a tow.

He parked his car in the private garage under his condo unit—probably, he could have walked home, but what fun was that?—and took the elevator to the top floor.

The mid-morning sun slanted in through the angled windows—part of the character of the penthouse—and burnished the parquet flooring. The place was warm, but he used his remote to turn on the gas fireplace anyway, then headed to the kitchen. He kept it clean, even with his house help, all his appliances and dishes behind onyx-black cabinets. It contrasted with the creamy white quartz countertops, and frankly, the place felt modern and sleek and...

Well, his agent had found it, and he was trying to grow into it.

Upstairs was the best—a master bedroom that overlooked

most of Vienna, and especially the towering Romanesque spires of St. Stephen's Cathedral. He could stand at his window and sometimes, on a good day, feel like he'd made it.

Seriously.

Aw, Iris in his head again. And not just when he'd agreed to take her home, but later, when their flight was delayed, and they landed with only an hour before his flight.

I can make it home on my own. My flat is an hour from here. What are you going to do, bring me home, order a pizza, tuck me in bed, and make it back by your flight?

She had a point there.

It still sat in his gut that he hadn't driven her home, hadn't seen her to her door.

But it wasn't like he was going to see her brothers ever again. And, like she said, she knew her way around Europe.

Maybe better than he did.

Now, he opened his fridge to see what Claudia had left him for dinner.

Potato goulash, with a note written in English, in a pot. He pulled it out and set it on the stove. Opened the top.

Potatoes, onions, bell peppers, sausages, paprika. His stomach woke up, roared.

Dinner, then a nap, and by then, maybe Iris would be out of his head.

He took out a long wooden spoon and was stirring when his Alexa rang. He answered it and grinned at his brother Harry's mug in the frame of his phone. His deep voice came through the surround sound speakers. "Hud. I just wanted to check in, make sure you were still alive after—"

"All good, bro."

He still had a hard time wrapping his head around the events of the past forty-eight hours.

"Good. Then happy birthday, mate. Twenty-eight."

"That's today?"

"Here it is. I think it was yesterday, your time. I know your life is bigger than birthdays—"

"Thanks. I appreciate the call. What time is it there?"

"Ten p.m. You home from practice?"

"Yeah. We have an exhibition game tomorrow with the Milano team."

"I saw you won your last game."

"Barely. The ref missed a pass interference call. Nearly cost us the game."

"Wait—that female ref? From America? What's her name again?"

"Iris Marshall. And yes, she missed the call."

"Wow, you just can't catch a break with her."

Oh, he had no idea. Still, maybe it wasn't her fault.

"I don't think she even remembers me."

Harry had the same short, dark-blond hair and pale blue-green eyes, but he wore a perpetual smile, the charmer that he was. Used it to his advantage when he needed to calm down the scared and hurting.

"Seriously? Her bad call nearly ended your career." Harry raised an eyebrow. "She seriously doesn't remember you?"

Well, she did now, but before... "I don't think so. But it doesn't matter. I'm here, now, and playing, and that's in the past."

Harry gave a closed-mouth nod.

"How's the new job? Like living back in Montana?"

"Yeah, the PEAK team is great. And now that we're getting into snow season, we've got more broken bones and falls in the mountains. Good thing the park closes soon."

"You say that like it's fun."

"Anything that gets me in a chopper, flying over the Rockies, is fun. Mostly."

"How's Mom and Dad?"

"Good. Mom's better. She's back to cooking for the bar S, and Dad just signed a three-year contract with them, so they might buy a fifth wheel. I'm trying to talk them into something more permanent, but you know Dad."

On the stove, the pot began to bubble.

"When are you comin' home next?"

"Christmas. We have a two-week practice break."

"Mom will love that." Behind Harry, in the background, a female voice lifted. "Oh, hey, I gotta run."

"It's ten at night. Who is over there?"

"I'm at work. Don't get excited. Still single."

"Yeah, me too."

He held up his fist and Hud bumped it, weirdly, through the screen.

He was hanging up when he heard it—a creak of the floorboards upstairs. Or maybe it was just his imagination, because—

Nope. Another creak, and he stilled. Held his breath.

Then he turned off the heat on his stew and grabbed a kitchen knife. Wished it were night and not high noon.

He stilled as feet came down his stairs. Booted feet, and then legs garbed in cargo pants, and then a black puffy parka, and finally, a sleek black ponytail.

"Ziggy?" He put down the knife as his handler—was that what he should call her?—walked into the room. "Can't you use the front door?"

Ziggy walked up to him with such an easy confidence it was a little unnerving. She carried a lethal aura about her, despite her smile. The woman could bring a dead man to life with her looks—that dusky skin, those sharp golden-brown eyes, the way her smile curved up, as if curious.

"You should know me better than that."

Yeah, he didn't know her at all. Just a phone call here and again, and recently, a midnight rescue of Tate Marshall. "Um. Do I?"

She raised an eyebrow, then sighed. "I don't want anyone knowing I'm here."

And that chilled him to the bone. "Why?"

She came up to the counter. "When's the last time you saw Iris Marshall?"

A beat. And he couldn't exactly lie, but the truth suddenly turned to acid in his chest. "Two days ago, around six p.m. in Milan." He took a breath. "Why?"

"I just came from her place. She's not there."

Oh. He set down the knife. She glanced at it, back to him.

"I don't know where she is."

"That's not good. Not good at all." Ziggy turned and walked to the window, stared out of it.

He didn't know why, but the action simply had his gut tightening.

And then she turned. "We need to find her. Because twenty-four hours ago, someone took a hit out on her."

He blinked at her. Tried to make out the words. "A hit. Like... someone is going to assassinate her?"

"Yep. And if we—and by that, I mean you—don't find her, my guess is that they'll put the blame on you."

"Why me?"

"Because you're the last person to be seen with her. And because your DNA and hers are all over a bloody hotel room in Prague."

OH, SHE WAS GOING TO DIE HERE, SHAE FELT IT IN HER bones.

She just had to face the truth...even if Ned found her, or if Uncle Ian ransomed her, it would be too late.

No more illusions, no more hands over her eyes or ears, no more hope that if she just kept her head down and kept digging, she might survive.

Because after today, well, she'd barely kept her toes, and not because the wind burned her ears and through her wool jacket and flimsy canvas jumpsuit. The pressed wool footwear turned out to be surprisingly warm, even when wet and muddy.

No, the death of her would be the enemy she'd somehow made in Vikka.

Vikka, who apparently had a favorite shovel.

Shae lay in her bunk, pressing her fists to her eyes. Her hands burned with blisters, and every muscle ached. She'd gotten a shower today, but the chill of the boat seeped through her wet head, down into her body, and she trembled, hard.

But she had to blame, too, the near miss of losing her toes today.

Eta moya lopata.

The woman had said it in Russian and then, because Shae wasn't looking at her and didn't understand a word she'd said, Vikka had said it again, this time in broken English—*Zhat is my shovel*—while an inch from her face.

This version, Shae understood.

What she didn't understand was her own crazy reaction. Maybe it was the result of sitting with Judah Lion at dinner last night and this morning at breakfast. The way that others sort of gave him berth, as if he might be scary or possess power. But even Vikka had found another table to terrorize.

Shae had started thinking that everything might be okay. That she would survive. It wasn't anything Judah said, either.

Just his presence. Sorta made her heart slow down, made her thoughts stop spiraling, stopped the constant thrum of fear.

But he worked on the pipes, welding the new pipes together or breaking open the old pipes to be lifted out of the trench, which left her alone with the diggers.

And Vikka.

And Shae's stupid, unfounded bravery.

"I like this shovel," she'd said.

Oh, what an idiot. Even as the words issued from her, she'd

wanted to grab them back. Especially when Vikka's face twisted—a sort of smile, almost—and she stepped back and—

The sharp end of her shovel came down right against the top of Shae's wool boot. So hard that it snipped off the finest layer of wool and dug a trench in the sand.

Toes. She needed those to run.

Shae handed over the shovel.

Vikka took it and then walked away, her shovel still standing guard in the dirt.

Around them, others had seen, many of them women, some of them men, but their expressions betrayed nothing.

Shae's stomach wanted to lose her kasha and brown bread breakfast. Somehow, she managed to keep her head down, keep digging, not look up, even when the tears came.

Just dig.

She'd foolishly pinned her hopes on seeing Judah after the workday. She'd gotten the rhythm, even after two days. Stack the shovels, line up by number, march back to the boat. Except Judah, and a number of the other welders, didn't join them.

She'd never felt so naked.

On the boat, she'd found number twenty-one, an older woman with gray-red hair and bony, strong hands who had spoken English on the first day when the whistle had blown and they'd needed to line up for lunch—bread and tea. "Move!"

So she'd leaned over and whispered, "Where are the others?"

The woman shook her head, glared at her.

Okay, then. Shae shoved her hands between her knees and tried not to let the sea upend her stomach as the boat motored them back to the hulking ship.

She'd climbed the stairs and lined up for dinner. Potatoes in a slimy gravy, two slices of brown bread, more tea.

She probably didn't want dinner anyway, but when Vikka sat down beside her, the idea of the woman stealing her supper rooted in her gut.

Then Twenty-Seven sat down next to her, and whatever verve she'd had died.

Twenty-Seven reached over and, with his grimy hands, grabbed her potatoes.

Vikka took the bread.

Another man, next to Vikka, grabbed the tea.

And when Shae tried to get up, to leave them to their thievery, Vikka grabbed her and pulled her back down. "Nyet."

She'd never quite felt so violated as when they ate her dinner in front of her, then piled up their plates for her to take to the scullery.

Or when Vikka then came up behind her, grabbed her around the neck and whispered something into her ear.

She hadn't a clue what it was, but just her breath on her skin made Shae want to retch.

And still no Judah.

The prisoners left the mess hall, a few of them smoking cigarettes they'd earned—or stolen. The guards then came out and made them line up on the deck, by number, in rows. She faced Vikka but stared out past her, to the horizon where the sun was setting over the far-away mountains. Behind her, the wind skimmed off the ocean, brutally cold, and she shivered, pulling her hat down lower.

Vikka eyed her. Smiled.

They stood on the deck in the cold while the guards finished their meals inside the cafeteria. Then they were marched down to their containers below deck.

Shae had never been so grateful to hear the doors slam, to be locked in the cold dungeon of her room.

Now, rolling over, she wrapped herself in the wool blanket, trying to ignore the press of hunger inside.

Footsteps, and more doors rolled open, then closed.

Silence, her heartbeat the only sound.

She wondered where Ned was. If he'd figured out she'd been moved yet. If Uncle Ian had gotten the demand.

Maybe, like Judah had said, he'd paid it, and it didn't matter.

Stop crying. Crying would get her nowhere.

Please, God, where are You? Send help.

"Twenty-Three." The voice wheedled through her, a whisper in the night.

She stilled.

"Shae, are you there?"

She sat up, looked at the barred window. Nope.

"Down here. Under your bed."

She leaned down, then rolled to the floor and reached to the wall.

There. A hole.

And reaching through the hole, a hand.

"Judah?"

"It's me."

She touched her fingers to his, the hole big enough to put her entire hand through. Somehow the touch of his hand, rough as it was, warmed her entire body. He gave her hand a squeeze, then let go.

She pulled her hand back through, then pressed her cheek to the floor, trying to see in the blackness. She barely made out the outline of his face.

"Are you okay?" he said.

"Where were you?"

"Number eighty-one tried to escape today. He was on the welding crew, so they took us all for questioning."

Her breath caught. "Are you hurt?"

"Not much. But good news—tomorrow I'll be on dig crew again."

She shouldn't want to cry with relief, but...

"What happened to Eighty-One?"

"He is in the infirmary. My guess is that by the end of the week he goes off the ship in a bag."

She closed her eyes. "Vikka and Twenty-Seven took my dinner."

"His name is Zurab. He's Georgian. The potatoes have wire worms, so they saved you from dysentery."

Oh.

"Listen, I need your help. The other twenty-three, the guy before you, was a friend, and he...he hid something in your container. I don't want you to get caught with it."

What?

"What is it?"

"It's blasting powder. They use it to get through rock. I steal a little at a time in my hat."

Brilliant. And, "That's dangerous."

"What are they going to do, kill me? I'm already a dead man in here."

"I don't want to hear that."

Silence. "That wasn't defeatist. I know my fate, and I've made peace with it. But that doesn't mean I am planning on sticking around, waiting for it to happen."

"Take me with you?"

"Absolutely. If and when I blow up the ship, you'll be the first to know."

She smiled at that. "Is that really your plan?"

Silence.

And she got that. Maybe it was for her benefit—she'd like to think so. Because if she didn't know anything, they couldn't get anything out of her. But then again, they might torture her to death trying, so...

"Where is it?"

"Inside your mattress."

"I've been sleeping on blasting powder?"

"Makes for a great pillow. You'll find a slit along the seam in front. The bag is in there."

She rolled out from under the bed and got up, then crawled to the front of the bed and searched the mattress.

Indeed, the seam opened up under the ribbing along the edge. And when she reached inside, she found a bag the size of a water bottle. She pulled it out. Crawled back under the bed. "How did he get that in there?"

"Took out the stuffing every time we got more powder, put it in his boots, then emptied his boots at the job site. Pretty soon we had a pretty big amount."

"Will this blow up the ship?"

A small, muffled snort. "My way it will. But it has to be at the right time or it won't work."

"When is that?"

"You'll know it when you see it."

The bag was thick plastic, sealed with glue. "Where did you get this?" She pushed it gently through the hole, between the containers.

He took it and eased it into his side. "We rotate duties. In a couple weeks, you'll be in the kitchen. And then KP. I stole it during my KP shift."

"So I won't dig forever?"

"No. You'll graduate to peeling potatoes. Thanks for the powder."

Wait— "Don't go...I..."

"Shh. I'm right here, Shae. Just a voice away." He stuck his hand through the opening again, and she found it, gripping it with both of hers.

Oh, she didn't want to be this afraid. "I'm trying to be brave."

Maybe he didn't hear her. Or maybe he did, because he squeezed her hand, then slowly pulled his back.

"Yea, though I walk through the valley of the shadow of death, I will fear no evil; for you are with me."

She drew in a breath. "That's from the Bible."

"Psalm twenty-three, verse four. You are not alone. And you are still safe."

He fell silent, but his words found her bones, and with them, Ned's voice, from years ago, when evil pursued them. *We are not alone, Shae. And we are still safe.*

No, no she wasn't.

But as she got on her cot and stared at the ceiling, as she ran the verse through her head, she stopped trembling.

In fact, as she lay there, a sort of warmth spread over her. Enveloped her. Held her.

No, she was not alone. And maybe she would survive just one more day.

And then, maybe, the next one after that.

Until finally, one day, she escaped.

Six

For the first time in his life, Ned could see why people questioned jumping out of a perfectly good airplane. The Gulfstream G700 just might be the most beautiful plane he'd ever HAHO'd out of, and frankly, he wasn't thrilled to leave the leather sofa, the smooth ride over the Aleutian Islands, for the frigid cold of the 12,000-foot jump.

But if it meant getting his feet on Kamchatka soil and getting onto the gulag ship that held Shae, getting them both safely out of Russia with Ranger's crazy plan, then, yes.

Get him out of luxury.

"Let me check your gear." Ranger's voice from behind him as Ned clipped on his helmet, then ran his hand over his equipment, re-memorizing the tac gear in his vest, his pants pockets. At least this time he wasn't going in naked. KA-BAR, a Sig handgun loaned to him by Ranger, plus a suppressor, a multi-tool, bolt cutter, flashlights, NVGs, and even an inflatable life vest and a personal EPRIB should they land in the sea. It only activated in water, so that wasn't going to happen.

But in case of tragedy and they did land in the drink, he carried a small pouch of fresh water, although even that wouldn't outlast the deep freeze of the Bering Sea. But the plan was not to get his feet wet, to let the High Altitude, High Open deployment carry him the extra forty miles to the Russian shore.

So far they'd traveled under radar, close to the deck, but for this last bit, Dodge and Moose would climb hard to their jump altitude of 12K. They'd offload into the sky, then the Gulfstream would bug home, outrunning, hopefully, any fighters, all the while playing dumb. *So sorry, Ivan, got a little lost.*

According to Moose, who ran SAR, even out this far, it could work.

"Testing," came Fraser's voice in the helmet.

Ned pressed on the com affixed to his vest, two clicks, then, "Confirm."

Two clicks back and Ned gave a thumbs-up. Then he checked his watch, the compass on the outside registering due west, and the GPS on his wrist. He wore three layers of thermals and a waterproof jumpsuit, but it was like wearing a baseball cap in a snowstorm. He pulled on his goggles.

"You're good," Ranger said, and turned him around. Held up the map. "I marked the entry points as well as where you should meet your contact." Then he bent and shoved the map, inside its plastic bag, into his leg pouch. "Fraser has the same map."

"Who's the contact?"

"His name is Pavel. He's a friend of Moose's—a fellow pilot. Learned how to fly from him, actually. He'll get you into the ship."

"How?"

"I don't know."

Ned met eyes with Fraser, whose mouth tightened.

"Can we trust this guy?" Fraser asked.

"Yes." Ranger glanced toward the cockpit. "Yes."

Which meant maybe, at best. But they hadn't had time to cobble together a better plan, so...

"Climbing," Moose said from over the speaker, which meant they were a hundred miles from the drop zone.

And deep in Russian territory.

Ned walked over to the door, across from the bathroom. The cockpit door was open, and he looked over, through the window.

In the distance, tiny lights prickled the shoreline. Petropavlovsk.

They had fifty miles to fly before they could land, or they'd freeze to death.

Hang on, Shae.

Fraser stepped up behind him.

From the cockpit, Dodge looked at Moose. "They're pinging us."

"Keep climbing," Moose said. "We're not at altitude yet."

Ned's ears began to pop, and he yawned, freeing the pressure. Ranger was doing the same, his gaze on the altimeter.

"They're warning us to turn around," Dodge said. Apparently, he spoke enough Russian to understand. Or maybe the warning came in English. Ned had heard that all Russian traffic controllers had to learn English, but what about the Russian military?

Yes, keep climbing, Moose. But hurry, because the faster they got off, the faster Moose bugged out, the less of a chance they'd deploy—

"They're threatening to shoot us out of the sky with anti-aircraft missiles."

Oh. "What's the range?" Fraser said.

"The S-400 Triumf has a range of four hundred kilometers." Dodge, from the cockpit.

"We're well within range," Ned said.

"Even if they have the next model down, it's a hundred fifty-five miles." This from Ranger.

"What's our altitude?"

"Just passing ten thousand," said Moose.

"Let's pull the trigger," said Fraser. "We'll just deploy immediately and let the wind take us." He clamped a hand on Ned's shoulder. "We'll make it."

Ned swallowed past the burr in his chest and nodded.

The plane leveled out, and Ranger opened the door. Not made for dumping out passengers over the ocean, the plane fought the sudden rush of air and bucked. Ned held on while Dodge and Moose evened her back out.

The stairway retracted into the body of the plane, and now Ned stepped out. Looked down. Darkness, the night black with clouds. That would help.

He pulled down his NVGs, gave a thumbs-up, covered up the glasses, and ran from the plane.

He cleared the wings, falling hard, and in a second, pulled the rip cord. The chute yanked him up, hard, and the fall arrested, the world turning instantly quiet.

"You good?" Fraser's voice in his helmet.

"Yes."

Above them, the Gulfstream had banked hard, was fleeing Russian airspace.

Run, boys, run.

He grabbed the toggles of his chute and steered the canopy west, barely making out Fraser in the darkness via the eerie green of his glasses.

"You there, bro?"

"Yep. I see you. Adjust a little to the northwest. Don't want you to miss the island."

Ned grinned. "Aw, I'd just end up in Japan, maybe grab some sushi."

Fraser laughed.

And weirdly, it sort of choked Ned up, the fact he was hanging here, in the sky, with his brother. "Fraser, I should probably say thanks, you know—"

"Not necessary, bro. It's what we do."

"Yeah, but you're not on the teams anymore, and—"

"No, Ned. It's what Marshalls do. One jumps, we all jump. I thought you'd figured out we had your back when Kostia jumped you."

Right. The bully from fifth grade. "That's one thing. Jumping onto a gulag ship in the middle of Siberia..."

A beat. "Thing is, Ned, I always thought it would be great to be on an op with you—well, maybe not one where we might die, but a training op, where we HALO'd out of a plane, landed on a rib, took it to shore, or better, dropped in and SCUBA'd in for a night infil, took out some CIA rubes, and then exfil'd to a local beach bar and hung out with our toes in the sand. Yeah, that."

"So instead, you decided to come to Siberia with me?"

"Not quite the sandy beach I was hoping for, but I can't let you have all the fun. Let's veer north a bit more. The winds has us, so we're still high, but if we ride it more, we'll land up shore, away from the city. I'm aiming for all that darkness ahead."

Ned spotted the place, still some six thousand feet below but coming up quickly. No lights, which hopefully meant nothing inhabited. "I don't mind hoofing it as long as we don't get wet."

"Me too."

Another pause. "Fraser, you need to know that if something goes south, you leave with Shae. No matter what."

"Ned. Nothing's going to happen. We're going to get Shae and get home."

"But if it does—"

"Not leaving you behind, so you can just put a cork in it."

Wow, and now he was getting way too choked up, and probably it was simply the tension of the last three days. He took a breath.

"Let's try not to hit the military base." He'd seen it on the map and now checked his GPS. "I think it's just west of us, near that peninsula."

"Roger. Okay, head south, stay on my six."

He could barely make out Fraser against the night with his black chute, dark clothing. But his heat signature helped, and he followed his brother down.

And then, just like that, the current they rode died.

He could feel it, the breath gone, his weight falling.

"Fraser?"

"We're still ten clicks out, easy."

"We won't survive a ten-mile swim."

"Toggle your chute and start circling. Let's see if we can find a current."

Fraser pulled on his toggle on one side of his chute, turning it in a circle. Ned toggled the other way. Then again, the opposite direction.

He felt it, the smallest gust, lifting him. "I got one. It's just south of you."

Fraser turned his chute, heading for Ned, but he'd lost too much air. "I can't grab it."

"Keep trying." Ned had fully caught the gust now, and it lifted him, carrying him northwest. He rode it, directing in toward land.

Fraser continued to fall.

Ned checked his GPS. They were still a good eight miles from land. But at this rate, he'd make it.

Fraser might land five miles out, maybe closer. But even a five mile swim...

Oh, God, Fraser could not freeze to death in the Bering Sea.

"Keep searching!"

"I'm trying, bro. But I'm too low."

Indeed, Fraser was dropping fast now.

"There's always a gust, right above the water. Grab that, and ride that as far as you can. I'll land and get to you."

"This is going to get chilly."

Ned's jaw tightened as he watched Fraser work his chute. Indeed, he caught a gust, the chute maybe fifty feet above the water, his feet nearly at depth. But, as if he might be kiting over some Caribbean sea, he skimmed the waves, angling the chute toward shore.

But this wasn't a parasail, and their chutes lacked the front edge wing shape that let kiters glide over the water.

Fraser dropped into the chop a mile from shore.

"Fraser!"

No answer. He was probably untangling himself from his lines and fighting to stay afloat.

Ned needed to get his feet on land.

And get a boat.

And...*oh, God, please,* Fraser couldn't die just off the Russian shore.

Ned sailed out of the gust and powered down to shore, scouring the shoreline for a boat, anything, even debris, but saw nothing but gray gravel shoreline.

He put down on a lip of shore, his feet sinking into the wet gravel. Trini would have called it a textbook landing.

He called it desperation. Especially as he shucked off his chute and didn't even bother to secure it. Instead, he did something painfully stupid.

The only thing he could think to do.

He unbuckled his tactical pack, tucked it with his gear, grabbed his life vest and headed into the water.

Stupid, stupid, but the waves would carry Fraser in, and if he could get to him, they'd get back together and—

He was already in the water, shouting against the cold that burned through his body, when he heard the motor. More like a buzz, but it thrummed through him, and he paused, eating waves, treading water. He was maybe three hundred feet from shore, his body already numb, when the light bumped over the water. Disappeared.

Flickered again.

The Russian military had found Fraser. Ned knew it in his bones, and shoot, he had no choice but to turn and flee to shore. He'd get his pack and run for the thick forest, hide in the mountains cape. Survive. And then in a few days, he'd find Pavel and—

The motor burned toward him.

What a colossally bad idea, flung from his desperation, and

now he'd gotten his brother killed along with himself, and Shae would be stuck—

He spotted the shoreline, some one hundred feet ahead, and with the surf pushing him, he might outswim the boat, now throttling toward him.

"Ned!"

He thought he heard his name, but maybe it was his own heartbeat—his feet hit shoreline and he swam-ran through the water—

"Ned!"

The voice jerked him, and he stopped, turned.

The boat road the waves, just beyond where he'd hit the shore and—

Fraser was in the water, holding on to a fishing boat just a little bigger than his father's bass boat.

Out here. In the *ocean*.

And at the helm was a man in a wool hat, a grimy jacket, waving at him.

What?

"Get your gear!"

Get his...? He stared at Fraser.

"It's Pavel! He picked me up."

At sea? What, did he have a...wait. "The EPRIB."

"Yeah. Dodge sent him our UINs. When I hit the water, it went off."

The unique identification number of their personal locater.

Not the usual SEAL gear, but thank you, Moose, who used it for all his rescue personnel.

Huh. Ned worked his way to shore, his heart thundering, grabbed his tac pack and his chute, then hauled it all back to the boat, shivering hard. He threw it in, and Fraser helped him aboard. Threw a blanket over him.

The man leaned away from the helm. "Pavel Dobrevich. Glad to meet you."

Yeah. "Glad to meet you too." That felt like an understatement.

He hunkered down then as the man threw down the throttle and sped alongshore, toward Petropavlovsk. Fraser sat beside him on the hard wooden seat, grinning.

Oh brother.

They sped by an uninhabited shoreline, just a few lights in the distance, which grew as they drew closer then rounded a peninsula into a massive bay. He wasn't sure what Pavel's plan might be, but he hoped it didn't include the KGB waiting for them on the dock.

Nope. Instead, they turned into a smaller bay and motored past a working shipyard. Then he slowed even more, passed a breakwater, and rounded yet another peninsula until he reached the end of the tiny bay. Pavel shut off his motor and glided them into a dock swathed in darkness.

He threw out a line to a figure standing at the end of the dock. A cigarette glowed in the darkness, then the person threw it away and reached for the line. The boat floated in.

Wan light, but as they got out, Pavel flicked on a flashlight, and the person helped him tie the knots. Ned and Fraser gathered their gear and climbed out. Ned glanced at Fraser and yep, he was shivering hard.

"Let's get you two inside," said a voice, and he looked to see a woman smiling at him—Pavel's dockhand.

"That would be great," Ned said.

Pavel came up. Put his arm around the woman. "My vife, Sasha."

Then he led them to a pickup truck parked in the dirt lot. They climbed in the back, trembling hard, and the man covered them with a burlap blanket and took off.

Don't sleep. And really, maybe the brutal journey helped, because every rut in the road found his hips, his spine.

"So, this is fun," Fraser said.

"We're alive."

"So far."

Right. He tried not to feel Fraser's words in his soul.

They finally stopped, and he heard a gate open, felt the truck lurch through, and then the gate closed.

The truck died with a cough, and the burlap came off.

They were in a small yard surrounded by a tall fence, a house sitting back from the drive. "You are safe now," said Pavel.

Yeah?

Ned hopped out of the truck, and the woman had walked up to the door, opened it. He followed her inside.

She turned on the light and shed her hat, her coat. She had dark hair, a sort of bowl cut, her body a little on the stout side. She turned to him. "Are you hungry?" She possessed good English. Interesting.

"I could eat," Ned said.

Fraser came in after him, and they both sat and took off their boots.

"You can change in the back bedroom," the man said. "Ve vill dry your clothes."

"Change into what?" Ned said.

"I vill get robes," said Sasha and headed to the back.

The place was small—an entryway, a kitchen off the main hallway, a family room with a large coal furnace pumping out heat in the middle, and two more rooms, bedrooms maybe, off the family room.

Small, but warm. Cozy. Artificial flowers were tacked to the wall in a string around the room, almost like a trellis, and a picture of a little boy, maybe age five, hung at an angle from a hook near the ceiling. Worn brown-patterned furniture, and a tall standing lamp, the light on, bathed the room.

Fraser turned to Pavel. "Thank you for saving us."

"Of course. Moose is my friend."

"I'm glad for that."

"And it is good you are here. Your vife is...she is in danger."

Ned didn't bother to correct him. "What do you mean?"

"She has made enemies at zhe prison," said Sasha as she came out carrying two thick woolen robes.

Ned took one, Fraser the other. Well, he wouldn't attack a ship in them, but they'd do for the night. "How do you know this?"

Pavel looked at his wife, back to them. "Because Sasha is a guard at ze prison. And she has a plan."

TODAY, SHE WOULD NOT DIE.

Shae stood under the sunshine of the day, her belly full of Kasha and tea, her hands wrapped in a pair of rags that were left by her door that morning, and decided that today, she would also believe in miracles.

Maybe it was the presence of Judah with her. He had ridden in the truck with her, and grabbed a shovel and handed it to her, and maybe it had been Vikka's, because the woman glared at him. He just met her gaze, then turned to Shae and gestured her toward the pit.

They had progressed maybe fifty feet as a group since they began digging four days ago. She couldn't imagine trying to dig a trench through Siberia. This stony ground fought their attack, much of it made of old lava, which took blasting to break through.

They dug the trench twenty feet deep and twenty feet wide to hold both the supports and the massive pipe, which they levered in with a crane, although Judah told her how they'd moved them by hand across much of Siberia.

"Where cranes fear to tread," he'd said as he dug. He was slow, methodical, and hummed as he worked.

Such a strange man. Unruffled by the guards who walked by them, armed, occasionally yelling. He seemed at peace in his world, although she knew firsthand that he was plotting an escape. And a violent one at that, probably.

They took a break at mid-morning, got hot tea from a barrel with a spicket. They had to share glasses—no paper here—and she stood in line for a glass, took it to where he sat. He had pulled his hat off, and she noticed how inside, it had been lined with plastic. He held it in his hand, like a busker, almost, waiting for alms as he drank his tea.

In the distance, the sky had turned pewter and the far away peaks white during the night. Smoke twined into the sky, and the wind carried the scent of smoke.

"It's going to storm," Judah said quietly. Someone walked by him, one of the men who packed the blasting caps for the lava banks, and he looked up, nodded at him.

Put his hat back on his head.

Oh, that was how it was done. So, Judah had a little team of rebels.

He looked over at her and smiled, his eyes seeming to twinkle.

"It reminds me of Montana. The air always felt almost thick with anticipation before a storm. I loved to watch the clouds roll over Glacier National Park."

"You grew up there?"

"Just after I was ten. Before that I lived in Dallas with my mother. But she was...she was an addict, and after a while, it got too hard for her to take care of me."

He raised an eyebrow. "Or too hard for you to take care of her?"

How did he do that? She lifted a shoulder. "I thought I'd end up in foster care, but my uncle Ian took me in. Told me that I'd never be afraid again, but of course that wasn't true."

Judah just looked at her.

"A few years later, I saw my boyfriend beaten to death by a man I trusted. And I was very afraid. I ran, and for five years started a new life, but...eventually I had to go back and face him."

Judah drew in a breath, looked beyond her, as if seeing something in his own past.

"Is that where you met Ned?"

Had she mentioned Ned? Probably. "No. I met him during a tornado, but yes, he was with me when I faced down the man who'd killed my boyfriend. He became a SEAL, and we've been dating for four years."

"That's a long time to date."

"He wanted to wait until he was in a stable place."

His mouth tweaked up at this.

"What?"

"Life is not safe. Not stable. You can't stop bad things from happening. You have to learn to live life in the middle of the danger. And trust that there's a bigger plan."

She drew up her legs. "Feels like danger follows me. I'm not sure it's a good idea for Ned to marry me."

He cocked his head, and it seemed he might be making to say something when Vikka walked past her. Turned.

And then, just like that, Vikka hit her. Right in the face, and the blow was so shocking, Shae simply jerked back, her hand over her mouth.

"Vikka!" Judah jumped up. Grabbed her just as her arm went back for another blow. "What are you—"

Then she rounded on him. But he blocked her hit and grabbed her arm. "Stop it!"

"Pomogee menye!" she shouted as one of the female guards ran over. She pulled Vikka away as Captain Boris charged in.

Judah held up his hands.

Boris sent Judah to his knees with a club to the gut.

Shae screamed. "No—leave him!"

Boris hit him again, this time across the head, and his hat fell off.

Oh! The blasting powder—if Boris found it.

She grabbed the hat even as Boris hit him again, this time across the ribs.

She shoved the cap into her jacket, then hit her knees. "Please, please, stop, please—"

Boris rounded on her and raised his club. She bent her hands over her head to protect herself and waited for a blow.

"Nyet! Nyet—" The female guard ran back—the pudgy one with the brown hair. Natasha. "D'vai."

Whatever that meant, but the woman pulled her up and away from Boris.

She shot a look at Judah, who lay on the ground, bleeding, his eyes closed.

What had just happened?

"Help him—someone needs to help him!"

Natasha shoved her into one of the passenger trucks. "Stay," she said, and Shae stilled, the woman's eyes hard in hers. "Don't move."

She nodded, but the moment she left, covered her face with her hands, hiccupping sobs. Then, scrambling to the back, she watched as a couple prisoners picked up Judah and half carried, half dragged him to another truck.

The infirmary truck.

A few minutes later, it drove away.

Judah.

She sat back. And never before had such a swell of darkness swept over her. It settled in her soul, gripped it and turned it to fire.

So, this was what hatred felt like.

She sat in the truck until lunch, when Natasha came to get her. Then they moved her to the lunch serving line. When Vikka came through, she met her eyes with a steel verve that she'd never felt before.

Vikka blinked at her, frowned.

Moved away, glancing back over her shoulder. And Shae wanted to say, that's right. You'd better watch your back.

But really, what was she going to do?

Something. Because Vikka wasn't going to terrorize her—or her friends—the rest of her life in gulag.

And the thought simply caught her up.

The. Rest of. Her *life*?

No. She was not staying here.

She was getting off this island, off that ship, and going home. Whatever it took.

She cleaned the dishes with the rest of the crew, then joined the line back to the boat, took the tug out to the ship, and climbed the stairs.

Judah was not at dinner. But neither did Vikka come by to harass her.

She ate her beet soup without incident and didn't care about wire worms in her potatoes. Or whatever that fat was floating on the surface.

She opted out of a shower and stayed in her container, on her bed. And when the doors closed, she got up, took out the blasting powder, and shoved it into her mattress.

Lay on her back and let tears drip into her ears.

The prisoners who'd showered returned to their cells, then the doors closed with a massive click, and all went dark.

She lay there, listening to her breathing. In. Out. Her heartbeat, pumping. Beat. Beat.

The rest. Of her. Life.

"Shae."

Her eyes shot open. She rolled off the bed and scooted under it. "Judah?"

"Oh, wow, I was so worried. Are you okay?"

His voice, saying her words. "Are you kidding me? I saw them put you in the infirmary truck. I thought you—you were really bleeding."

"Head wounds bleed a lot."

"And your ribs and—"

"Shh. I'm fine. Or will be. But look, I got this." He reached his hand through the hole, and she found it.

Into her palm he pressed a key card.

What?

"I pulled it off Boris when he hit me."

"You did *what*?"

"It was perfect. He came over, and there it was, in his shirt. Bam. Street tricks I learned too long ago."

Street tricks?

"I want you to take it and get out of here."

She stilled. "What?"

"Yeah. I did go to the infirmary today. And Eighty-One died a couple hours ago. He'll be in that black bag tomorrow morning when they drop it into the sea. You should be in it too."

What? "Get in the bag with a dead person?"

"He'll cushion your fall into the sea, and then just cut yourself out."

"With what?"

"This." He handed her a spoon, but chiseled at one end was a point.

"What is this, a shiv?"

"No. It's a tool. For getting out of a body bag."

"How long have you been planning this?"

"I've been here for a while. But the body bag trick—just since we got to the ship."

"Why don't I just go down the stairs?"

"They lower a metal gate in front of them at night. There's no way off."

Except in a body bag.

She let that sink in for a moment.

"Oh, by the way. I have your hat." She rolled out and opened the mattress, grabbed his hat and the powder, then shoved it through the hole.

Silence. Then, "Shae, you're fantastic."

She didn't know why his words found her bones, galvanized her. But, "I can't leave you, Judah."

A pause. "I'm going to pretend you didn't say that and

instead said, Wow, Judah, thanks for letting Boris hit you so you could grab this for me and I can get off this ship and go live my life."

Her eyes filled. "Yeah. That's what I meant. But...how do I get out of the container?"

"Every door comes with a keypad lock to the inner door. You just need to open it on the backside and put in the code."

"I don't—"

"The panel is already loose—previous twenty-three did exactly what I'm telling you. He took off the lock and put in the code."

"What's the code?"

"I don't know. He said he wrote it inside your container."

Wrote it? She didn't remember seeing—wait. The numbers, scratched into the wall. She rolled out and ran her hand over the wall, gently.

Found the etching and carefully traced her finger over it. Two. Three. Zero. Four.

She scooted back under the bed. "I found it. So, when I get the door open, what do I do?"

"Go to the elevator. Use the master code and get on it. Ride it up to level one of the superstructure. The infirmary is there. And next door is the morgue."

Oh, gross, so gross. But... "And then what?"

"And then you have a little faith. There'll be someone waiting."

Someone waiting?

"Judah—"

"That's all I know, Shae."

"I don't understand."

"You have about twenty minutes before the first guard does patrol. Go."

Go.

She closed her eyes. Took a breath. Then, "Thank you, Judah."

"Go be free, Shae. Be free."

She rolled out from under the bed and went to the door. Using the spoon, she took off the pad that covered the lock. The bolt was slid into place, but it allowed for her to reach in with the spoon and access the numbers. She simply had to depress the locking mechanism code to release the bolt.

Taking the spoon, she bent it back, the bowl side in, reached in and tried to visualize the pad. Two and three weren't hard, and she heard them click. Was zero at the bottom or the top? She guessed bottom and that, too, clicked, and then four, beside three.

The last mechanism clicked, and she then used her fingers to pull back the bolt.

It worked. She drew in a breath. But how long had it taken her? She didn't have time for a goodbye, but pushed the door open, then stepped out into the dark corridor and shut the door. Then she hunkered down and sprinted toward the elevator at the far end of the ship.

Swiped the master key across the keypad and called the elevator.

Oh, this could be a colossal mistake—what if the guards came down with it?

She stood to the side, in the shadows, just in case, but like a miracle—and she was believing in miracles today—it arrived empty.

Level two—or did he say one? Oh! One—one—

She chose level one, and the doors slid shut.

The elevator rattled through the cargo hold, up to the upper deck, then to level one.

Opened.

The hallway was dark, no light spilling out any of the windows. She stepped out and scampered down the hall, suddenly deeply grateful for her wool boots, like slippers on the metal floors.

She peered into windows and finally spotted the infirmary. A couple men lay in cots, but the room was dark.

And next door...she eased the big door open and slipped inside.

Eighty-One lay already in his bag, on a table, the form sending a shiver up her back. He wasn't a big man, but frankly, the idea of crawling inside with him...

Nope. Nope—

The rest. Of her. *Life.*

She swallowed hard. Okay, yes, just...do it.

Zipping it open, she saw that they'd wrapped the man in a sheet. She made a face and climbed on top of him. Oh, he was board hard and smelly and...

And the bag wouldn't zip over both of them.

So much for Judah's brilliant plan.

Except, what if it wasn't Eighty-One in the bag? She got off him, shook the willies off herself, and looked around.

The corpse room was nothing more than an old bunk room, and yes, probably an extension of the infirmary. But it still contained the bunks.

And compartments under the bunks for storage.

Probably Eighty-One could fit in one of those?

She grabbed the man by his shoulders and worked him off the edge of the gurney. He dropped onto the floor like a brick. Sorry. And hopefully no one heard her.

Then she dragged him over to the bottom bunk, pushing the bed up with her foot. Then she pushed him into the compartment, dragging him up, turning him. Oh, he barely fit, but she managed to get the bed down over him.

They'd find him in a few days, but by then, hopefully, she'd be long gone.

She straightened out the bag. Tried not to think of the corpse inside and then got in.

But as she was zipping it up, Judah's words came back to her. *He'll cushion your fall into the sea.*

Without the corpse, she'd hit the sea with a bone-crunching smack.

And what was the difference, then, between just jumping overboard or being dropped in a bag?

No. This was stupid.

She climbed out of the bag. Zipped it up.

Let them think Eighty-One was walking around as a ghost.

Then she slipped out of the infirmary and down the hall. Stopped when she heard voices, but they dissipated.

She took the stairs down to the main deck.

Oh, this ship was big. She looked down the deck to the forecastle, the cafeteria built above the cargo hold. It was dark, but that didn't mean Captain Boris and his men weren't having tea—or vodka—nearby.

Going to the edge, she looked down.

Fifty feet, maybe more, and the sea looked angry, the wind from the storm blowing in against the hull. The banging she heard.

So, not her heartbeat.

She could do this. For freedom she could do this.

Voices. She ducked back and spotted a couple guards with flashlights. But they didn't venture this direction, the prisoners being held nearer the front of the ship.

But it did give her a view to stairs, behind the superstructure and right in front of the getaway lifeboat, stuck at an angle as if wanting to leap off.

Yeah, get in line.

She scrambled toward the stairs and took them down.

Another level, with an outside walkway.

Closer to the water some twenty feet. From here, a thirty-foot survivable jump.

Cold, but survivable.

"Perestan!" The voice rose, and she looked over to see a guard heading toward her.

She threw her leg over, grabbed the rail.

"Perestan!"

Nope. She put her other leg over. Stood, holding the rail with both hands.

She could do this. She could—

"Stop!" The guard was running full-out now.

Nope. Not going back.

She looked down at the darkness, the thrashing waves, took a breath, and pushed off.

An arm snaked around her waist, catching her, slamming her against his chest. Another clamped over her mouth. And a voice found her ear.

"Gotcha."

SEVEN

A submarine could drive through the holes in Sasha's crazy swiss-cheese escape plan.

Ned had sat at the table, eating meat dumplings slathered in mayonnaise, dressed in the fat wool robe, finally warm, listening to Sasha's big idea...his gut tightening with every word.

Jump into the harbor in a cadaver bag? Fight her way out only to have him rescue her? With what? He didn't have any swim gear here—no dry suit for the extra cold water, no air tanks—and in the murky dark water, how exactly was he supposed to find her?

And what if she couldn't cut herself out? Those bags were sturdy, meant to transport the dead.

No, no, no.

Fraser had listened with a grim expression also, his fingers drumming on the table. If Ned looked as ridiculous as Fraser did, probably none of them should have any confidence in this mission. Fraser's bare legs stuck out from the bathrobe, his feet in a pair of slippers, his dark-blond hair rucked up, and he sported a four-day beard, his eyes a little reddened.

And neither of them had quite finished shivering.

"Zhere is no other vay off zhe ship," Sasha said, her English surprisingly good. "Zhey block off the stairway at night, and during the day, everyone is counted and recounted. zhey vould know in moments if she had escaped."

"But there are a million places to hide on a boat."

"Not zhis one. All zhe cargo compartments have been cleaned out. Zhe machinery room is locked, and zhe forecastle holds kitchen supplies. And it's also locked. Everything is locked."

"Then how is she supposed to get into the infirmary if everything is locked?"

"The key cards. There is one for the superstructure, and a different one for the kitchen, and yet another for engineering. But the master has access to everything, and only the captain has that."

She sat down then, holding her tea. "But I have a plan." And then she smiled.

Gold teeth, but something warm and even alive in her eyes. Pavel covered her hand with his, squeezed.

"Why are you helping us?" Fraser put down his own tea. "I know you're friends with Moose, but this is dangerous. If you cross the Petrov Bratva—"

"Zhey killed our son," Pavel said quietly. "It started vith a job vorking for ze gas company, vorking security, and zhen he vas promoted to vorking private security for Lukka Petrov, who oversees ze production here. Lukka is Arkady Petrov's son, and soon Alexi vas flying all over in his Gulfstream. And zen he got a look at vat Lukka vas into. Trafficking women, guns, drugs, and he vas sick. He zhought he vas a patriot; instead, he'd turned into a zhug. He tried to get out, and Lukka sent him to oversee a project last summer in Mongolia. Turns out it vas a biological weapon. Somehow Alexi got exposed, and he died of smallpox."

Fraser's jaw tightened. "I'm so sorry to hear that."

"Lukka Petrov is the son of the devil, and so is his gulag ship. He runs it like a Siberian work camp, starving the inmates, vorking zhem to zheir bone, and pitting zhem against each other for food," Sasha said. "Shae came in four days ago, scared to death. I vas zhere for her processing, and vhile she tried to be brave, I heard her crying in her container."

"Container?" Ned tried not to let the words dig into his soul. *Hang on, Shae. I'm on my way.*

"The prisoners are all kept in private tree-meter-by-two-meter containers equipped vith a cot and a blanket. It gets very cold in the ship at night." Sasha sighed. "And now Shae has an enemy. Vikka Morozova. She vas a former girlfriend of Lukka's and crossed him by getting involved vith one of his bodyguards. Instead of killing her, he sent her to Sevvostlag."

"What does she want with Shae?"

"I don't know. Perhaps it is because she is American. But zhis is good."

"How?" Ned had stopped trembling, finally. But now his body buzzed with every word Sasha spoke.

"We use Vikka to get zhe card away from Captain Orlov," Pavel said.

"You see, Shae has also made a friend. A man named Judah. He's a longtime prisoner—I'm not sure vhy he is zhere, really. But he has been looking out for her a bit, and I believe he vill help her escape by getting zhe card. I just need to make it happen." Sasha's face twisted. "Unfortunately, it might mean roughing up your vife a little."

Fraser's hand found Ned's shoulder, even as his breath tightened.

"How much is a little?"

"Every day, the prisoners are transported to a work site. Shae has already had an altercation vith Vikka, but tomorrow, Vikka vill bully her, and Judah vill step in. Ve vill make sure Captain Orlov is nearby—he particularly hates Judah—and Judah can grab his key card."

"Your man can do this?" Fraser said. "Without getting himself killed?"

Pavel smiled. "Judah has skills. It is not ze first time he has gotten someone off ze ship zis way, although, yes, it is not vithout danger."

Ned didn't like it. Not at all. Especially when Sasha went on to detail the rest—Shae's escape from her container, the break-in of the infirmary, the use of the cadaver bag—

"There are too many what-ifs," Ned said. "The biggest being—what if the impact to the water knocks her out, or kills her? What if she can't get out—or I can't get her out?" He'd gotten up then, carried his bowl to the kitchen sink. "No."

"Then what do you propose?" Fraser said as Sasha picked up his bowl.

He looked at Pavel and Fraser, then returned to his chair. "I propose we get aboard the ship, find her container, and spring her before she does something that is going to get her killed."

Sasha gave him a look then that turned his veins to ice. "I believe it is too late for zhat. Zhe plan is already in motion."

Already in motion.

Ned went to bed with those words burning through his head and slept not at all. It didn't help that he and Fraser shared a bed little bigger than a twin-size and his brother took up most of the room. Ned had finally gotten up before dawn and taken a chair across the room, staring down the day.

He'd just have to get on the ship before it all went down.

And that meant inserting himself into the story long before anyone realized it.

Which was how he and Fraser, garbed in the standard blue uniform as prisoner guards, after a raiding of their hosts' son's closet, fur hats, and gloves, along with Russian boots, joined the security forces at the Petrov gas pipeline project.

Only Fraser's hand on his arm—and yes, a big picture view of the op—kept him from jumping in when Vikka hit Shae.

He watched Shae go down, and every cell in his body ached.

Then, as expected, or hoped, or maybe planned, Judah jumped in, and in the chaos, Fraser and Ned slipped into the crowd, freshly shaved, wearing the fur caps of the guards, faces solemn, eyes down.

They picked up a bleeding and damaged Judah and brought him to the infirmary truck. Climbed inside, and as the truck carried them back to the gulag ship, Fraser tried to staunch his head wound.

"You're the Americans," Judah had whispered, so quietly Ned had to put his head down to the man's ear. "You're here for Shae?"

Ned nodded. "I'm her fiancé, Ned," he said, and Judah smiled.

"She said you would come for her."

That heated him through, filled his veins and kept him from jumping off the truck and running full sprint to Shae, being held captive in another truck.

Stay on the plan.

Judah then closed his eyes, and Ned suffered a moment of panic thinking the man had expired. But when he shook him, Judah opened one eye. Smiled. "At least someone cares."

Huh. Who was this guy? But he'd taken a beating to free Shae, and frankly, seemed the answer to Ned's prayers, so he kept his finger on the pulse at Judah's neck, jostling him awake now and then as they transported back to the boat, then onto the ship, and deposited him in the infirmary.

They walked out to questions by the medic, an air of aloofness to cover their lack of language, then headed upstairs to the weapons locker using the card Sasha had given them.

"Now I can breathe," Ned said, checking, then chambering the AK-47. He hung it combat-style across his chest. "Let's take a tour."

They used their card to stroll the ship, taking in the layout, starting with the superstructure, then down to the main deck, the stern of the boat, including what looked like a makeshift helicopter pad with containers bolted together and a metal platform created on top with stairs down to the deck.

They checked out the lifeboat and rescue boat. Ned pointed out a rusty hole in the bottom of the rescue boat.

They finally went down to the lower cargo hold. The odor of unwashed bodies, rust, and metal, the scent of desperation, could almost knock him over. And he'd lived with himself for six weeks in BUD/s, so that was saying something.

He walked by container twenty-three, the door open, and stood there.

Hang on, Shae.

"Let's take position," Fraser said, and he and Ned headed back to the deck and climbed up to the bow, hid in plain sight. Front sentries, just minding their own business.

He didn't like being this exposed, but according to Sasha, no one would notice them up here, and yet, if they did, their attention would wander right past. Then they waited as the sun set over the water.

"How bad do you think she was hurt?" Ned finally said, quietly.

"The better question is...did you see the look on her face when Vikka hit her friend? For a second, I thought she'd jump her."

He'd only seen her get on the ground, pick up Judah's hat—as if that mattered—then plead for his life. If Ned didn't know her better, he might be jealous.

But he did know her.

"Hopefully she doesn't do something stupid."

"What, like try and escape?" Fraser looked at him. "We'll get to her first."

As the sun sank in the west, casting a fiery glow over the deep platinum sky, Ned spotted the boat returning. Then he watched from his sentry position as the prisoners returned. Shae walked in line, looking unhurt, her face solemn, no blood or cuts, and that settled his gut a little.

Then they'd eaten, a full fifteen minutes for dinner, and assembled on the deck as the last of the sunlight winked out.

"The cargo hold must be pitch black."

Fraser nodded, patted his pocket where he'd detached his NVG scope and stored it. He also carried, along with Ned, his

KA-BAR, his Sig, and the multi-tool, along with zip ties and a roll of tape—just a few accessories they'd brought to the party.

They waited thirty minutes until they spotted Sasha on deck. She disembarked with a handful of other guards, and then the stairs were blocked with a tall metal plate.

And all went quiet.

"Let's go."

They descended the bow stairs onto the main deck, then headed over to the cargo hold access, unscrewed it, and opened a hatch with a ladder that led into the bow section of the hold.

"Ready?"

"Go," said Fraser, and Ned hooked his feet on either side of the ladder and slid down. He landed on the floor with a quiet thump, then backed away as Fraser landed beside him.

No movement in the darkness. He moved toward a doorway that led to the cargo hold, one unsecured by the card—clearly, not a passage often used—and opened it. It groaned on its hinges, and he stopped.

"The waves are hitting the boat," Fraser said, and indeed, down here, the thunder of the surf against the hull made it reverberate.

He timed the door with the thunder, masking it as he urged it open, and finally slipped through.

Then he pulled out his night vision scope. Put it to his eye, closed the other one and got a lay of the area. He'd memorized the layout—four rows of containers, two passageways, and hers was near the end of the first row.

He headed over to her container. Peered through the bars with his scope.

Her bed was empty. He scanned the container, but nowhere really for her to hide.

He looked at Fraser and shook his head.

Fraser used his hand to indicate the stairs, and back they went, into the compartment.

"She's gone," Ned whispered. "Where now? The infirmary?"

Fraser nodded.

Ned scampered up the ladder, back to the deck. The wind had started to really blow, cutting through his jacket.

No way she'd survive going into the water. Especially in a cadaver bag.

Fraser joined him and they closed the hatch.

"Patrols on both sides of the ship," Fraser said, looking through his scope. "And guards on the superstructure."

"How do we get to the infirmary?"

"Carefully."

Right.

"On me," Fraser said and got up, headed toward the mess hall. The structure had been added to the deck long after the ship had come to port—no working cargo ship would have their mess area located on deck. But given the condition of the ship, while it might be afloat, it certainly wasn't seaworthy. They clung to the darkness and worked their way past the hall to the massive broken crane that sat in the center of the boat.

Another fifty meters to the superstructure, and nothing between them but open space.

And a handful of guards. One of them perched inconveniently in front of the elevator.

"There are stairs in the aft of the boat. We go there," Fraser said. "We'll leapfrog. Ready?"

Ned pocketed his night scope and maneuvered the Russian gun to his eye. "Go."

Fraser sprinted toward the rail and took cover near a windlass.

Then Ned watched as Fraser grabbed a guard and pulled him into a choke hold. The man was down in a moment, and Fraser rolled him over, fumbled a little with the zip tie, but got it on and then motioned for Ned.

Not bad for a guy in a cast. But Fraser probably needed to ease up on the hand-to-hand combat there, bro.

Now, Ned followed his brother and took position at the windlass. Fraser moved up to a bolt for a mooring line. Crouched there while waiting for another guard, then brought him to the deck, same maneuver.

So far, no lives lost.

Ned chased him up the deck of the ship, leaving behind a trail of guards, zip-tied and gagged. It might slow them down.

They reached the superstructure and took cover under the walkway leading to the stern. Here, more windlasses and bolts and lines offered protection, and they moved quickly. Apparently, security on board didn't expect an attack on the ship—so they went unharassed.

"Stairs," said Ned, and Fraser scooted toward them, quickly ascending.

Ned followed, and then they were on the first level.

No card reader here—Ned simply opened the door and found himself in the inner hallways. He spotted a map, memorized the route, and in moments, they reached the infirmary.

Dark, abandoned—so much for the doctor on staff. Two patients, both of them locked to their beds. Neither of them was Judah.

Fraser hissed, then motioned, and Ned headed for another door and followed Fraser in.

The cadaver cover sat on a gurney. Empty. *What?*

"She didn't make it."

"Do we go back to the cargo bay?" Fraser said.

Ned stared at the cover. There was no way he'd get in that thing—even if he did think it might get him off the ship. The claustrophobia of it, the helplessness...nope.

And he wasn't the only one who didn't like being helpless.

"If it were me, and I was free, I'd get off this ship any way, any how."

Fraser looked at him. "Take your chances with the sea?"

Ned was out the door and headed to the rail. He took the stairs down to the deck the way he'd come.

They were dockside, away from the ocean side. But here, too, there was boat clutter and harbor debris.

But if she jumped on the other side, the waves would bash her against the ship.

"This is a bad idea."

"She's not on this side," Fraser said, using his scope now to scan the port side. "Let's try starboard."

They crossed over the back of the ship, near the lifeboat and broken rescue boat, and Fraser scanned the rail. "No joy."

A shout lifted, echoing into the night. Russian.

Fraser pointed toward the stairs, and Ned slid down them, picked up his gun.

A guard ran full speed at a figure standing at the rail.

Shae!

He took off. *Do not go over. Do not—*

She put her leg over. The guard yelled at her again.

Oh, that stubborn woman put other leg over. Held on.

"Stop!" Not his voice, but he wanted to shout it.

Stop, Shae!

Below, the waves thundered against the hull.

He leaped at her just as she pushed off.

His arm grabbed her, slammed her hard against the rail, himself. Without thinking, he clamped his hand over her mouth. "Gotcha."

Behind him, Fraser met the guard head-on.

Ned heard the scuffle behind him but didn't look as he pulled Shae over the rail, set her down.

She rounded on him, her fist cocked. He grabbed her wrist—

"It's me. It's me—"

It took a full second, the slam of one heartbeat, an indrawn breath and then— "Ned?"

Who else did she expect?

And then she launched herself at him, her arms around his neck, her legs wrapped around him, shaking so hard he staggered back against the wall.

Then he just held her too.

Shae. Smelly, grimy, crying, nearly cutting off his air supply, but *Shae*.

He wanted to cry too.

"It's okay, honey. I'm here. I'm right here."

"We have company," Fraser said. "Let's go." He grabbed Shae and pulled her off Ned.

"Honey, we gotta run."

She stared at Fraser, then back at Ned, wide-eyed.

Ned took her hand. "C'mon."

And this was where his big exfil plan had Fraser's eyes widening. Because, yeah, it might not be much different than taking a header off the side of the boat.

But this way, they might not freeze to death.

Fraser turned and cuffed one of the guards, and Ned heard his jaw break as he went down. Then, "Go—go!"

"Stay behind me!"

She nodded, and he fixed her hand onto his jacket pocket. "Don't let go."

Then he took off, Shae in step with him, down the gangway, toward the stern of the ship. They rounded the back, toward the dockside, and there, below, he spotted Pavel's little fishing boat.

He pulled out a flashlight and turned it on. Pointed it down, across the water.

Pavel's boat came to life.

"Now what?" Shae said. "Jump?"

"What is with you and jumping? This is five stories up. You'll break your legs."

Fraser came running up. "Just where she said she'd leave it." He carried a fraying but still intact mooring line from their fishing boat.

He looped it around a bolt, tied it off, then Ned picked it up. He wrapped the rope around his back, then down between his leg, then up again in his other hand.

"I'm going to step over the side, and then I want you to climb aboard."

Shouting, and somewhere in the bow of the boat, a light went on. Perfect.

Fraser stood guard near the bolt.

"Climb aboard what?"

But he didn't wait to explain. He simply went over the side, his feet balanced on the hull.

"Grab her, bro."

Fraser swooped her up, then leaned over and set her down, right on his chest, her legs on either side of his waist.

"Hold on to me."

Her wide eyes affixed to his, terror in them.

"Maybe close your eyes too." He was already moving down the side of the boat, his entire body tensed, ignoring the burn of the rope around his waist, on his thigh. He quick-walked down, grunting, ignoring the shots firing on deck.

His feed hand slipped once, and Shae screamed, but he caught himself, let out enough rope to reposition his hand.

Pavel caught him and pulled him into the boat.

A few shots hit the water.

"Go!"

Fraser was over the side, and Ned picked up his gun. "Get down, Shae!" He returned fire, and in a moment, the attack ceased.

Fraser hit the boat, Ned pulled him in, and then they were lying in the belly as Pavel hit it. The boat cut through the dark water, shots in its wake but, in the darkness, futile.

And then they were out in the bay, racing through the darkness, the cold spray hitting them.

Ned rolled over, found his feet and searched for Shae.

She was huddled in the back of the boat, her knees up to her chest, her arms wrapped around her legs.

"Shae."

He stumbled over to her, sat down next to her, and pulled her into his arms.

"I've got you, babe. I've got you."

She simply put her head into his chest, held on, and wept.

THREE DAYS FROM THE STUPIDEST THING SHE'D EVER done, and Iris still couldn't shake it from her brain.

See, didn't want to be a spy, never wanted to be a spy, and what was she doing pretending to be a spy? She probably needed to hit her knees and thank Jesus that she hadn't done something *really* stupid and gotten herself killed.

But she'd lived, and it was over, and diving into some retail therapy had seemed the only answer when she'd gotten off the plane with Hudson Bly.

Her *babysitter.*

Sheesh.

"It's just up here, a few blocks down, then take a right." She directed her Uber driver in Italian as he drove north to Lake Como.

The sun hung low over the mountains rising across the lake, the fiery descent glowing upon the water. A glorious place to live.

Even if it might be a little lonely.

But next time she thought about spicing up her life, it wouldn't be by becoming some idiot for a fake-CIA.

How desperate could she be? She just wanted to keel over with the horror of it all.

"What was that, honey?"

"Sorry, Mom, I'm listening. I just had to direct the driver." She wore an ear bud, held on to her smartphone, and listened to her mother talk about the tasting of their recently uncorked 2019 La Crescent Gold.

"Your dad is so excited about this varietal. It has notes of stone fruit and even pineapple, which is crazy. He's sent bottles away to some reviewers...Iris, are you okay? You sound...quiet."

She sighed and imagined her mother, Jenny, her blonde hair

pulled back in a headband, wearing a pair of jeans and a sweatshirt, sitting in their family room back at their century-old farmhouse in Minnesota. Plush leather furniture, a stone hearth—probably with a fire going—the fields full of empty Marquette and Frontenac cold-weather grape vines.

"I'm fine, Mom. I spent the last three days shopping in Milan."

"Oh, my, you sound like it's just another day at the mall. Milan. Was it amazing?"

Amazing. And expensive. She had done some serious damage to her savings. But frankly, she'd just had to disappear, and she was a little tired of her zebra wardrobe.

"Yes. I shopped at the Via Monte Napoleone." Alone. "And had coffee at Corso Vittorio Emanuele II." Alone. "Had king crab at Langosteria and spaghettoni alla tamarro at Dongiò."

All, of course, alone.

"No pizza?"

Iris laughed. "Right. I did have an artichoke and olive pizza in my hotel room." Watching the Vienna Vikings and Milano exhibition match. And yelling at a couple missed penalties.

"Sounds exotic," her mother said. "I made some stew for Pippa and Princess Imani."

"Anything you put with the word *princess* makes your life infinitely more exciting than mine."

Her mother laughed. Iris sighed.

"What is it, honey?"

"I don't know. Sometimes I wonder if maybe I should have stuck it out. You know, in the NCAA. Then maybe tried to ref for the NFL."

"Iris. You made a wise choice at the time. But you know, you can come home anytime."

"Yeah. I know. I just..."

"You need a boyfriend."

Iris laughed. "Mom. The last thing I need is a boyfriend."

Silence on the other end of the line.

"What?"

"I know that Rocky really hurt you—"

"I don't want to talk about it, Mom."

"Not every football player is a jerk."

She made a sound to that. So far...and maybe, okay, she wouldn't include Hudson in that category.

Or at least, the Hudson that seemed to morph into a responsible, albeit annoying, babysitter. But before that—

"No, Mom. No football players for me, European or otherwise. I'm happily single. It's just...hard to meet people when I travel so much."

"I get that. I'm still feeling jet-lagged after our trip to France."

The driver had slowed as he came down her street, cobblestones flanked on either side by ocher-yellow and burnt-pink or orange stucco homes, most with Juliet balconies, many with bicycles parked outside. Planters with lemon trees or geraniums cordoned off the sidewalk, and the bistro near her house had attached their plastic tenting, adding warmth to the chilly evening.

"Mom, it's been at least two weeks, and you're still tired?"

"I'm fine, honey. Although, I am a little worried about your brothers. Ned and Fraser left in such a hurry about a week ago—I know Fraser is retired and Ned is on leave, but I got the sense that they were about to deploy on some secret op." She finished with a chuckle, but Iris only drew in a breath.

So, the boys had left their mother—and maybe their father—out of the loop. Interesting.

But the boys had always been a little protective of their mother.

And her.

Her mouth tightened, thinking of Fraser's words to Hud. *Take her home.*

Poor man hadn't even been given a choice. Even when she protested.

But that was Fraser. Bossy. Made her feel invisible most of the time.

"I know that Jonas sometimes stops by, so if you happen to see the boys, can you have them call home? I don't like to bother them, but..." She sighed.

"I'm sure they're fine, Mom," she said, hating that she'd suddenly taken sides with the boys. The driver pulled up outside her apartment block. Hers sat on the end, a two-story townhome with an inner gated courtyard and a view of the lake. She'd renovated it herself, adding an Italian tiled bathroom and finishing the attic.

"When is your next game?"

"Not for a week. I'm flying to Spain for a week of practices with the Barcelona Dragons. Then they play the Vienna Vikings."

And oh goody, she'd see Hudson.

Given the way she'd left him, he wasn't likely to be in a great hurry to see her again either.

She might have been a little nicer to him, given that he'd taken a plane with her all the way to Milan and might have even called them a cab and driven her all the way home if she hadn't intervened.

I can make it home on my own. My flat is an hour from here. What are you going to do, bring me home, order a pizza, tuck me in bed, and make it back by your flight?

And even after that, he'd stood there, considering her for a long, way too long, moment. A moment where she had sort of stopped and considered it also.

Because he had been about to attack her brother, thinking he was an evil spy sent there to hurt her. And no one, ever, had gone to the mattresses with one of her brothers over her. It had sparked something inside that she hadn't realized was there.

Hudson, in that moment, had made her feel *not* invisible.

And it helped that he was, in a word, gorgeous, in a made-for-action sort of way. Shorter dark-blond hair, a body made of steel, and when he'd looked at her at the airport with those gray-blue eyes, she'd seen in them something of a storm, as if he warred with himself.

Again, over her.

Oh brother. Maybe her mother was right.

Nope. Not going there again. "I gotta run, Mom. I'm home. But I promise—if I talk to the boys, I'll have them call."

"Take care of yourself, Iris. I love you."

"Love you too." She hung up, then gathered her bags and got out. The driver popped the trunk, and she grabbed her backpack and carry-on.

"Need help, ma'am?" The driver was a younger man, Italian, with dark hair, well-dressed. Very Milano.

"No, thank you," she said, strapping the bags over her carry-on handle before putting on the backpack. She tipped him, then pocketed her phone, then schlepped her bag up to her gate entrance. She could enter the front door, but it opened on the street level, a tiny alcove with just a place to hang her coat and store her shoes before a steep flight of stairs led to the main level.

Instead, she unlocked the wrought iron gate that led to her tiny cobblestone garden. A table with chairs, a few planters with geraniums spilling out in desperate need of pruning.

She used her key and opened the back door and hung her keys on the rack near the door. In the semidarkness, she set her bags on the small island in the kitchen. Then she headed toward the stairs.

Nearly tripped on a book in the middle of her floor.

What? Walking over to the wall, she flicked on the light.

Stilled.

She'd been robbed. Or maybe not, because at first glance, it seemed she had the big stuff—the flat-screen television, the Bose stereo system.

But her bookcase had been emptied, most of her collection on the floor. And the cushions were off her sofa.

She froze, listening. Nothing but the thundering of her heartbeat. Still, she grabbed her Japanese chef's knife out of the drawer. Swallowed.

Then she crept upstairs.

Her upper floors weren't big—a master and guest room-slash-office on the second floor, and another guest room in the attic.

The stairs creaked, and she stopped.

No intake of breath, no creaking of the floorboards. She held her knife up, took another step—silent—and kept going.

She reached the landing—it overlooked the open room below—then eased her way to her bedroom.

The mattress was off the frame, the sheets torn from the bed, and the contents of her closet lay on the floor—shoes, dresses, pants, belts, jackets. The drawer to her dresser hung open, also emptied.

Her gut knotted at the destruction. Even her nightstand drawer had been pulled out, upended, her toiletries on the bare mattress.

No, not a robbery either, because her jewelry case lay open, pawed through, the jewelry there, although not fancy, still in puddles on her dresser top.

She closed the door and kept going.

The guest room was in the same condition, mattress tossed, the bedclothes on the floor, only now the pillows spilled out foam pieces, stabbed and empty.

Now a heat added to the knot. For the love—why her pillows? From America, no less.

Jerk. Whatever the thief had wanted, it hadn't been her Anatoly Metlan original oil of Portofino that hung over the bed, so that was good.

She took a breath, then turned and headed up the stairs to the attic.

She'd heard from Jonas that he and Fraser had stayed here a month or so ago while Fraser had been on his runabout through Europe looking for Princess Imani. She'd missed him by a day or two.

The room stood untouched, the single beds still covered with white duvets, pillows. Nothing of value here except the view, really.

She stood at the window as the last of the sun departed the sky. The moon was already rising, its beam upon the dark waters of Lake Como. Then she pulled her phone from her pocket.

"Don't do it."

She stilled, then rounded, the blade up.

The outline stood in the door, nearly filling the frame. Huge, with wide shoulders and a voice that she recognized.

Maybe.

"Stay where you are."

He held up his hands. "Calm down."

"Calm down? You're in my house. I'm calling 9-1-1—"

"I think in Italy it's 1-1-2."

Jerk!

"Not that I call emergency services that often, but our coach makes us learn the numbers for every country."

And if she'd had any doubt, his sentence confirmed it.

"What are you doing here, Hudson?"

He flicked on the light.

She blinked against the brightness.

Yep, Hudson Bly stood in the doorframe, big, bold, and unwelcome. He pointed at her chef's knife. "Put down the knife and I'll tell you."

"Ha. You'll tell me now."

"What are you going to do, carve me up for steak?"

"I might."

"I'm all muscle. I wouldn't taste good." He smiled then, a poster boy for the Vienna Vikings.

Oh, the jerk!

"Yeah, well, the village dogs don't care."

His smile dimmed a little.

But really, yeah, what was she going to do? She lowered the knife. And then— "Wait. Were you the one who tossed my house?"

"Tossed? What is this, *CSI*?"

"*Law and Order*, thank you, and you didn't answer the question."

"No, I didn't toss your place. But I did get here earlier and see the mess. Thought you were just a really bad housekeeper."

"Now you can leave." She stabbed the knife at him.

"Yeah, nope, sorry." He still held up his hands, but now stepped into the room, all sense of a grin gone. "Where have you been?"

"Where have I—that's none of your business!"

"I think it's a little of my business. You were supposed to go home. And yet, I see shopping bags from Milan downstairs." He lowered his hands. "Unless you call Giorgio Armani home now."

"Funny." But she lowered the knife. "I just needed some... shopping therapy."

"For three days?"

"I ate too!"

He ran a hand behind his neck, blew out breath.

"Why? What's going on—wait. Is it something with Tate? I thought Ziggy got him to the hospital in time."

"No, he's fine."

Oh, and she shouldn't ask. She was done with this craziness— Aw, "You talked to Ziggy?"

"Yeah, she showed up inside my house in Vienna."

"It's a trend, I see."

"Your door was open."

"Which door? I came in the sliding door."

"The one on your street?"

Oh. She hadn't even checked. A tremble started at her core. "There could have been someone in here, waiting for you."

"No, waiting for *you*. But there wasn't, because I came in and checked the place."

A beat, and then, "What *are* you doing here, Hud?"

And suddenly it occurred to her that maybe... "Did you come here to *protect* me?"

He made a sound, deep inside his chest, as if he didn't want to agree but couldn't help himself. "Ziggy thinks you're in trouble."

She stared at him, at the way his mouth tightened as if not wanting the words to spill out.

"Okay, just tell me already. What kind of trouble?"

He suddenly looked at her, his eyes widened, then he took two steps and pulled her away from the window. She shook out of his grip.

"What was that for?"

"I'm not great at this game—but you shouldn't stand in front of open windows."

"Why not—I'll get sick? A little breeze—"

"You'll get shot."

She had nothing. Just...nothing.

"Sorry. That came out worse than I meant, or...I dunno. Maybe not." He met her gaze. "According to Ziggy, there's a hit out on you."

"A hit? Like—"

"Someone wants you dead. And is hoping to hire someone to do it."

She just stared at him.

Then, outside, a bang sounded.

And just like that, Hudson grabbed her, pulled her to himself, turned and shoved her against the wall.

Braced his arms around her.

Okay, yes, her heart pounded against her chest, but really— "It's a *car*, Hudson."

"Oh." He stared down at her.

She hadn't quite realized how big he was. Just...enormous. And for a second, she felt very, very safe.

And very, very noticed.

No, no... She ducked under his arm and headed out the door and down the stairs, away from the attic window and into the relative safely of her hallway. But then again, she had windows along one entire side of her house, so it wouldn't be hard for a sniper to find her.

"Keep the lights off," she said as Hud came out of the room behind her.

"No duh," Hudson said. He'd already turned off the attic lights, and now followed her down the stairs.

She stopped in the hallway, clutching the knife to herself.

Hudson halted beside her.

She looked up at him. "So, wait. Ziggy told you that someone might be trying to kill me, so you jumped on a plane to find me?"

"I had an exhibition in Milan last night. Thought I'd stop by..." He shrugged.

She narrowed her eyes at him. "What, are we partners now?"

"No. Calm down there, Ref," he said. "I just wanted to make sure you were okay. After all, you made me a promise to get home safely."

"I did not promise—"

"Fine. I made a promise to your brothers."

Her mouth tightened. "Okay, well, home safe."

He gave a chuckle from deep inside. Sounded more like a train rumble. "Hardly. Have you seen this place? Someone was looking for something. Any idea *what*?"

"Actually, not a clue."

He drew in a long breath. "Okay then. Let's go."

"Let's—no. I'm not going anywhere."

He had stopped at the top of the landing. "What—hey. My job is to keep you safe—"

"Since *when*?"

"Since Paris, when...your brother asked me to...well, he implied that I was supposed to take care of you."

She blinked at him.

He held up a hand. "Okay, fine. I do remember the part where you said you could take care of yourself, and yes, you probably can, but—look at this place. You can't possibly think you're safe."

Shoot, he made sense. Ridiculous, perfect sense.

"Listen. I have a place in Greece. Just a little time-share, but maybe we just go there, lay low for a few days while Ziggy tracks down the source of this hit on you. And then figures out a way to get it lifted."

She narrowed her eyes at him.

"It's on the beach. I have room service and a cook."

Of course he did.

"And two bedrooms, and I promise to pretend I don't know you."

"Good, because if we're seen together, we'll probably get reprimanded by ELF."

"Probably."

"We're just headed to the same place."

"Not together. But on my boat."

"Coincidentally."

"I don't even know you. Who are you?"

She smiled. "Fine. My bags are in the kitchen. I want to grab a couple things."

"Now, or after a shooter takes you out while you're trying on Gucci?"

She glared at him.

"Just checking. Wasn't sure how important those shoes were."

"Let's go. And, very important."

But she followed him down the stairs, grabbed her bags—and yes, grabbed the Gucci and Armani bags, thank you—then followed him out the back door.

Hoping, again, she wasn't doing something stupid.

STOP SHAKING.

She was fine. Just fine.

She hadn't gone over the side of the ship into frigid, Titanic waters, hadn't been shot while rappelling down the side of a ship,

146

and most of all, hadn't betrayed her terror—at least much—when Ned introduced her to the woman who'd masterminded her escape.

Natasha, aka Sasha, who'd smiled at her, not quite an apology for treating her like a zoo animal. But with Ned's arm around her, Shae had managed to keep a lid on the roiling emotions and thank her.

All this while she stood in the small but warm home, the wind starting to howl outside as a storm began to sweep over the ocean.

She wouldn't have survived going over the side. That reality had hit her bones and turned them brittle as she and Ned and Fraser—wow, she was a little humbled, but not at all surprised that he'd showed up to rescue her too—had escaped in the tiny fishing boat. The spray from the waves had hit her face like pellets and it'd only made her hold onto Ned more.

She might never let go.

How had he found her? The thought just kept circling her mind as she finally released him and then followed Sasha to a real bathroom, with a real shower and a fresh towel and a purple velour leisure suit and warm socks.

Sasha had stood at the door, something of sadness on her face. "I am sorry you suffered."

Then she'd closed the door, and Shae had just stood there, letting the steam rise around her.

She was sorry she suffered? What about letting Vikka hit her? Her cheekbone still burned with the punch.

Except, Ned had sort of filled her in, how the master plan had been to get the key card, and by the time she got out of the shower, having washed her hair twice, scrubbed herself nearly raw, she'd decided that maybe she needed to forgive.

In twenty-four hours, she'd be home, hopefully, this entire horror behind her, and then what? She'd lie in bed at night harboring fury?

Nope. She'd been down that road. Holding on to anger was

like eating poison and expecting the other person to get sick. Or at least she'd heard that somewhere.

So, she put on the velour jumpsuit, zipped it up, wadded the prison clothes into a ball, and shoved them into the garbage.

Then she came out of the bathroom, her hair wet, wearing wool socks, the main room warm with the heat of the coal furnace. The house was small but cozy, with bare rugs on the floor, worn sofas, and a faux trellis of flowers along the wall. Reminded her a little of one of her childhood homes, probably a boyfriend her mother moved in with.

The smell of roasting meat, maybe soup, filtered from the kitchen. Outside, the wind howled, banging against the windows.

Oh, it would get so cold tonight on the ship. That thought took her, held her captive.

Ned got up from the sofa. "Babe, you feeling a little better now?"

Her gaze went to him and, oh, Ned had never looked so handsome. Dark hair, those blue eyes, and he'd filled out over the years, turned from a boy to a man with wide shoulders, a thick chest, powerful body.

Now he pulled her against himself, holding on, his hands cupping her shoulders, the move so secure she just sank into his warmth.

What she wanted was to be alone with him. To tell him she was sorry for being so...well, for being so easily offended. And independent. And for giving him back his ring—oh!

"Ned, do you still have the ring?" She lifted her head, looked up at him.

He blinked at her. "Yeah. It's in my gear, back at Air One in Alaska. Of course I have it."

Her eyes filled.

"So maybe we'll give you guys some space," Fraser said and got up from an armchair. Pavel followed him into the kitchen.

Ned held her face in his hands. Met her eyes. "I am so sorry—"

"Stop."

His eyes widened.

"This is not on you." She drew in a breath. "I was so stupid. So...stupid."

"Shae."

"No." She broke away from him, walking over to the massive furnace. Held her hands over it. "I should have known that Dana was bad. I just didn't want to believe it. I am so...stupid."

She closed her eyes, and Ned's arms went around her, his chest to her back. He pressed a kiss to her neck. "No, you're not. You can't live your life constantly suspicious of others."

She turned in his arms, put hers up around his neck. "It's more than that. I...I was almost proud of myself that I didn't need you. That I didn't pressure you to marry me. That we were this team of independent people...but the truth is, I've always been a little afraid that if I married you, then...well, then when something happened, my life would be in shambles."

"Nothing it going to—"

She put her hand over his mouth. "My life is already in shambles without you."

His gaze found hers, fixed on it, so much in his eyes she didn't know how to read it all.

He kissed her. Simply lowered his mouth to hers and took her in. Hungry, as if he'd been holding back, and he wasn't particularly gentle either—not with so much urgency and desperation in his touch. He picked her up, and she put her legs around his waist, and he stood there, his legs braced, simply devouring her.

And she devoured him back, her arms tight around his neck, holding on with everything inside her, tasting him, smelling the night and the sea on him, the power and danger that was her man.

The man who'd followed her to Siberia to save her.

She lifted her head and met his eyes, and his were wet. "You really scared me," he whispered.

Oh, Ned. "I knew you'd find me." Or at least, she'd hoped it with everything inside her.

"Always," he said, his voice a little broken.

Then he kissed her again, this time slower, taking his time, the reality sinking in.

She'd survived. They'd both survived.

He held onto her and walked her over to the sofa and sat down, settling her on his lap, and she held his face, deepening her kiss.

Yes, she wanted to marry this man. Right here, right now.

Go home with him, build a life with him, have his children.

Live happily ever after.

She leaned back and smiled.

"What?" he said, resting his head back on the sofa.

"Gotcha," she said softly.

He grinned. "Didn't know what else to say."

She laughed, and then he pulled her close, holding her as she wrapped her arms around his neck and held him back. "Never let go."

"Never leave me."

"Deal." She turned her face to his neck, rested her lips there. Closed her eyes.

"I hate to interrupt, but anybody hungry?"

Ned's entire body sighed, and she pulled away, looked over at Fraser. "Please tell me it's not kasha, or wormy potatoes, or cold noodles."

"How does borscht sound?"

"Whatever that is, as long as it matches that smell, I'm in." She pushed off Ned but took his hand as he got up.

The soup was a deep red, with fresh bread piled in the middle of the table, and she wanted to weep with the smell, the fresh dill, the homemade mayonnaise, the hot tea.

She sat down on a bench, Ned beside her, and then, to her shock, Pavel took Sasha's hand.

"Grace?"

Ned took her hand, and she took Fraser's. He took Sasha's and bowed his head.

Okay. Sure.

"Lord, zhank you for safety tonight. For a varm home. For soup and bread. For family, khere and across zhe ocean. For never leaving us, even in ze darkest moments. You are Emmanuel, and ve are grateful. Amin."

Pavel looked up, grinned. "I still have my English."

"Where did you learn it?" Fraser said as he reached for a piece of bread. Shae lifted her spoon. Hearty chunks of meat, chunks of potatoes and beets, carrots and onions. Pavel dolloped mayonnaise on his soup.

"I met a missionary, years ago, vhen he landed here. The first flight to Russia from Alaska in a small plane. His name vas Dwayne and he invited me to fly vith him. I was already pilot for Aeroflot, but I vanted to fly small planes in Alaska. I got visa and spent one summer in Copper Mountain, flying. He showed me Jesus and I became believer. And so did Sasha. And I zhink..." He reached out and took Sasha's hand. "Alexi." His mouth closed, and she swallowed.

Clearly, she'd missed something.

But the soup was filling all the nooks and crannies of her body, and she couldn't stop eating. Ned seemed to enjoy it too, given the sounds emitting from him.

"Still eats like a grizzly bear," said Fraser.

Sasha laughed. "My Alexi vould do the same."

Ned turned to her, his voice low. "Their son died working for Lukka Petrov and their organization."

Shae looked over at Sasha. "I am so sorry."

Sasha nodded. "Is a terrible mafia. Much vorse zhan Bratva. They steal vomen—and sell zhem on ze black market." She looked at Ned. "It is good you found her, because I hear Lukka make deal for her."

Beside her, the men stilled, and even Shae put down her spoon. "They were going to sell me?"

"Da. And Vikka too. And a couple other vomen—zhe young ones."

She might be ill.

"Shae?"

"I'm okay. I just..." She closed her eyes.

Ned's hand covered hers. "It's the number one reason women go missing."

Except. She opened her eyes. "I don't think that's why Dana took me. At least, not the initial reason."

"What do you mean?" Fraser said.

"I was held first at a compound, a big house in a forest. I think it might have been owned by the Petrovs—it used to be a palace, maybe. Anyway, the elder Petrov—"

"Arkady," Pavel said. "General Arkady."

Yes, that felt right, given the way he'd held himself. "He had all the contents of my backpack on the table out, including my very expensive five-thousand-dollar camera, the one I use for my job, and after he questioned me—which wasn't much—he told me they already had everything they needed. And that's when Lukka suggested sending me to the gulag ship."

"Probably to secure a deal for you."

"But what did they get from kidnapping me that was everything they needed? It's not like I was carrying national secrets. I mean, Ned tells me nothing of his missions. Not even where he goes."

"He can't," Fraser said.

"I know. And probably this very reason is why. But they got what they wanted, so...what was that?"

"Did they take your phone?"

"Yes. But again, nothing important was on it. My banking app, social media, a few phone numbers, some photos. And even those aren't much. I use my camera for anything I really want to capture. And, of course, for work."

"He had your camera out...what was on it?" Fraser asked.

"Shots of my latest projects. Nothing that would blow up national security."

"What were your latest projects?" Ned asked, and she frowned at him. Did he not remember?

"I was in Lauchtenland, taking pictures of Titus Stadium. It's their big futbol and rugby pitch and where they hold all their concerts and even the parade grounds. There's a big event coming up, and I was hired to take shots of Port Fressa, as well as the stadium, for some tourist hype."

"You still have the pictures?"

"I sent them in already to the agency, but they were on my digital roll too. But I also took pictures of, you know, the mountains I climbed, and Geneva, and even took pictures of Creed's track event—hey, did he ever get that mess with his girlfriend figured out?"

Fraser raised an eyebrow. "Still working on that."

"Is he okay?"

"Well, he wasn't captured by Russians and put in a Siberian gulag ship, so..."

"Not everyone can have my level of adventure."

Silence, and then she shook her head. "Too soon?"

Ned grinned. Winked.

She laughed and felt it down to her soul.

She might live. Find herself again.

"After dinner, I vill take your brother to my barn and ve can contact Moose on zhe radio. Arrange for him to pick you up."

"There's a plan?" Shae said.

Ned looked at her. "Of course there's a plan." His gaze then went to Fraser.

"Of course there's a plan," Fraser said.

She nodded and took another sip of soup.

See. Really, she could stop shaking.

Everything was going to be just fine.

Just. Fine.

EIGHT

S hould he be worried that Fraser wasn't back yet?

Ned stretched out on the sofa, Shae snuggled beside him, her body lost in slumber, her arm around his chest, his own around her waist.

He should stop worrying. Apparently, the barn was on their dacha outside the city—a garden plot carved out of the woods, but where Pavel communicated with Dwayne and, more recently, Moose.

Someplace the Russian government couldn't track him down, maybe.

So yes, with the storm, Ned guessed it might take some time to travel there in Pavel's old truck, get ahold of Moose, and travel back.

But three hours?

Calm. Down.

"Your heartbeat is being funny," Shae said, her eyes closed. "You okay?"

He'd suggested she go to bed in the other room, but she didn't want to be away from him, and frankly, he didn't exactly trust himself, locked in the other room with the woman he wanted to marry. Tonight. Right now.

Especially after that kiss. He'd very much lost himself there and hadn't cared. And that scared him a little, because he wasn't a guy who let himself off his leash.

Was a guy who liked rules and parameters and plans. How he loved plans.

Such an idiot to drop into Russia without a solid exfil. But he'd been, well, desperate, and really, Moose had assured him that Carpie would let them use the boat.

So, yeah, his plan was hope, and right now it was dying a little in the storm.

Shae raised her head. Met his eyes. Oh, she had such beautiful eyes, and they *trusted* him. *I knew you'd find me.*

That tore into him, settled into his bones.

What if he hadn't? What if he couldn't get to her?

"Ned. Your heartbeat again." She pushed herself up. "Talk to me."

He sighed. "I just…I don't like being helpless."

She raised an eyebrow. "Does anyone?"

"No, I suppose not, but…I don't know. Just the thought of you in that container, cold and scared and me not able to get to you—" He drew in a shaky breath. "And we're not out of the woods yet."

"But you did get to me, so—"

"If Moose's plan worked. But who knows…" Oh, he shouldn't have said that, because her eyes widened.

He pulled her down, held her. "I'll get you out of Russia. No matter what it takes."

"Get *us* out of Russia," she said softly.

Yeah. He ran his hand down her hair.

"Ned?"

"Yes. Of course. Us, babe."

Silence, and she pressed her hand on his chest, her hand warm over his heart.

Fraser, where are you?

"When I was about six years old, I was playing in the backyard by myself. It was fall, and the leaves were out—my parents were hauling in pumpkins. I remember that. We had this old cellar on the farm. It was built into this little hill, with a heavy wooden door and steps leading down to this earthen cave with wooden shelving filled with canned goods—peaches and pears and apples and pumpkin and beans and bins of potatoes. But most of all, we'd store apples down there. And I loved apples."

Outside, the rain had started to subside, the wind dying a little. Maybe the road had been washed out.

He kissed the top of Shae's head. Yes, he should have married her long ago. "So, on this day, when my parents were picking pumpkins and my brothers were out in the field—I have no idea where Iris was. Maybe out with them, but I was left to run around the yard, and I got in my head that I was hungry. And I needed an apple. So I went into the cellar. But I also wasn't allowed to go in, so I pulled the door closed. And immediately, it was dark. I couldn't see the apples, and I don't know what I'd been thinking. I tried to open the door, but the latch had fallen down on the lock, and it wouldn't move. I was trapped."

"And you were six?"

"Yeah. And I know that when you were six you were eating out of garbage cans and trying to survive—"

"Ned. We don't have to compare survival stories. Your story can be just as traumatic as mine. Probably more so because I never felt safe." She lifted her head. "Until now."

Until now.

Aw, what was he going to do with that. He caught her head and kissed her. Sweetly, but also turning so he could hold her better, both arms around her. She sank into him, and he simply slowed down and savored the smell of her—something floral, from her shower, her hair silky between his fingers, her mouth soft on his.

She broke away slowly. Met his eyes. "How long were you trapped?"

Oh. "It doesn't matter." He bent to kiss her again, but she put her hand to his mouth.

"How long?"

"Until late that night. Mom and Dad came home, couldn't find me, and they spent the next six hours looking. I was freezing and scared, and I'd wet my pants by the time my dad figured it out. I couldn't stop crying. But most of all, I was just...mad. Mad that I couldn't get myself out. I'd spent hours kicking the door, trying to pry it open, ripped off a fingernail doing it, and the fact that in the end, I had to be rescued just...yeah. I hate being helpless."

"And now you're a SEAL."

"And I do the rescuing. Although, we're a team too, so it's not just me."

Where are you Fraser?

"But right now, you're freaking out, aren't you?"

He sighed.

"So, I met this guy in gulag, and I can't stop thinking about him. His name was Judah. Lion. Weird name, huh?"

"I know—Sasha told us about him. He's been there a long time."

"He stood up for me—distracted Vikka and then—"

"I know, babe. I watched the whole thing."

She stilled. "You were there?"

"It was part of the plan."

She made a grim line with her mouth. "I'll bet that was hard."

"Yep. And I felt almost as helpless, but not quite, because I knew we were going to get you. So I stayed the course. And... gotcha." He brushed his hand over her cheek. "But I'm sorry you were hurt."

"It's okay. But Judah is still in there. And he really got hurt."

"Shae. We can't get him out. I'm sorry—"

"I know. I...know. But he said something to me that helped. He said that life is not safe, and that we can't stop bad things from happening. That we have to learn to live despite the danger, believing there's a bigger plan."

"Maybe that's the hard part for me. I have trouble not being in charge of the bigger plan." He rolled back over and lifted his arm, settling it over his head.

"Yeah. I can't help but think that just being around me, you're going to get hurt, or killed."

"C'mon. You're not *bad luck.*"

She made a face at him.

"Really, that's what you think?"

"I don't know—I just feel like being around me...maybe...bad things happen."

"And it's not your fault."

"I think—"

"You have a choice, just like me. You can be a victim of your circumstances, or you can be a victor. From where I'm sitting, you had a lot of bad stuff happen to you and around you, but not *because* of you. And you survived. You are amazing, and smart and strong and *not* a victim. In fact, you're the best thing that's ever happened to—"

Pounding at the door made him sit up.

"Otkroi dver!"

She froze.

Ned didn't. He pulled her up and reached for the Sig he'd put in his backpack. "Get behind me."

She jumped on the sofa as Sasha emerged from her bedroom. Sasha motioned to the other room, and Ned grabbed Shae and pulled her into the room with him. Closed the door.

Paced. Think, think.

"Otkroi!"

The sound of the door shuttering open was shattered by shouts, all in Russian and then—

A shot.

Ned turned, searching for a way out. The window. But it had bars on the outside.

"Get in the closet." He opened the door to a standing wardrobe and practically shoved her inside.

"Ned—"

"Get in and stay quiet."

Then he shut the door on her.

Pounding at the door, and he knelt, aimed at the door. First man through would die.

And then everyone after that.

"Ve have your brother!"

He stilled. Closed his eyes.

"Open, or he dies."

No. No.

"Ned, open the door!"

He glanced over and spotted Shae peeking out. Tightened his jaw. "Get back—"

The door slammed open, and he turned, pulled off a shot.

It hit a man in Kevlar, who went down, and then the men were on him, too many for him to fight—he got a hit in, then another, but they had him down, clubbing him, and then one of them tased him.

His entire body tightened, and for a second he thought his heart had stopped. He couldn't breathe, couldn't move—

And then suddenly, air filled his lungs. But his entire body turned to fire, and he lay there, unable to move.

A big man flipped him over and zip-tied his hands. Then hauled him up and threw him on the bed. He still couldn't move.

Sheesh, talk about helpless. He growled, though, fighting. C'mon legs. He could get out of the cuffs, but—

"Ver is she?" Big guy, hairy, black hair.

"Who!"

He got a fist in his face, blood pooled in his mouth. He spat it out at the man.

"Let us try zis—you tell us vere she is or you die." The man pressed the barrel of Ned's own gun to his temple.

Ned ground his teeth, shook his head—

"I'm here." Shae pushed open the door. Stepped out. "I'm right here."

The man smiled.

Then he grabbed Shae around the neck and pulled her to himself. She closed her eyes, but he shook her. "Look at khim!"

Her shoulders rose, fell, and she opened her eyes, staring at Ned.

He had his hands back, feeling returning to his arms. C'mon body, *work.*

And, wait—where was Fraser?

Oh no. Maybe they'd already killed him. He refused to go there, simply shut down the thought.

"You vant your voman to live?"

Very much, but he just stared at the big man.

"Zen ve make a deal."

A deal. He could do a deal. His toes worked. If only he had his boots on— "What deal?"

"You get ze caesium back. Ze caesium you stole from us."

He blinked at the man. What? "The caesium?"

"In Slovenia. You vere zere. Ve know. And ve know you can get it back."

Actually, um, "I don't know where it is."

"Zen she dies." The man tightened his hold around Shae's neck. She ground her jaw.

"Fine. Yes, I'll do it. I'll find it." He looked at Shae, then the man. "Let her go. C'mon, man, she needs to breathe."

The man considered him a moment, then smiled.

And then he let Shae go.

She fell to the floor, hit her knees, then scrambled over to Ned. Tears filmed her eyes. "Ned—"

"Shh. Babe." He had his hands now, but there were three in the room, all with weapons, and his chances of them both getting out alive— "I'll do this. And then I'll come back and I'll get you." He looked at Big Man. "Right? I do this, you'll let her go?" He didn't want to say a word about Fraser. Couldn't actually think about Fraser. Not without something breaking inside.

Later.

A moment, then, "Yes. Ve vill let her go."

Ah, not without a fight, but he'd cross that bridge later too. And Shae didn't have to know that. He met her eyes again. "See? It'll be fine. Just fine. Just...stay alive." His voice broke as he said it. "I will come for you."

"I love you, but—"

The man grabbed her, yanked her back. "You have three days."

Then he reached into his pocket and pulled out a phone. He tossed it on the bed beside Ned. "Three days. No call, hmm, no vife."

Then he dragged Shae from the room.

Ned lay there, closed his eyes and listened to them leave, his chest raw and open.

Then he rolled off the bed, broke the zip ties, staggered to his feet and let out a sound that emanated from a place he didn't recognize.

Or maybe he did. Once upon a time in a root cellar.

He leaned over, grasped his knees, caught his breath, and tried to keep the panic from spiraling out.

Three days.

He scooped up the phone and headed out into the living room. Sasha lay on the floor of her entryway, a shot to her head, and he looked away.

At least Fraser wasn't in the foyer with her, shot in the head. Ned wanted to look for him, but he was burning time.

Still, he stuck his head out the door, into the night. The yard was dark.

No truck.

No Fraser.

Choices.

Everything inside him turned to stone as he put on his boots, grabbed his jacket and his tac gear.

Three days.

He headed out into the dark, rainy night.

"IT'S TOO BAD THAT GREECE DOESN'T HAVE AN American football team."

Hudson looked up at Iris's words, spoken as she studied the breakfast buffet menu on a card. She sat opposite from him on the eighth-floor restaurant of Athens Gate, a hotel in the historic district of Athens, overlooking the ruins of the Temple of Olympian Zeus.

It was chilly this morning, in the mid-sixties, and the sun had yet to warm the open spaces, but the waiter had lit an outside heater, and Iris seemed nonplussed at the slight chill. She'd even taken off her jacket.

Seemed right, her being from Minnesota.

He hadn't needed the heater either, really, given he still wore his jacket, but his head pounded this morning, and frankly, he wished he were back under the Egyptian cotton sheets, the drapes closed despite the view.

The headache had started last night, on the red-eye to Athens. Now, he rubbed his temple.

Iris looked up. Frowned. "You okay?"

"Just...a headache. Yeah, I'm fine."

She put down her menu as a waiter came over. He wore a long white apron and carried a couple fluted glasses of orange juice. As he set them on the table, "Help yourself to the buffet."

Iris picked up her glass. "I can admit, these are better digs than what the ELF contracts for."

He grinned at that. "Yeah. I usually stay here while I wait for my boat to be delivered."

She eyed him, one eyebrow up.

"It's not like that. I rent it. But it's a nice boat, and the drive takes about three hours. You can take a high-speed ferry—it's about five hours—but I like to drive."

"Must be nice." She took a sip. "Refs don't make that kind of money. And we spend most of our time traveling, reviewing tape for missed or questionable calls, and even training."

"You sound like an athlete."

She cocked her head at him. "I am. I have to run down the field as fast as you do so I can see the play—or penalty—accurately. I have to dodge you. I have to make sure I'm not interfering with the play at all. Basically, I have to be omnipresent yet invisible."

Right. "Sorry. I hadn't really thought of it that way."

"Mostly because the only time you see us—or me—is when we have to call you out. Or don't call out the other team. Or when you make a mistake."

Aw, she was right. "You're not the most favorite person on the field."

"I am if I call it a catch, or a touchdown." She smiled at him. "Listen, I like my job. But don't think for a second that I don't have to be in shape."

He could attest to that. She had muscles and curves and seemed pretty able to take care of herself. No wonder she'd been a little peeved at her brother's request for Hudson to babysit her.

Maybe that ran through her mind, too, because she set down her glass. "You really think I'm being hunted by a killer?"

"I don't love how you put that."

"Well—?"

"Ziggy said that the hit hadn't been accepted yet—at least a couple days ago when I last talked to her." He took a sip of his own juice.

"So, maybe I'm safe—"

"Or maybe you need to stay the course, lay low with me until we get the all-clear from Ziggy."

"She's interesting. Gorgeous, but you definitely have the sense that she is dangerous."

"To the wrong people. She knew what to do with Tate."

"How'd you meet her?"

"At a bar, after a game. She came up to me, bought me a

drink, told me that she had big plans for me."

Iris cocked her head. Oh, she had this way of looking at him that made him feel a little naked. "Big plans?"

"Nothing happened. Just...she asked me to courier some information around once in a while. For the country."

"Right. Same song, different verse."

"Huh?"

"It's what Alfonzo said to me. Such a liar."

He stared at her. "What did he say to you to get you out on that bridge?"

She took another sip of her juice. "Just...that you were a spy."

"And you believed him?"

"No—" She sighed. "Okay, maybe I didn't know, okay?"

"Why? Because I left my country to go play football?"

"No." Her mouth pinched closed. "Listen, I know a lot of guys who play football in the ELF. But you, Hud—you were about to be a first- or second-round draft pick. And then you just...you dropped out. Disappeared. And then you reappear three years later in the ELF."

"I played a year of arena ball."

"Again—I mean, sure, I like arena ball. It's scrappy and fun for the locals, and a great way for a player to keep playing the game he loves. Maybe even get called up to the league. But then you get picked for ELF and suddenly you're a star again. So, what happened?"

He just stared at her. Because, hello, and really? His mouth opened. Closed.

Incredible. "Because I—"

The waiter came up, brought them silverware and a plate of cheeses. "Compliments of the chef. He says he's a big fan."

Hudson looked at the waiter, who smiled. "A fan?"

"Vienna Vikings? You are Hudson Bly, right?"

Huh.

"Tell him thank you." He looked at her. Okay, calm down. Because even if his career hadn't been destroyed with a targeting hit, even if he had landed a first- or second-round pick in the NFL, who knew but he wouldn't be riding the bench, just like so many of the first-rounders.

Here, he was a star. At least for now.

"You what?" Iris said.

She was pretty today, her dark-blonde hair down, blue eyes. She wore a pair of jeans and a cute off-the-shoulder shirt, bare neck.

Completely not at all the ref he knew on the field.

"I was...injured. And had a bit of a hard time coming back." Like, seeing double. And the ringing in his ears. Oh, yeah, and he'd forgotten his own name for a bit. So, "But I'm better than ever." He gave a big smile.

"Well, you certainly have fans. And if you keep playing like you did against the Milano Seamen, you have a future. That last catch—one-handed. Beautiful."

Huh.

"Even if you were over the line."

"What?"

She laughed. "Gotcha."

Okay, whatever. "I'm hungry. And we have four hours before the boat is ready." He pushed out his chair, got up.

The world tilted at him, coming up fast, and he staggered, catching himself on the table. The force of it tilted the table, the glasses spilling over. Iris caught them, set them right.

"Are you okay?"

He pressed his hand to his temple. "Whoa. Head rush."

But she stood there, frowning at him. "You sure? You don't look great."

"Thanks for that."

"I mean—okay, hotshot. You're just too big for me to drag back to your hotel room."

He raised an eyebrow.

"You know what I mean. Sheesh. Okay, clearly, you're fine." She headed to the buffet.

Maybe not so fine. A sweat prickled his skin. The room still spun, just a little, so he kept his eyes on her, following her to the long, overflowing breakfast buffet.

"Are you kidding me? There's like, twenty different pastries, then there's breads, and is that homemade yogurt? Probably. And olives and...oh, wow, you picked wisely, Indy."

He knew that line. From somewhere, but he couldn't place it. "A movie reference?"

"Please." She picked up a plate from the stack. Handed it to him. It was warm. "Did you grow up under a rock? That's a clear *Indiana Jones and the Last Crusade* reference."

"Australia—at least, until I was nine."

"No movies in Australia?"

"Not in the outback. But yeah, I did see that. I think."

"For the love, I hope so. Life isn't right without being able to quote Indiana Jones. Or really, any of the Harrison Ford movies. Pick a blockbuster, you'll find Harrison Ford. Oh my—is that bougatsa?"

She picked up a phyllo pastry filled with cheese. "I'm in heaven."

He loaded his plate with olives and tzatziki and fresh crusty bread, and another phyllo pastry called tiropita, and some hot spanakopita along with honey-coated feta cheese, and finished with dolmades.

"I've never had stuffed grape leaves," Iris said, her plate high as she headed back to the table.

"They're really...good..." He slowed his step behind her, the world angling around him. His skin turned prickly, his entire body rushed with heat. He might have emitted a groan, because she turned.

Her eyes widened. "Hud. You're bleeding."

She set down her plate on a nearby table and swiped up a cloth napkin. Stepped up to him and pressed the napkin to his nose while retrieving his plate with the other hand.

"Hud?"

He fell to his knees, taking her with him. She wrapped her hand around the back of his neck, kept holding the napkin to his face. "What's going on?"

"I...think..." He might retch. But he didn't really haven't anything in his stomach. And the floor just kept getting closer.

He put his hand down.

"Help! I need help over here!"

Iris was right there with him, her eyes holding his.

Wow, she had pretty eyes. Blue, with gold in the middle and...

"Hud!"

The world faded, and then everything went dark.

SHAE BRACED HERSELF AGAINST THE WALL, HER HEAD down, her breath held.

Stay alive.

The water hit her, stinging, brutal, but she didn't move, just let it sweep over her, hit her hair, her shoulder blades, her back, her thighs.

Stay. Alive.

"Povernees," said Ivanka, the blonde with the short hair.

Shae turned. Folded her arms, looked away. Braced herself.

Didn't flinch.

They gave her twenty-three again.

Could be worse. She could be eighty-one.

Big Captain Boris had locked her in his office until the female guards came on duty, and while the rest of the inmates ate breakfast, she was washed, changed, and given new wool boots, a coat, a hat.

She found her spot in line just in time to be counted.

The sky had stopped spitting upon them, just a haze in the air and over the water. It filtered into her jumpsuit, the collar of her jacket, but at least her wet head was warm from the fur hat.

And her stomach still digesting the hot borscht.

She blinked away images of Sasha and balled her fists at her side.

"Twenty-Three, what are you doing here?"

Judah's voice. She said nothing, raised her chin. But her gaze flickered to Vikka, standing across from her. The woman glanced over, and her jaw tightened.

Shae had spent most of the night handcuffed to a desk, so yeah, she'd had plenty of time to think.

If Sasha had asked Vikka to clobber her in order for Judah to pull Boris's key card, then she knew Sasha was at the helm of the jailbreak.

Dollars to donuts it was Vikka who'd ratted them out and sent the Bratva to Pavel's doorstep.

Pavel. She hadn't seen him when they'd dragged her away, when they'd made her step over Sasha's body, but she feared he, like Fraser, was already dead. Probably ambushed on their way back to the house.

She couldn't think about Fraser. Not and keep her wits about her. But...oh...

And she couldn't begin to imagine what Ned was going through right now. She'd seen the look in his eyes, the way something has simply flickered off, and in its place a coldness, a resolve.

He was coming back for her. But to do it, he'd have to commit, well, *treason* was the word that came to mind. Because he couldn't steal caesium-137, nuclear waste, and give it to Russians without being called a traitor, right?

And last time she checked, treason was punishable by...execution.

I love you, but—

She hadn't finished her sentence. *But don't come back.*

She was finished with people dying to rescue her, to set her free.

What had he said about her not being unlucky?

Whatever.

However, she *was* angry. Very angry.

And as they formed ranks and walked down the stairway, as she sat down next to Judah, who glanced at her with a look of worry, she knew one thing.

She very much intended on staying alive. No matter what it took.

Because she was leaving this place. With or without Ned.

"Are you okay?" Judah leaned over to her.

"Yep," she said and climbed onto the boat. She sat on the bench, and Judah sat beside her.

"I thought—"

"We were betrayed." She stared at Vikka, who met her gaze, until finally Vikka looked away.

"Shae, don't be afraid."

"I'm not." She looked at Judah. He looked rough, his beating showing on his terribly purpled, swollen cheek. It ran all the way to his eyes.

But those eyes looked at her with such concern she sighed. "How soon before your...pillow is ready for use?"

He blinked at her, frowned. "The time has not yet come."

"Hurry up," she said, and looked away. "Because I'm going to help you get off this ship."

The boat pulled up to the dock, and she got out, stood in line, then filed into the truck.

Again, Judah sat beside her. "Is Ned—"

"He's alive. But Sasha is dead, and maybe also Fraser, his brother. And probably Pavel."

"I see," he said quietly as the truck bumped them along rutted roads.

She tucked her hands between her knees, warming them. She'd lost her rags for her hands, but they were tougher now, so maybe she didn't need them.

"Tell me how I can help get what you need," she said to Judah before they exited the truck.

169

He just looked at her, his mouth a grim line.

She grabbed a shovel from the pile and started for the pit. Spotted Vikka and didn't know why, but something just swept through her and, in a moment, she'd stepped in front of her, turning.

She brought her shovel down hard an inch from Vikka's foot and met her eyes.

Vikka recoiled, frowned. Then her eyes narrowed.

"I know what you did," Shae said quietly. "And I won't forget it. Here's the new rules. You stay away from me, and I'll stay away from you. But you get in my face, and I don't care what kind of beating you try and give me, I won't go down."

Maybe Vikka understood her, maybe she didn't, and maybe the words were just for Shae, but she'd found the little girl who'd saved her mother from an abusive boyfriend, stolen a car, and lived for a month on the streets of Dallas.

She needed that girl if she hoped to survive.

Vikka tried to push past her, but Shae stepped in her path again. Vikka glanced away, probably looking for Twenty-Seven.

Shae spotted him over Vikka's bony shoulder.

Judah stood in front of him. Huh.

Finally, Shae moved away, and Vikka spat at her, then kept walking.

Whatever.

A guard shouted, maybe at her, maybe at someone else, but she walked over to the edge of their ditch and set her shovel in the ground. It was heavy from last night's rain.

Judah came over to her. "Shae—?"

"I never had a father," she said, lifting the dirt. She grunted and dumped it into a nearby wooden wheelbarrow. "And I desperately wanted one. My mom went through a series of boyfriends, and none of them took until we met this guy named Hardy. He fixed cars and smoked pot, but he was kind to me."

She stuck her shovel again into the dirt. "Hardy took me to the park sometimes, and we'd sit on the sofa together and watch

Buffy the Vampire Slayer. I'm not sure why he liked that show, but I wanted to be Buffy. Tough and standing up against evil. And...and then he became evil."

Her dirt splattered in the wheelbarrow. "He lost his job and started drinking and then, one day, he hit my mom. So hard that she lost a tooth. I'll never forget that, seeing her front tooth gone. It made her...weak, I guess."

The wheelbarrow was full, so the prisoner went to dump it and Shae turned to look at Judah.

"I decided I'd never be that weak."

"I'm sorry."

"She stayed with him for three years. Two of those were good. One wasn't. And I saw my mom change from a person of hope to a person of fear. I don't want to be a person of fear."

She glanced over at Vikka, digging the trench farther down. "I won't let it rule me."

Judah nodded. "But don't let hate rule you either."

She frowned at him.

"Don't let circumstances tell you who you are. They are simply opportunities for you to choose who you will be."

"I choose to be brave."

He glanced at Vikka. Back to her. "Everyone has a story."

The man with the wheelbarrow had returned, and Judah set his shovel back into the dirt. "You might find that you two are not all that different."

Hardly. "I don't go around threatening people."

Judah glanced at her, tossed his dirt into the wheelbarrow.

"If I'm going to survive here, I'm going to need my kasha."

He nodded, then sank his shovel into the dirt again. The soil was thicker here, redder, like clay. Heavy.

"Are you saying I shouldn't defend myself?"

"No. But you might be surprised what a little compassion gets you."

For Vikka? "She practically murdered Sasha. And Fraser. And now Ned is out there, committing treason to save my life. Which probably won't work because Lukka is planning on selling me—and Vikka, for that matter—into slavery, so, really, Judah?"

He leaned on his shovel, gave her a soft look. "You know what comes after 'Yea, though I walk through the valley of the shadow of death, I will fear no evil: for thou art with me'?"

She, too, stopped shoveling as the wheelbarrow man dragged the dirt away. "Enlighten me."

"'Thou preparest a table before me in the presence of mine enemies: Thou hast anointed my head with oil; My cup runneth over.'"

"What does that mean?"

"It means that in the middle of battle, when we're surrounded on all sides, God still provides for us. In fact, he blesses us with more than we even need. We are still his chosen ones."

She blinked at him, her jaw tightening, and shoot, tears filmed her eyes, burning them. "I've never been his chosen one."

"Never?" he said quietly. "He's never shown up for you? Been with you in trouble?"

The wind picked up and blew against them, around them, and the flaps on Judah's grimy fur hat lifted, little wings on either side of his bearded face. His mouth offered a grim smile.

Maybe. Uncle Ian. Ned. The PEAK Rescue team in Montana. Ned's family.

Judah.

"You are not alone, Shae. And you are still safe."

The words shook through her, took ahold of her bones, turned them weak. Her mouth opened— "Who are you?"

He smiled, then turned back to the dirt. "We have all the blasting powder we need to get out of here. We just need the moment to be right."

She still stared at him. "And what moment is that?"

He looked over and winked at her. "You'll know it when you see it. Until then, dig."

The guard shouted behind her, and she jerked.

Then she set her shovel into the ground.

Nine

The answer was simple.

Really, Ned had no choice. He'd come to that in a split second, watching Shae struggle for breath.

He could spend the rest of his life in Leavenworth if it meant she lived.

So, done. Yes.

He'd commit treason.

Ned sat on a hill that overlooked the Gorleben mine in Germany, the former-but-still-current location of the caesium-137. Forest surrounded him on all sides—he sat under a massive black pine, a scope to his eye, watching the movements inside and around the facility.

His plan was simple, really—the simplicity of it almost comical. Since his team had been the ones who'd transported the containers of the radioactive waste to this location, or at least had ridden shotgun as a team of NATO nuclear waste specialists oversaw the transfer, it hadn't been super hard to find his way back here.

At least physically. Mentally, Ned had wrestled with himself from Kamchatka Airport to Moscow to Berlin, where he'd rented a car and then found his way to Gorleben, just a three-hour drive.

And by the time he arrived, the resolve had settled in his chest like a boulder.

He'd drive in, steal the caesium, rescue Shae, then turn himself in. Confess, and spill everything he knew.

And pray hard that millions of people weren't murdered.

There went his gut again, clenching.

But you gotta keep praying until this knot goes away.

His throat thickened. *I'm sorry, Fraser.* He'd gotten his brother into this mess.

At least once he'd picked up his phone to call his parents, but really, what was he going to say? He had no proof Fraser was dead.

Except, of course, the dread in his soul.

But maybe he was right about the praying part.

God, please, give me wisdom. Keep Shae alive. Help me do this terrible thing...

No, that didn't feel right.

Sorry. But he couldn't take it back. Not when he was in this far over his head.

The sun was just sinking into the surrounding mountains, casting long shadows on the complex—not much security, but then again, their status as "inactive" created its own form of security. Still, a chain-link fence with rolled barbed wiring encircled the compound with plenty of open space between the forest and the grounds. High lights, probably motion-operated. In the middle, like a keep, a number of buildings surrounded a massive center tower that housed an elevator that led to the deep salt mines under the earth.

2,755 feet deep, to be exact.

But probably, the caesium-137 hadn't been moved to the depths yet. Ned's best guess was that it still sat in one of the concrete temporary storage buildings, right where the team had left it.

He didn't see any armed guards—but a security officer at the gate checked passes as workers moved in and out during the day.

He reached for the ham sandwich in his pack, something he'd

picked up in Wittenberge, some thirty clicks away. He'd also refreshed his water and washed his face. A couple bruises from the licks he'd taken, but nothing serious.

This didn't have to be hard. He still had his clearance, and really, could walk right through the gate. And with the right paperwork, could probably roll out of the place with the canisters in the back of a truck.

Maybe.

Take the packages to Lübeck Airport. A plane will be waiting.

He'd gotten the voice mail on his contraband phone when he'd gotten off the plane in Moscow.

And then what? Fly back to Kamchatka and retrieve Shae? In his wildest, denial-was-his-friend dreams.

She wasn't already dead—he knew that much. They had to keep her alive just in case he wanted proof of life before he handed over the nuclear waste.

But then what? He'd been ticking around that problem for the past nearly twenty-four hours.

Wow, he hated not having an exfil plan.

The sandwich was warm, the water tepid and did nothing to soothe the knot in his gut. But he finished eating, took another long look-see at the facility, then picked up his pack.

A twig snapped behind him, and he whirled around, crouched.

A shadow, and it slipped behind a tree.

He pulled out his KA-BAR. See, this was why he needed a real plan—flying by the seat of his pants only left him half naked, no one watching his six—

"I'd prefer not to be stabbed, thanks."

Ned stilled—what? He lowered the knife just as—wow. Ned had nothing as Fraser rolled out from behind the tree.

Silence dropped between them, just the terrible thump of Ned's heart. And the filling of his throat. He swallowed. Put the knife away. Took a breath. "Where have you been?"

"Getting donuts. My nails done. You know." He smiled, but sadness sat in his eyes. "Sorry I was late."

"It's better than dead." His throat thickened.

"Yeah." He sighed. "I'm sorry I wasn't there—"

Ned took a step toward him, and Fraser grabbed his outstretched hand and pulled him in for a quick hug.

"Glad you're not dead," Ned said quietly.

"Back at ya." He pushed Ned away. "It took hours to get ahold of Moose. He'd gotten the crabbing boat, and that's how I got out. But if I had been there—"

"No, bro. No shoulda-wouldas."

Fraser's mouth made a tight line. "Brought you this." He held out Ned's pack from Alaska. "Went the long way around."

"How'd you find me?"

"Coco pinged your GPS." He glanced past Ned to the facility in the valley below. "I'm afraid to ask."

"They'll trade Shae for the caesium-137."

Fraser's mouth tightened. Then he ran a hand over his mouth as if thinking.

"I have no choice."

"Mm-hmm," Fraser said, a noncommittal sound if Ned ever heard one.

"I can't let—"

Fraser held up his hand, then took a step closer. "You're going to use your security clearance to get in?"

"And then, hopefully, out."

"And then where?"

"Lübeck Airport. My guess is that the Bratva has an aircraft there. The airfield is close enough to fly to Moscow or wherever they want to land."

"And then the nuclear waste is back in Petrov hands, ready for use in a dirty bomb."

"Not lovin' the way you put that."

"Just speaking the truth." Fraser looked at him then with the barest hint of a smile. "Which is perfect."

Ned frowned.

"Your guys still around here?"

"You mean my team? I dunno. I've been on leave—"

"Gimme your phone. I need to talk to Trini." Fraser held out his hand.

Ned just looked at him. "Are you kidding me? The last thing I need is to pull my team into this. It goes south either way—they help me, they're accomplices; they don't, and someone gets hurt, because there is no way I'm walking away—"

"Calm down." Fraser still had his hand out, waiting for the phone. "I'm on your team, Ned. I promise."

Ned considered him. Then shook his head and walked away, back to his perch.

Silence, and then pine needles crunched behind him. "What's going on?"

"You shouldn't be here," Ned said. "I mean—yeah, I'm glad you're not dead, and I'd really like to know how exactly you're not dead, but...this is my burden, my crime. I'm the one who screwed up."

"How did you screw up, exactly?"

Ned turned. "If we'd had a decent exfil plan—"

"Stop. We had one—things just got messed up. And you, better than anyone, know that plans can get shot. It's the way of life. You can't blame yourself."

"I gotta blame someone!" He cut himself off from shouting, but just barely. His voice shook, his entire body lit as he stared at Fraser. "Otherwise, I don't know how to fix this. I just—"

"Can't fix it, Ned." Fraser met Ned's eyes. "Not on your own."

Ned's jaw tightened. "If you mean call the team—"

"I mean, you need to call God. As in 'Help, God, I'm in over my head.'"

Ned stared at him. "What do you think I've been doing for twenty-four hours! Sheesh, Fraze, I thought you were dead. And Shae is...who knows what is happening to her, and I'm about to destroy my entire career and maybe cause thousands of people to be irradiated—I don't know, so don't you think I've been praying?"

"For God to help you, or for you to help God?"

Ned's eyes narrowed.

"How about praying for you to get out of the way? To yield, and let God be God."

"I..."

"Don't yield. I know this about you, Ned. You don't give up. You don't surrender. And yeah, that's a good thing. Until it comes to God. See, He doesn't need a partner, bro. He needs a soldier, a warrior, someone who sets himself behind God, not equal with Him. You two are not co-leaders. And you're not supposed to be—that's what He means by 'Come to Me all who labor and are heavy laden. I will give you rest.' You don't have to carry the answers, or even the troubles."

Ned took a breath. "I have no idea how to...I don't know, put it all down, or whatever."

The sun had fallen, nearly to darkness in the forest. The breath of snow hinted the air. A chill ran down Ned's back.

"You just let go. You just...let it drop. And then you wait for God to show up."

Ned stared at him. Then slowly shook his head. "I have thirty-six hours to spring the caesium, get it to the Russians, and get back to Shae. I'm sorry, bro, but I don't have time to wait for God's plan."

Fraser lifted an eyebrow.

"What if this is His plan? What if...I don't know...He's trying to make me suffer?"

"Why would he do that?"

"I don't know. Because..." Ned looked at him.

"Because you don't need Him enough."

Ned frowned at him. "I need God."

"Not as much as you need yourself."

Ned's chest rose and fell. Then he picked up his pack. "I gotta go. You in, or is this your exit?"

Fraser nodded. "I'm in."

"Great. Because I have a plan." He set out for the rental parked a half mile away, on the road.

"Oh goody," Fraser said.

It was dark by the time they arrived at the rental car.

"A BMW station wagon?"

"I got upgraded." Ned drove them back to Wittenberge and checked into the Airbnb he'd rented on his app while waiting for his car in Berlin.

An old house, really, outside the city on a grassy plot of land, cows in a nearby pasture. It sat on a lake, the fog rising to hover above as he and Fraser pulled up. The place had a thatched roof, brick exterior, beams on the ceiling, wooden floor.

He dropped his gear and made a fire in the stove in the family room while Fraser heated up some ramen noodles. An overstuffed sofa, a trestle table with benches, and one bedroom, which he gave to Fraser since he wasn't going to sleep anyway.

He outlined his grand plan to Fraser as they ate dinner.

"I bought a suit coat at the airport. I clean up a little, flash my military creds, and say I'm checking on our delivery. The team brought it in—I might be already in the system at the facility. I drive in and find the caesium. The waste is all in cylinder containers that fit into about three checked bags. I'll just load them into the truck and drive away."

"Just like that." Fraser was slurping his soup. "What about the guard at the place?"

"He won't know the orders. And if he slows me down when I leave, I'll make a run for it. By the time they figure it out, I'll be long gone. I can do this."

Fraser considered him. His spoon clinked in his bowl. "Okay. And where am I?"

"Overwatch. And the guy on the other end of the phone should someone decide to call NATO."

"You're going to end up in some dark CIA prison." Fraser dropped his bowl in the sink and ran water in it.

"If something goes south, I need you to get the caesium and bring it to Lübeck Airfield. There will be a plane there."

"And then I'll get to join you in that CIA hole."

Ned swallowed. "Yeah. Okay, you can—"

"Stop. Of course I'll help you." Fraser met his eyes.

A beat passed between them.

Then Fraser headed to the bedroom and shut the door.

Come to Me all who are weary and heavy laden, and I will give you rest.

The words from Fraser dogged Ned as he washed the dishes, then lay on the sofa, watching the night close in over the lake.

Yeah, well, if God was going to show up and enact a plan, He'd better do it soon.

Because the only rest for Ned was going to be in a cold, dark cell.

"STAY IN THAT BED. STAY IN—HUDSON BLY, YOU STAY in that bed!"

Iris was already out of her chair even before he sat up, before he started to pull off the electrodes pasted to his body—a rather impressive body—stop. She wasn't going there.

She'd seen more of Hudson Bly over the past twenty-four hours than he probably wanted her to see. But that was what happened when a guy collapsed in her arms in the middle of a high-end restaurant. When she had to play girlfriend to get any information from the doctor in the Henry Dunant Hospital Center, a private hospital that the hotel recommended.

Indeed, the place was clean, high-tech, and the doctor of neurology, a Doctor Ioannis, spoke impeccable English.

"You can't tell me what to do," Hudson said, taking from his head the electrodes that also monitored his brain activity.

"I think, as your girlfriend and as the person who is making medical decisions for you, I probably can." She'd come over to the bed and tried to put the electrodes back on. They'd shaved his glorious hair in a few places—he looked a little rough. But that's what he got for keeping his, um, history of concussions from her.

And probably the entire European League of Football. Hel-*lo*. "My *girlfriend*?"

"How else do you think they let me in here, by your bedside, schlepping Jell-Os for you for the past twenty-four hours?"

"I wasn't that out of it. I would have noticed the Jell-O."

"Uh, flag on the play. You practically had a brain bleed there, champ. They caught it, gave you some anti-stroke meds, but no way are you getting out of that bed."

It was a little like holding back the sun. He even eased the IV out of his arm. "Let's go."

"If you think I'm giving you your clothes—"

He stood up, out of the covers, wearing just his green hospital gown.

She stood there. "It's going to get breezy."

"I've been walking around naked in locker rooms for most of my life. Down hallways, into training rooms—you think a little breeze is going to hold me back?"

He stared at her.

She met his gaze.

"Okay, then, sweetheart, you ready to roll?" He held out his hand.

"Oh, for the love. Fine. But what's the hurry?"

"Um, aside from the fact that someone is hunting you?"

"Give me a break." She'd walked over to the tall closet where she'd hung his clothes. "By the way, the EMTs wanted to cut your clothes off. I told them this was Armani and that you'd take them apart."

He was smiling when she turned holding his shirt, his jeans.

"And I saved your ultra-cool Magnannis when they took them off at the restaurant." She handed him the shoes. "I like the buckle."

"Thanks. I got them on sale." He had pulled on his jeans under his pajamas, then pulled off the gown, giving her another view of those abs, a fairly hairless chest, just the finest field of dark-blond hair.

Avert. Eyes.

She looked out the window. The hospital sat in the middle of the metropolitan area. Sure, a large park stretched out across the street, but no cool Greek ruins or city gates. Just a Starbucks across the street—praises—and a couple of fast food places. She'd picked up a pork gyro yesterday for dinner, and then this morning, while they ran tests, she'd found a place that made flat bread and had a gözleme with spinach and feta cheese.

So, she wasn't suffering.

Outside, puffy clouds floated in a perfectly blue sky. Probably, Jonas would know the word for those clouds, but to her, it looked like a perfect day.

Not the kind of day to die.

"Are you sure this is a good idea? Your tests haven't come back yet, and..."

"It's a good idea."

When she looked back at him, he had his shirt mostly buttoned. She hadn't noticed until now, but he hadn't shaved, and he now wore a smattering of dark whiskers with reddish hints.

That and his fancy shoes, the white shirt—the man belonged in Greece, some sort of resurrected mythological hero.

He grabbed his jacket and turned to her. "Let's go before they figure out I'm leaving." He even touched her elbow, and then, crazily, slipped his hand into hers.

"What are you doing?"

"Walking out of here with my *girlfriend*."

"We can be dating without holding hands."

"Not in my world." Then he pulled her out of the room,

strolling along, all the way to the elevator. Smiled at a few passersby. Then leaned one hand against the wall, facing her.

"What's happening here?"

"Just pretend you like me."

"Why?"

"Really? Not even a little bit of 'Hey, yeah, Hudson, of course I like you'?"

"I'd like you more if you stayed in the hospital where you and your leaky head belong."

"I guess that means we're breaking up?"

"If you get in that elevator, we are."

"See, no one wants to get in the middle of a squabbling couple." He smiled, and the elevator dinged, and then he grabbed her hand and pulled her in.

He sighed, however, and let her go as soon as the doors closed. Stepped back and leaned against the wall of the elevator, his eyes closed.

"You're scaring me. I'm not going to have to drag you into the ER again, am I?"

"I thought you said you were athletic." He didn't open his eyes.

"I am. But there's a difference between dodging wide receivers and dragging two hundred pounds of—"

"Pure muscle."

"—pure stupidity across the hospital."

The elevator dinged and he stood up, walked toward the door. Grabbed her hand again.

"Just keep your head down."

"You're not that famous."

"But we are walking out of here without an official discharge, so…"

"If I drop to the floor and scream that really loud, what will you do?"

He looked at her then, and instead of smiling or joking, a muscle pulled in his jaw. "Please don't do that."

Oh. Uh. "I was kidding."

He made that sound again, deep in his chest, and she just held onto his hand until they got outside.

Then he dropped it again—and maybe she was just a little sad about that—and breathed in the fresh air. Deep breaths, long exhales.

"What are you doing?"

"Living one more day." He then looked at her. And smiled.

It was such a slow, mysterious, authentic smile, she had nothing for it. "What is going on?"

"Just..." He turned to her, then, "I had a TBI from a targeting hit a few years ago, and...I'm fine. But—"

"You shouldn't be playing football."

"I'm not on the line—"

"You're a wide receiver. You get hit, hard."

He held up his hand. "I was cleared by the Vikings' medical staff to play. And even before that, in America, before I tried out for arena ball."

But she was putting together his last few games, the way— "You tripped on the field last week. During the exhibition. Were you dizzy?"

His mouth tightened. "Let's just go." He turned.

She put her hand on his arm. "Hudson."

"I don't want to talk about it!"

Oh.

He'd rounded on her and now drew in a breath, clearly schooling his words. "Sorry. Let's just get the boat and get to the resort and then..."

"You'll tell me what's going on?" She kept her voice low.

He stared at her, his chest rising and falling. "Maybe."

"Okay. That's good enough for now."

Then she took his hand.

"What's this for?"

"So you don't face-plant."

"I'm not dizzy."

Yeah, well, she might be. Still, he didn't let go, his hand big and safe and warm in hers as they walked down the sidewalk. They took cover in a Starbucks—like the medical staff would hunt them down. But he also needed coffee.

Then, while he sipped a trenta caramel macchiato, she called an Uber.

Meanwhile, he called the boat rental company. "They released our boat. We need to lay low until tomorrow while we wait."

They made it back to the hotel still dating, but when he got out of the Uber, he let go of her hand. "I think I'm going to get some shut-eye."

"Not on your life."

He looked at her.

"You can't sleep."

"What, is that a crime here? No sleeping in the daytime?" He pushed into the hotel.

"You have a concussion!" She grabbed his arm, turned him just inside the lobby.

He raised an eyebrow. "I don't currently have a concussion. And what, I can never sleep again?"

She narrowed her eyes at him. "I'm...coming with you."

He shook his head, walking past the sleek wooden front desk, a table with a massive spray of exotic flowers.

"To my room? To do what?" He smiled then. "I mean, you may be taking this girlfriend thing further than—"

"Calm down there, buck. I'm going to watch you sleep."

He punched the elevator button. "That'll be high fun. Listen, here's the highlight reel. I breathe. In. Then out. And then...wait for it—in again."

"Perfect. Maybe I'll catch up on a football game. I heard the Sea Devils' game against the Vienna Vikings was a keeper."

"Hilarious. I dropped two passes in that game."

"I know. I can't wait."

"I really am breaking up with you."

"Good. I need to date someone with a better reception record."

He narrowed his eyes at her. "Fine."

"Does your head still hurt?"

"No. I'm just...tired. And sore. They woke me up every three hours to take my blood pressure."

"I know. I was there."

He opened his eyes. Looked at her. "Yes. Yes, you were. Thanks for that."

She didn't know why his words sort of just wheedled into her bones, warmed them. Maybe it was the way his gaze stayed on her.

Seeing her.

The doors opened and he got out. Different floor than hers. She'd called and extended her stay a few days, hoping—

Uh oh.

He'd reached his door. Pulled out his key. Ran it over the door lock.

The light beeped red.

"What?" He tried again.

Beep. "Aw—"

"Sorry, Hudson. I extended my stay, but I forgot to do yours."

He leaned his forehead against his door. "And my clothes?"

"Probably at the front desk?"

He sighed, turned, his shoulder against the door. "Can I..."

"C'mon. I'm a sucker for the homeless."

He followed her to the elevator and took it down to the fourth floor. "It's not the penthouse suite, but..."

"I don't care. I'll sleep on the sofa."

"Actually, I don't have a sofa. Just that boring budget room. But it does have a double bed, and a small balcony, and in the meantime, I'll see if they have any more rooms."

"I could kiss you."

"Yeah, you homeless men are all the same."

But his words sat with her anyway.

She opened her door and let him in.

186

Suddenly, that budget room seemed way too small. He barely fit into the tiny entryway between the door and the closet.

But the bedroom also held a couple chairs, and he plopped into one.

"Oh, for Pete's sake—lie on the bed. I'll take the chair. Like I said, I'm watching television anyway. And I need to catch up on my YouTube videos."

He'd already toed off his shoes. "You sure?"

"Want me to tell you a bedtime story?"

"Can you sing to me?"

"The wheels on the bus—"

"Okay. I take it back." He climbed onto the bed, stomach down, pulling the pillow under his head, his eyes closed. "Tell me if I stop breathing."

She looked at him.

He smiled. "Kidding." Then, "But no, really."

"I got this, Bly. I don't miss things."

"Mm-hmm."

Then he was just...out.

And she picked up her phone, hooked to the hotel internet, and began to google. *Montana Griz football player. TBI. Targeting.*

She was scrolling through a list of results when a knock came at her door. She dropped the phone into the chair and headed to the door.

Peeked out.

It took a second for the recognition to click in.

She glanced at Hudson, now out like a bulldozer, snores and all. Oh, she didn't want to wake him.

But. Okay. She opened the door and stepped out into the hall. Looked at the woman standing there, wearing a leather jacket, cargo pants, and boots, her hair pulled back in a dark ponytail.

"Hey, Ziggy. What's going on?"

It was Vikka's fault she'd ended up in the infirmary.

Well, they both had. And because of that, she looked over at Vikka and smiled.

"It worked," Vikka said.

Shae leaned her head back against the wall, closed her eyes. "Maybe, hopefully."

Her jaw still hurt from Vikka's punch, but Vikka sported a fat lip.

"You hit good."

"My boyfriend taught me that."

Probably had saved her life, really, last night when Vikka approached her in the showers.

And to think she'd actually had a day where she'd thought she might survive. Vikka had carved a wide path around her since her return. Maybe Shae had gotten too confident.

Whatever it was, she'd stood in the shower, her eyes closed— probably a bad move—and let the lukewarm water wash away the dirt. She had a clean jumpsuit waiting, too, thanks to the laundry.

At least with the cold, the fleas and ticks couldn't survive.

"You're escaping, and you're taking me with you."

She'd opened her eyes, and Vikka stood in front of her, her eyes red, her voice low. Naked.

"You speak English."

"Yes." Her voice cut low. "And I heard you and Twenty-Four talking. I know what you are doing. And I want to go with you."

Shae had turned off the water, grabbed the tiny towel they'd given her, and held it in front of herself. "Maybe we do this with clothes on."

Vikka's eyes narrowed. Shae pushed past her to her hanging, clean jumpsuit. She pulled it on, then dried her hair.

Vikka did the same, pushing her dark hair back away from her face. Then, "I know he steals blasting powder. And if you do not take me, I tell the guards."

Oh, Shae didn't like her. "I don't know when he's leaving."

"How is he leaving?" Most of the other prisoners had finished, moving to their containers. Shae had refused to shower with men, so she'd waited until the last of them had moved out.

The room was nearly empty, which meant the guards would be back soon.

"Tell me." Vikka glanced at the lone woman leaving the shower area, her voice low.

Shae shook her head. "You betrayed Sasha and Ned and—"

"They were going to kill Zurab."

"Twenty-Seven. Who is he—your lover?"

Her mouth tightened. "My brother. He is...not well. And he needs me."

"So you're just going to leave him?"

She closed her eyes. "They are going to sell me." Her gaze met Shae's. "And you."

"No, Ned is coming back for me—"

"You are a fool. The moment he comes back, he is a dead man. Even more than that, if your man is military, then he is worth something. Maybe even more than you. But you are both going to be sold. The Petrovs do not just set people free." Vikka's eyes brimmed, and she looked away. "They kill who you love."

Shae nearly cared. Footsteps sounded outside.

"What is his plan?"

His plan. The one she'd finally wheedled out from Judah as she lay under her bed last night. She stared at Vikka, the dark eyes, a desperation in her expression, and then.... "Okay. I'll tell you. But only if you promise to pick a fight with me."

Vikka frowned.

"Judah will put the blasting powder into the oven after dinner. Then, while the prisoners are assembled on the deck, the guards will light the stove for tea and..." She made a gesture with her hands. "Boom."

Vikka's eyes widened. "Boom."

"Yes, but he needs a distraction."

Vikka smiled slowly. "A distraction."

"In the chaos, and before the stairs go up, we escape. With so many running, we'll have time to get away. Everyone for himself."

"And then what will you do?"

And it sounded crazy, but, "Judah has a plan. He says he can get us away."

Vikka just stared at her. Then, suddenly, laughed. "You trust him? He has been here longer than any of us. Why has he not escaped before? Because he is a cra-*zy*. That is why everyone avoids him."

Shae stilled. She hadn't thought of that.

But Judah didn't seem crazy. He seemed sane. Calm. Kind.

In a Russian gulag? Yeah, suddenly that did sound crazy. "I believe him."

Maybe it was her tone, the way she met Vikka's gaze. But Vikka stopped laughing, considered her a moment.

"Fine. What can it hurt? I am doomed anyway. So da, I will beat you good."

Shae didn't flinch. "I'll fight back."

"I hope so."

Vikka patted her cheek, then walked away. "See you at dinner."

See you at dinner.

Then she just had to convince Judah that the time was right.

He'd turned quiet a long time after she'd whispered the plan to him through the hole on her floor. She lay in her blanket like a burrito and found that the floor wasn't any worse than the cot. And frankly, having Judah right there, a whisper away, seemed to keep her thoughts from spiraling out, from believing Ned dead, or in custody as a traitor, or...

"We need to do it tomorrow night, at dinner," she whispered. "Because Vikka thinks we're going to be sold, and even if not, I need to get ahold of Ned and tell him not to come for me—because Vikka is right. They won't let us go. No way."

"It's not time yet."

"Then when is time, Judah? You've been here for three years. When are you going to enact this plan? Or is it just a crazy fantasy—"

"It's not crazy. It will work."

"And then what? You say have faith, but I need to know how—"

"I'm a spy, Shae. An American, undercover here, but it's time I leave. I have people on the other side—I just need you to have faith."

That had sort of shut her down.

They might actually do this.

Now, twenty-four hours later, sitting in the infirmary, well, maybe not as much.

"It was not a bad plan," Vikka said in the darkness. Their wrists were both secured with zip-ties. Although, frankly, Ned had taught her how to get out of those, so that wasn't an issue.

The bigger issue was the man outside the door.

And, of course, the fate of Judah, who had been caught in the kitchen, despite their epic, Chuck Norris-style fight with thrown furniture, a food fight, and yes, some blood.

But he'd been holding a couple potatoes, as if stealing food, so...

"I cannot believe he wore blasting powder on himself all day."

"Wore it in a pillowcase around his neck, under his jacket."

"I told you he was crazy."

"Mm-hmm." She twisted her wrists. Maybe, but she'd used his trick to steal a spoon from the table. Now it sat in her boot, ready to be sharpened.

Just in case she didn't get off this ship anytime soon.

"Did he put the package in the...place?"

"I don't know."

The door opened, and the guards dragged someone in, threw him on the bed.

Shae stilled.

"Judah," Vikka said.

He lay without moving as they zip-tied him, hand and foot, to the bed. In the wan light, Shae saw blood, shiny on his face.

She closed her eyes, unable to look.

"Zhenshina! Dvatset-tree!"

Twenty-three. She looked up. One of the guards held a phone. He snapped her picture.

What—?

"Proof of life," Vikka said when he left.

She looked at Judah. Then she drew up her knees, put her head down.

What life?

Her breath began to hiccup.

"Nyet," Vikka said from the other bed. "No cry. No. Cry."

Shae looked up, blinked.

No cry.

Yea, though I walk through the valley of the shadow of death, I will fear no evil.

She swallowed and watched Judah in the dusky glow of moonlight. He lay on the bed, spread-eagle, bloodied, unmoving.

But in the darkness, she thought she heard a voice.

Have faith.

Right. Maybe faith was the only thing she had left when desperation moved into her soul. Because without it, there was only darkness.

Please, God, keep Ned safe. Be with him. With me. And help me to trust You.

"You are not alone, Shae. And you are still safe."

She looked over.

Judah's eyes were open.

"You're alive."

"Mm-hmm. And..." He smiled, glanced at Vikka, back at her.

192

"It worked. Better than I hoped." He then snapped his wrist free, the other one, then his legs.

"Do you need help?"

Vikka snapped off her tie.

Shae shook her head, then pulled the tie down with her teeth and pulled her hands down, hard.

The ties broke. "Let's go."

"Nope." Judah climbed under the wool blanket and closed his eyes.

"So...when—"

"Shh," Judah said, his eyes still closed. "You'll know when. For now, get some sleep. It's going to get cold tonight, and we have heat and blankets."

Yes. Yes, they did.

Blankets and maybe, well, hope.

She pulled up the blanket, rolled over.

And maybe for the first time in weeks, really slept.

TEN

Today Ned committed treason, and he didn't care.

Because Shae was still alive. And if he played this right, in twenty-four hours, she'd be free.

So yeah, denial was his friend.

Even though she looked rough.

Alive, but rough.

Her face bruised, a welt on her cheek, her eye blackened a little, but still alive. And almost...angry?

Ned couldn't tell by the picture on his phone, but he stared at it a long time before he heard Fraser's feet shuffle from the bedroom.

He opened the door. "Ready?" Fraser stood there in a pair 5.11 tactical pants, a pullover, a jacket, his backpack over his shoulder.

"You are," Ned said. He'd changed into jeans and a shirt, a suit jacket, even a tie. The getup felt stupid, but maybe this entire plan was stupid.

Thankfully, Fraser said nothing as he gulped down a container of juice and a croissant, a little stale from last night's bakery run on the way to the Airbnb.

Ned couldn't risk anything in his stomach, thanks.

Fraser said nothing as they drove to the site, and Ned dropped him off where he'd parked the car yesterday. Fraser got out, carrying with him their communications gear, confirming contact when he got into position.

Ned confirmed back, then set the earpiece in the glove compartment.

He drove up to the gate.

Here went nothing.

The complex wasn't heavily populated this morning. But it was early, the sun still rising to shine upon the containment tower, the few parked cars in the lot.

Ned showed his passport—his real passport—and his military ID to the guard. "I'm here to talk to Director Shumann."

Just a little homework had netted him that name.

The guard let him through, and he parked near the building as the gate closed. Then the guard headed back to his station.

Ned pulled out and drove around back, behind the building, to the containment area.

No security, which felt eerie. A massive metal rolldown door was secured at the bottom. He affixed his earpiece.

"Any movement?"

"Nothing. Bright sunny day. Hurry up."

He got out, opened the back of the wagon, lifted the flooring, and pulled out a pair of bolt cutters. Then he snapped the two locks securing the door and raised it.

No dogs, no soldiers with AK-47s...yeah, something definitely felt off, and it sorta needled him as he walked inside.

Apparently, NATO and the US Military weren't the only ones using this facility. Along the walls, in protective 91 CASTOR or TN85 metal containers were hundreds, maybe thousands of waste products, from radioactive sludge to scrap metal to fuel elements to reprocessed waste.

Yeah, there should definitely be more security running around here.

He shoved it to the back of his brain and went hunting.

He found the three suitcases with the caesium sitting in a temporary intake area near the back of the massive building, probably where the team had dropped it off.

Just to be sure, he opened up one of the cases. He'd helped pack them, so he used the code he'd locked it with and, bingo, the case opened.

Inside sat the metal containers of caesium-137, enough product to infect a small nation.

Then he took out his phone and slipped it into the case, behind the padding.

He closed the case and loaded them onto a wooden flatbed, then headed toward the entrance, the daylight like a beacon.

Just load it in, cover it up with the blanket he'd taken from the Airbnb—they could keep his cleaning deposit—and then drive away. Through the gate, to the airport. Deliver the goods.

Get on a plane.

Find Shae.

Live happily ever after.

Yeah, big denial. But he was buying in because that was all he had.

He pushed the flatbed out to the wagon. Still no guards.

He loaded the suitcases into the back seat, then covered them with the blanket.

Yeah, like that wasn't obvious.

And yet, still no guards.

He pulled down the door, then stowed the bolt cutters.

Then he got into the front seat. "Package acquired," he said into his coms.

"A few cars arriving. Hold."

Ned put the car into drive and slowly moved around the building, away from the container. He parked next to a waste container and watched as said cars pulled in and parked.

"All clear."

He drove around to the front, then up to the entrance. Raised his hand to the guard and offered a smile.

The guard buzzed him through, and the gate opened.

Really? But maybe that was the thing—who wanted to take home radioactive waste?

Maybe he'd hyped this way up in his head.

He pulled out and headed toward the pickup spot. "Meet me on the road."

No answer from Fraser. Weird, but Ned kept driving. Fraser stood by the side of the road. He raised his hand, smiled, like, *Hey, bro, pick me up.*

Ned slowed. Stopped. "Get—"

As Fraser opened the door, behind him, from the forest, emerged—ah, he should have guessed it—Master Chief Trini, dressed in full tactical gear, pointing his M-16 at the car, and behind him, his XO, Marsh, their cousin Ford. And then, to his starboard, there was Mac—Riley McCord—and Sonny...

"Don't do it, bro." Fraser looked at him.

"Seriously—?"

"Hands up, off the wheel!" Trini shouted.

"C'mon!"

"Now, Bull!" This from Mac, closing in on the driver's side.

Ned lifted his hands. "Everybody just stay calm—"

"Get out." Mac yanked the door open, grabbed his jacket.

Ned jerked his arm up and back, broke the hold. "Back. Off!"

Mac wore an expression of betrayal, and Ned shook his head, hands up. "Just—hear me out."

As soon as he stepped out, Mac grabbed him, shoved him against the car, kicked out his legs.

"Watch it."

Mac pulled his KA-BAR off him.

Ned whirled around. "I'll need that back—"

Mac yanked it up, away from his reach, peddled back.

Ned held up his hands, turned around. "Is anyone going to listen—"

"I'm listening," Trini said and held up his hand to Mac, then Sonny and Cruz.

Fraser, too, had stepped away from the car.

Now Ned looked at him. "You had to call the entire team?"

"That was Trini's choice," Fraser said.

"We were already in country." The Master Chief lowered his weapon. "Talk."

"What's there to talk about?" Mac said.

"Easy there, Mac," Trini said.

"He's about to put back into play what we nearly died securing? I don't think so—" Mac reached for Ned, and Ned slammed his hand down on Mac's wrist.

"Hey! Hey—just, everyone take a breath. Let's just talk about this." Fraser, his hands also up, but more to calm everyone down. "Trini, I told you the score."

"I know." Trini looked in the back seat, back to Ned. "But we can't let you take the caesium, Ned."

Ned closed his eyes. "Except, what if we could?"

Ford had also lowered his gun. "I'm listening."

"What if we tracked it?" Ned said, glancing at Ford. "It's already done. My phone is in the case."

Fraser looked at him. Then smiled. "Really?"

"Came to me in the middle of the night. I dreamed I was in the middle of the ocean, at night, and suddenly someone found me."

"Huh," Fraser said. "Naw, couldn't happen."

"I woke up and thought—what if we could track it?"

"And you were going to tell me this, when?" Fraser glanced at Trini, who was nodding.

"Now. Right now, after you trusted me enough to let me do this." He looked at Trini. "Wait. Why was there no security at the containment facility?"

"We wanted to see if you'd walk away with it," Mac said. "And you did." He opened the back seat and pulled out one of the suitcases. "I want to see that phone."

Ned stepped back from the car. "It's in the back. I'm not sure which one."

Mac opened the case and stuck his hand in around the foam. Pulled out Ned's phone.

Ned shrugged.

"All right," Mac said, and finally smiled. "I won't kill you."

"Thanks."

Mac turned to Ford. "Tell him."

Ford smiled. "Fraser and Master Chief had the same idea. I'm tired of the Petrov's beating us. They are always one step ahead. and when Fraser told us your plans, we thought...what if..." He touched his nose, then pointed at Ned. "What if we put a tracking device on this and let it go?"

"I gotta get to the airport, fellas," Ned said. He grabbed the phone.

"Nope. That's going to die," Sonny said. "Let's use actual tracking devices." He pulled out a package while Mac opened the cases. They affixed the devices inside.

"Here's how this is going down," Trini said as they shoved the cases back into the wagon. "You're going to deliver the caesium, and we're going to track it. Believe me when I say that no one is disappearing into Siberia with nuclear waste."

Ned nodded.

"But maybe we get our eyes on who is behind all this. See if the caesium leads us to bigger fish and maybe a glimpse at what they're planning with it," Ford added.

"Who knows, Ned? You just might end up being a hero." Trini smiled at him, shaking his head.

"I just want my fiancée back." He climbed back into the driver's seat.

Fraser got back in the car.

"What are you doing?"

"I'm going with you."

"No, you're not. I need you in Alaska, getting me a ride home."

"That's your plan?"

"That's all I got."

Fraser made a sound, deep in his chest. Then nodded. "Stay alive. God will come up with something." Then he got out of the car.

Ned left him in the road with his team.

Hang on, Shae. I'm on my way.

"No, absolutely not, over my very large, angry, dead body." Yes, Hudson might be a little crabby, but no way, no how, was he going to follow Ziggy's crazy, hair-brained plan and— "That's a great way to get her killed."

He stood over Ziggy and Iris, who both looked at him like *he* might be the crazy one here.

But he was also the only one with a good eight hours of sleep under his belt. Although, honestly, it'd been a long time coming. And he'd had to work for it.

He couldn't believe that Iris had thought she could just sneak out of their hotel room. Oops, *her* hotel room. But whatever, he'd heard her leave, with a click of the door, and in a second, knew something wasn't right.

Mostly because he'd gotten used to the sound of her breathing. Weird, but he definitely remembered, or had maybe sensed, her presence in his hospital room while the nurses jabbed him and took his blood pressure, and he'd become keenly aware of her in the corner, on a recliner, just hanging out.

Watching him sleep. But he hadn't hated it. Not sure why.

And when she'd left, he'd sort of just...yeah, sensed it.

Which was why he'd forced himself off the bed and to the door and—

"Ziggy, what are you doing here?" He'd stared at the two in the hallway, Ziggy dressed in her usual spy attire, Iris in her jeans and cute top, and they'd stared up at him, wide-eyed, as if caught in some drug hand-off.

Maybe worse, because, "I found out who put the hit on Iris."

"Nice. Maybe you could announce it right here in the hallway." He'd opened the door and practically pushed the ladies into the crowded room.

"First, we need to move you. And then I have a plan," Ziggy said.

Iris had grabbed her roller bag, still mostly packed, and thrown her toiletries into it. "It's that guy, isn't it? Alfonzo. I'll bet he's angry that I didn't text him back."

Ziggy had just frowned at her, then looked at Hud, but he'd just shrugged. "No idea."

"You were supposed to text Alfonzo? Or rather, Alan Martin?"

"Yeah. I still have the phone." She'd walked over to her bag and pulled out the flip phone.

And that's when things had gotten a little crazy. Ziggy got on her phone with someone named Logan, who then activated a hacker who then called Ziggy, and by the time Iris was packed and they were headed downstairs, Ziggy had dialed her hacker friend to take control of the phone.

He'd gotten his clothing back—in his suitcase—tipped the concierge, and ordered an Uber. And while Ziggy had made Iris tell her everything she knew about Alfonzo, he'd lined them up a new hotel room.

This time a suite, with two bedrooms and a nice big living room and room service.

They'd ended up in the Presidential Suite at the Athens Plaza, with a view of the Acropolis and enough king-sized beds for a crowd. Or three people.

He'd ordered room service—moussaka and stuffed eggplant—then sat on the sofa nursing a sparkling water while Ziggy gave them both a rundown of the scariest man he'd ever heard of.

"Alan Martin is a rogue CIA agent. He and the former VP-elect, Reba Jackson, along with some of their ilk who we're still trying to uncover and the Petrov Bratva, tried to kill the president, twice. Most recently a few months ago by disabling Air Force One."

"Like the movie with Harrison Ford?"

Ziggy frowned at him, and Iris gave him a side-eye.

"What? She mentioned him. And now I have Harrison Ford on the brain."

"Not really, but a little, yes," Ziggy said. "And they tried to unleash a lethal strain of smallpox into our country."

He stopped thinking about Harrison Ford.

"We stopped them, but Arkady Petrov is up to something. Or so we think. About a month ago, a large amount of radioactive waste was stolen from a nuclear storage facility in Switzerland and then deployed in a training event over Slovenia. Thankfully, your brother Jonas"—she pointed at Iris—"figured it out, and a SEAL team stopped them."

"Ned was on that team."

Ziggy nodded. "Yep, I met him too." She stood up, stalking the room.

Nice room, with a plush velvet sectional, a huge flat-screen, and two big bedrooms located upstairs for an even more stellar view. It came with a kitchen, a dining area for ten, and a marble bathroom, along with views of Athens and even the Saronic Gulf.

Ziggy stood at the window.

Iris got up. "I'll text Martin. Tell him to meet me."

Ziggy turned, her mouth open. "I like it."

And this was where Hud had first stood up with a resounding *Nope. Never. Not gonna happen.*

He might have gotten a little worked up, but that's when dinner showed up, and Ziggy had shut up about it and he'd nearly dropped off to sleep in his mashed potatoes.

So he'd gone to bed.

And he thought they had too.

Apparently not, because this morning, when he came downstairs showered and dressed and ready to not do whatever crazy, dangerous thing Ziggy had cooked up, he found the ladies also dressed and ready to enact Ziggy and Iris's Crazy Plan That Would Get Iris Killed.

So now he looked at them again, at their nonplussed expressions, and said, "Do I need to repeat myself? Over. My. Dead. Body."

"Just calm down, Hud," Iris said. "I'm not actually going to meet him. Ziggy's team can ping his phone, and they'll track him. But they need him to text me back first."

"And this is the guy who you think put a hit out on her?" He turned to Ziggy.

"We're not sure. There's an organization called the Orphans who broker hits—"

"Seriously. An organization? Why don't they call themselves, Assassins R Us?"

"It's a little on the nose, don't you think?" Iris said. "Maybe 1-800 Kill Me?"

He just stared at her. Shook his head.

"I'm kidding, Hudson. Take a breath."

He'd breathe when they were safely on Santorini. "So, these Orphans, they know who is trying to kill her?"

"I'm in touch with the leader, a woman named Raisa Yukachova who has helped us out in the past," Ziggy said. "She's looking into the source, but's it's difficult to nail down. Often the hit has to be completed and the payment made before they can track it down."

"Perfect. Just...yep. I'm getting the boat." Hudson got up.

"Hudson—"

"No!" He rounded on Ziggy. "I rue the day I met you at that bar. I even bought you a drink! What was I thinking? I'm an idiot—"

"It's possible the information that you helped deliver will save Shae's life."

He looked to Iris, back to Ziggy. Then, "But I don't want it to cost Iris hers."

And it was probably more emotional and weirdly possessive

than he meant, but...well, she *had* sat at the hospital with him for a day. Or two.

He looked at Iris. "Listen. I'm sorry I got you into this. I'm not James Bond. I'm not even Tom Cruise."

She frowned.

"I'm just a lousy wide receiver with a leaky brain who needs to get off this roller-coaster ride. And I think you should come with me."

Ziggy looked away.

Iris, however, met his gaze. Then looked at Ziggy.

Then, surprisingly, she got up. "He's right. I never wanted this life. I don't need to do something brave and spectacular like my brothers, and most of all..." She turned to Hudson. "I don't want to get you in trouble."

"I'll be fine." He met her eyes, so fixed to his, and it seemed he'd sort of made a pact with her.

Keep her safe.

Or maybe it was just with himself, but whatever. "And so will you. I promise."

Ziggy's jaw tightened. "Fine. Okay. It's probably better this way. I can text him, pretending to be you..."

"Hello, am I the only one with a functioning brain here? Why didn't we think of this sooner? Sheesh."

Ziggy gave him a smile. "Your country thanks you, Hudson."

"Yeah, well, my country better be paying for this hotel room, because it's *expeeeensive.*"

She laughed.

He turned to Iris. "Get your stuff. We're going to a Greek island. And we're not coming back until the world is at peace."

"That's a never, then?" Iris said, heading toward the stairs.

That might work for him.

He turned to Ziggy. "You call me if there's trouble, okay?"

She nodded. "But you be careful. These Marshalls...they have a way of getting in over their heads. And bringing the people around them in with them."

"I got this, Coach."

Ziggy picked up her backpack. "Okay. Hopefully your greatest tragedy will be a sunburn."

IT PROBABLY DIDN'T BODE WELL THAT THE GUARDS HAD taken both Vikka and Judah out of the infirmary in the morning for work.

And left Shae locked in the infirmary.

She'd met Judah's eyes as he left. He gave her a small shake of his head, his mouth a tight line. But something of confidence, almost peace, radiated from him.

You are not alone. You are still safe. She heard those words in her head, held on to them.

And maybe he was right, because with rain and snow spitting from the sky, she didn't mind staying huddled under her blanket, like Judah had suggested.

That, and she'd spent the better part of the day honing the end of the spoon into a sharp point.

The sea outside her window had turned dark, angry, frothy as it came into the harbor and thundered against the ship. The sky was a deep red as the sun set, the overhead clouds nearly black, the horizon bleeding out over the waves.

Still, despite the words, a knot grew in her gut all day.

One of the prisoners brought her kasha, some tea, and she ignored the weevils—they were dead anyway—and ate it down.

It sat like a brick in her gut.

Especially when the door lock turned and it opened to Captain Boris standing there. He said not a word about the fact her ties were broken and yanked her up by her arm.

"No trouble," he said as he pulled her down the hallway and then forced her down the stairs.

The deck looked slick, snow accumulating along the rails. The works crews had returned and now sat in the mess hall. The air shucked out her breath, the cold moving over her, down the back of her jacket, into her jumpsuit. She huffed out and her breath formed before her.

A hum tremored the air, and she looked up to see a helicopter moving overhead.

"Idti!" Boris jerked her and she stumbled, nearly fell on the wet deck.

"Hey!"

And that's when she looked up. And standing on the deck of the ship, flanked by a couple guards, radiating fury, confidence, maybe even a little revenge in his eyes—Ned.

Ned!

She jerked away from Boris, despite his hold on her, and took off.

Boris shouted, but she didn't care.

She slammed into Ned, her arms flinging around his neck. "You came back! You came back."

He grabbed her up tight, just for a second, then put her down, pushing her behind him. "We're not out of this yet."

Right.

Boris came up to them. Gestured with his chin.

No. It couldn't be that easy. But Ned's hand closed over hers and he took a step back. "We're just going to go down the stairs," he said softly.

She glanced behind her and spotted the prisoners emerging from the mess hall, forming lines on the deck.

And then her gaze caught on Judah. He stood by the rail of the ship, just watching, a strange look on his face. Sort of a smile? As if he'd known this would work out? Next to him stood Vikka.

She met Shae's eyes, lifted her chin as if in a nod, then brought a cigarette to her mouth.

Ned took another step back.

"Perestan!"

The voice came from near the superstructure, shouted out from the deck.

Shae froze as Lukka emerged along with a contingency of guards.

What—?

If your man is military, then he is worth something. Maybe even more than you. But you are both going to be sold. The Petrovs do not just set people free.

"Run," Ned said as he turned, grabbing her.

A shot zipped by them, and Ned yanked her toward the stairway.

The massive metal door came down over the stairway, blocking them in.

It barely slowed Ned down. He still had a grip on her arm and now pushed her behind a massive winch on the deck.

"Stay put."

Then he stood over her, his arms braced on either side of her. He was breathing hard, his chest rising and falling, the presence of him big and solid, and despite the shooting, she just wanted to turn and cling to him.

His mouth was by her ear. "We're going to have to go into the ocean."

More shots, and now there was yelling on the deck.

"Can you do that?"

You can be a victim of your circumstances, or you can be a victor.

"I can do that."

"Okay, let's—"

And that's as far as he got before someone grabbed him from behind. He shouted, rounded, but the guard was there—Boris. How he'd gotten there, she couldn't guess, but he had Ned on the ground, Ned fighting even as Boris slammed his rifle into his spine.

Ned roared, and another man jumped on him, caught him around the neck.

"Stop!" She held up her hands. "Stop!"

Ned looked at her with such agony she had to look away. Especially as they hauled him up and dragged her and Ned toward the deck.

Toward Lukka, who stood there with a small group of security. He wore a pair of black pants, a fur coat, a wool hat, and arrogance in his smile.

"Where do you think you're going?" Lukka said. "We're not done with you yet."

Then a hood went over Ned's head. He jerked, trying to fight the hands that worked to secure his arms.

No. No, it couldn't end this way. Could not—

Boom!

The entire ship convulsed, a blast tearing through the twilight. It knocked Shae to her knees, toppled Lukka and a few of his men.

Ned tore away from his captor and ripped off his hood. "C'mon!"

Of course a guy who detonated breacher charges, kicked in doors, and threw grenades for a living might not be rocked by the fact that the entire mess area exploded into flames.

She grabbed his hand, let him pull her up.

And couldn't help it—glanced over where Vikka had been standing.

The woman was gone.

But just for a moment, she thought she saw Judah. Standing in front of the flames, his eyes in hers.

If and when I blow up the ship, you'll be the first to know.

He smiled.

And then black smoke billowed over the ship, and he was lost.

"Run, Shae!"

Ned grabbed her hand, taking off across the deck toward the smoke. A few shouts, but shots went wide and he directed her down the passageway toward the stern of the ship.

And then she got it. "What about the lifeboat?"

"Good call—go! Go!"

More shots, but they'd made ground, and she sprinted toward the massive boat, held at a launch angle at the stern. An orange tub, it held maybe a dozen people, max, and looked like it had been last attached during the time of Stalin.

But beggars...

She scrambled up the stairs.

"Get inside! I'll unhook the lashing line!" Ned said.

She removed the safety pin and unlatched the door as he unhooked the battery cable.

"It's stuck!" She yanked on the door latch again.

More shots, and she ducked as Ned came behind her and wrenched the door open.

"In!"

She nearly fell in, catching herself on one of the chairs. They faced backward, toward the back door.

"Strap in!" Ned followed her, his feet on the chairs, holding himself up as he latched the doors.

A barrage of shots.

"We need to get off before they shred this thing!" Ned grabbed her, pulled her into the seat. "Belt in!"

Then he climbed up to the cockpit above.

She belted in, a cross strap over her body.

"Hold on to the seat in front of you!"

She grabbed her seat and looked up to see him belted in, then pumping a release handle.

Go, go—

More shots fired, and she wanted to scream, but they didn't seem to penetrate the boat.

"Hold on!"

They didn't move.

"Ned?"

"The brakes are still on—"

She watched as he broke an acrylic cover off a gear, then grabbed a bolt and inserted it onto one of the gears.

Pounding on the outside of the door, and the latch wiggled—

"They're coming—"

The boat released. Just like that, it slid, then picked up speed.

"Hold—"

They slammed into the water so hard she jerked in her seat. Then suddenly, they were floating, thrashing in the waves, but...

Off. The. Ship.

Shae unbuckled and climbed up next to Ned in the cockpit. He was trying to start the engine. "C'mon, honey, c'mon."

He glanced at her.

And for the briefest moment, smiled.

She smiled back.

"Gotcha," he said. Then turned back to the engine. It whined. Sputtered. He turned it off. Outside, the wind was pushing them back, toward the ship.

Shots fired down to the water.

"We're a duck in the water," he said.

She climbed down to the floor.

"What are you doing?"

"I'm looking for the engine." She pulled up a hook in the flooring.

The engine sat inside the compartment. "We used to live in this 1974 Volkswagen Rabbit. When it sat for a long time, the fuel would gum up, and it would need to be primed." She hunted around for the pump. "Found it."

More shots, and the waves knocked her over. She grabbed the seat, then got on her knees and braced herself. Then she unlatched the pump. Gave it a number of vigorous pumps. "Try it now!"

The engine nearly caught, sputtered. She kept pumping.

The motor roared to life, angry and coughing.

"Brace!"

She held on as Ned put the throttle down.

The lifeboat churned in the water, fighting for motion.

"Not quite the jet boat you'd hoped," she said and closed the hatch. Then she climbed up next to him. The night had fallen like a curtain, and in the distance, maybe forty yards away, the massive gulag ship rose against the darkness, the fire lighting up the sky, debris falling into the water. Hopefully, the prisoners had gotten off the ship—at the very least, the fire would create chaos, give them a fighting chance.

Shots still reported in the darkness, although at this distance, maybe the lifeboat was already in shadow.

The motor had slowly started to move them, pushing them through the waves toward the far harbor lights, the choppy water rocking them hard. Ned kept the throttle down, his feet braced like he might be Captain Ahab. His dark hair had been mowed back by the wind and rain, his parka soaked. Only now did she notice he wore a tactical vest under his jacket.

"You did it, didn't you?"

He glanced at her. "Did what?"

"Stole the caesium-137."

"Sort of." He looked back out the window. "It's under control."

She touched his arm. "Thank you for coming back for me."

He frowned, even as they cleared the harbor lights. "I'd never leave you, Shae."

She leaned up and kissed his cheek. "Ditto."

He didn't smile as they headed out into the choppy, rough sea. "But we have about five hundred miles to go before we're safe."

A massive explosion shook the air, and she looked back to see the entire ship engulfed in flames, the bow sinking into the depths.

Judah.

I know my fate, and I've made peace with it.

Thank you.

Then darkness closed in around them as Ned pointed them out to sea.

ELEVEN

I t had worked. Ned couldn't believe it.

In truth, he'd given their chances of getting off the ship alive about point seven percent.

But desperation made for blind faith, maybe.

He just needed to tell that to his heart, still back on the ship, a hood over his head, seeing his future unwind into a cell in some Chinese prison.

Tortured for information until he begged to die.

"Ned, you okay?"

Over the last few hours, Shae had found lights, powered by the generator, which was powered by the motor, and had been down below, digging around in the compartments under the seats, calling out when she uncovered items, like "C-Rations," and "drinking water," and "thermal suits."

Even, "There's instructions on how to launch the life raft. I think it's attached to the backside of the boat."

Good to know.

"Hey! There's toothpaste!"

Meanwhile, he'd been staring out at the black sea, wishing for stars, pretty sure he might be driving them in a circle.

She popped her head up into the hatch that sat above the

main section. "Hungry?" She handed up a wrapped candy bar, Cyrillic written on the outside.

"I think I'll pass. My stomach is already roiling."

"How much longer before we find land?"

"Five or six days?" If they were headed the right direction. For all he knew, he was pointing them due south, headed out to the Pacific Ocean.

Maybe they'd get picked up by a Japanese trawler.

But just as easily, a Russian cargo ship, headed back to Vladivostok or Sakhalin Island. But given Russia and America weren't at war yet, maybe he'd take his chances.

"Do we have enough fuel for that?"

Oh, she'd been brilliant with that fuel pump.

"I don't know. We've been out here for two hours, and the needle hasn't moved. I'm afraid it's stuck there."

"Which means it could die any moment?"

"And we turn into a bobber."

"As long we don't sink. We could probably live for a month down here, with all these rations."

"I've been radioing Alaska, but I'm not sure anyone is hearing me."

"Is that where we're going?"

"I'm hoping the coast guard has picked up our signal, but if not, I'm aiming for an island in the Aleutian chain. But at this point, I'd be happy to be on board a crabbing boat. It would help if the stars would come out. I'm just relying on my watch, and so far, it's pointing due west."

So maybe he wasn't going in a circle—

Shae touched his face. "Ned."

He looked at her, and for the first time really saw the bruises on her face. He ran his thumb over her cheek. "They sent me a picture of you like this, and...did they beat you?"

"I got into a fight."

He frowned. "You did *what*?"

"It was the only way Judah could get the blasting powder into

213

the kitchen, although with the explosion, maybe he put it near the propane tanks." Her eyes widened. "Vikka was smoking—I'll bet she put the cigarette in the blasting powder."

Ned just stared at her. "Who are you?"

She grinned. "Not a victim."

He laughed. "No, no, you're not." He cupped her face with his hands. "You are not."

Then he kissed her. Not a crazy kiss, nothing of desperation, but the kind of kiss that said maybe he'd underestimated her. A kiss of respect and appreciation, one that spoke of partnership and maybe, yes, a little need.

More need, the longer he kissed her. She tasted of the toothpaste she'd used, and smelled of the earth, and he wasn't repulsed in the least by it. In fact, maybe he smelled a little rough too, but she still wrapped her arms around his neck and held on, kissing him right back.

Maybe a growing need in her touch too.

He turned and drew her up against himself, pulling her closer, deepening his kiss. The boat's motor hummed, the sea rough, but right here, with Shae in his arms...

Maybe this was safety. Maybe it wasn't about tucking her away someplace without problems or trouble but knowing... knowing that they could face it all together.

Maybe it was about trusting her. Just like she trusted him.

Not independent people, but one flesh.

At least in his heart, and someday soon, in body.

And most of all, both of them trusting God.

He leaned up, met her beautiful eyes, searching them. "I still have that ring."

"What? Here? I thought it was in Alaska."

"Fraser brought it."

A beat. Oops.

"He's alive?" Her eyes filled. "Oh, Ned." She reached for him, her body wracking a little with what he guessed was relief.

She finally leaned back, and he unzipped his jacket. Then he opened his utility shirt to reveal his vest and ripped open the Velcro.

And inside that, in a plastic pouch, he dug out the ring. A beautiful one carat solitaire, no frills, just the simple beauty of an almost flawless diamond.

He held it out to her.

"Yes."

He put it on her finger. She nodded. "It never comes off again."

The boat rocked hard as it fell into a trough, and she gripped his jacket, holding on.

He put his hand on the wheel. "It's getting rougher out there."

"And colder. I'm going to put on a thermal suit."

She disappeared below, started rooting around. He picked up the radio again. "Mayday, mayday. Is anyone receiving this?"

He heard grunting and looked down. She lay on a bench, sliding into the rubber thermal suit. "Good thing I lost a few pounds. Sheesh."

He laughed.

The engine sputtered out.

"Shoot."

"I'll take a look," Shae said and opened up the hatch.

Water filled the hatch, the engine partially drowned.

"Ned?"

"Yeah, I see it. There's a bilge pump in the back." He climbed down and found the pump attached to the wall.

She put the hatch cover back on as he pumped.

"Get on the radio and keep calling for help."

The seas had roughened, the storm tossing them, and he fought to keep his balance as he pumped.

"It's not working!"

Whether Shae was referring to the radio or the bilge pump, he didn't know, because no, nothing was working.

The lights flickered off, the generator power dead.

So much for the radio.

Shae slipped down next to him. A sweat swept down his spine, despite the cold.

"Get a suit on," she said. "I'll pump."

Probably a good idea. He found the biggest one, slipped off his shoes and put it on, taking off his vest and parka to get it over his body and shoulders.

He zipped it up. All one piece, it included booties—a giant onesie.

He stepped down.

The water had breached the compartment, now ankle deep in the well between the seats. But the thermal suit warded off the icy water.

"Good idea, Shae."

"It probably won't last us long, but it's a start."

Outside, the sea raged, and he'd seen his fair share of *Deadliest Catch*. The swells in the Bering Sea could be thirty feet high, maybe more.

He'd give them another hour, maybe.

"Ned?"

He hadn't realized he'd been standing there, listening to his heartbeat, until Shae put her hands on his chest.

Then she simply moved them around his neck and held on.

Quiet. In the darkness.

He closed his eyes. No. Not like this. Not after everything.

"Let's deploy the life raft."

"It's probably got holes—"

"I don't know what else to do!"

He'd scared her maybe, because she loosened her hold. Pulled back. Aw, but— "I'm sorry, Shae. I'm so sorry. I thought...I thought I could get you out of this. Us out of this. But really, we're just going to die here in the middle of—"

She kissed him. And not a gentle kiss but something hard and purposeful and clearly to shut him up.

Fine. He kissed her back. Because frankly, it might be their last kiss, and if he was going to die—okay, he'd do it right there. In her arms. So he kissed her well and with everything inside him.

When the water sloshed over the benches, he broke away.

"Let's deploy the life raft. At least then we might have a chance."

She said nothing. Probably a good thing they had no lights.

Here went nothing. He unlatched the door. It swung open, the sea tossing them, filling their compartment as it splashed.

He stepped out onto the back and found the suitcase-sized raft attached to the back. Not a huge case, so that didn't bode well for room in the boat, but it was just the two of them.

"It'll float away!" Shae said.

"It's attached with a painter line. It connects the container to the lifeboat. As soon as the boat sinks, it will detach from the life raft and free it."

In theory.

He unlatched the unit from the boat, and it splashed into the darkness.

C'mon, *c'mon*.

Shae leaned out with him. That woman was going to go right into the sea. "Is it going to—"

With a pop, not unlike bread dough popping from a can, the life raft deployed, self-inflating into a small floating tent, the doors open.

He hauled it toward the boat, hanging on to the painter line as the sea pitched him. "Get a life jacket on!"

Shae appeared at the door a moment later, strapped in a massive life jacket, her hood up, mittens on her hands. She shoved a life jacket into his hands. "You too."

"Get on the boat."

"Not until you have your life jacket on."

He took it, shoved it over his head. "Get on!"

She stepped up beside him. In the darkness, he could barely make out the raft, despite its now-activated LED lights, and with the waves and the sea spitting at them—

He tied the line to the door, then lay, straddling the boat, reaching out for the life raft. Found the opening, the sea turning his hands to ice.

"Follow my arms. I've got the door!"

"You're right behind me, right?"

"Yes! I'm right behind you! Get in the raft, Shae!"

She climbed over him, then held on to the railing of the lifeboat, and shoved her feet into the hole.

He pushed her in.

She fell, landed hard.

The force of it yanked his knot free. The raft spiraled out into the ocean, still attached by the painter line.

He'd have to get wet to get in the boat.

"C'mon, Ned!" He barely heard Shae's scream over the pull of the sea.

He pushed back, turning to grab his tac vest—and ripping off the life vest.

He felt the swell a full ten seconds before it happened. The boat rode up the side, and the water filling the boat sloshed hard to port. Ned reached for a chair and got his hands on a pole running across the ceiling.

And then the boat flipped. Just like that, like the half-sunk bobber it was, right over onto its back.

The water filled the ceiling and Ned scrambled to right himself.

Shae.

Please let her still be afloat.

He grabbed his life jacket floating in the water and shoved it on. Tied it. So much for his tac gear. Water had flooded inside his onesie, but he put up the hood, fighting the cold, and headed for the door.

Closed.

He pushed against it, but the swell of the ocean had flooded the boat, pushed him farther into the sea, and the pressure outside jammed the door shut.

No.

He put his back to it, his feet against the chairs and managed to move it open, just a little, but when he turned around to push through, the water slammed it shut.

And of course, he'd managed to spill half the ocean into the boat. He was treading water now, the ocean up to his shoulders, the cold finding his bones.

He'd last about ten minutes in this sea.

Two minutes once the boat went under.

So at least his death would be quick.

No—not like this. Not without getting Shae to safety—

He pushed against the door again.

Nothing, the sea unmoving. He pressed up to the top—really, the bottom—of the boat and gulped air.

Slammed his fist into the ceiling. Not. Like. This!

He kicked the door, then again put his back to it, but everything shook.

Yeah, his death would be quick.

He shoved his mouth up against the slip of air still remaining. And something inside him just broke.

Not. Like. This.

He closed his eyes. Not like this, Lord.

Stay alive. God will come up with something.

Fraser's words. He winced at his own. *I'm sorry, bro, but I don't have time to wait for God's plan.*

Aw, yeah, he was an idiot. And now, he got to stand before God and admit it. Perfect.

Still—I'm sorry, Lord. I...

Come to Me, Ned. You, who labor and are heavy laden, and I will give you rest.

He stilled, and it seemed the words came from inside him. Or maybe not, but what else did he have?

He closed his eyes and took a long breath as the sea overtook him.

And then, he waited.

Ned wasn't right behind her.

Wasn't right behind her!

Shae righted herself from where she'd hit the side of the flimsy life raft tent. The wave had caught her, but instead of rolling her, she'd ridden over the top while the lifeboat overturned. It made a massive *thunk,* and now her raft flashed wan LED lights on it, bleeding out over the water. The outline of the orange boat reflected the light, a giant bobber in the water.

"Ned!" She stared out at the water, at the boat, overturned, breathing hard.

The line to the lifeboat had miraculously held, and now she reached out along it, hoping to feel his hand holding on.

Nothing.

"Ned!" The wind ate her voice.

No. This was not happening. Not happening.

Not after he'd rescued her, twice, from gulag. Not after she— after she'd fought her way free.

It was happening again. Life reaching out to steal the people she loved.

To steal Ned.

Ned was trapped inside. She knew it with every bone in her body. And no, she wasn't a victim, but she wasn't a SEAL either.

Oh God! She closed her eyes, holding on to the rope, every muscle in her body seizing.

Psalm twenty-three, verse four. You are not alone. And you are still safe.

"Ned!"

Everywhere she looked, darkness, the waves tossing her into valleys, the sea confused.

Yea, though I walk through the valley of the shadow of death, I will fear no evil; for you are with me.

Oh, she hoped so.

"Ned!"

Then, her very life came crashing over her as the lifeboat sank beneath the waves.

"No! Ned!"

She screamed, splashing the water, watching it go down.

Ned's voice came back to her, the bit about the rope connecting the raft to the lifeboat.

And how if it sank, it would detach.

She waited, watching the ghost of the boat vanish under the waves.

Ned—

She had to get him.

Not a victim. Not a victim—

The life jacket would keep her afloat. She unsnapped it, about to go over the edge.

Stay alive.

Ned's voice practically rumbled through her, to her bones.

No! But after everything he'd done for her—

Then the line drew taut. The raft started to fight it, to drag in the water.

No—what?

And this was it—survive or be dragged down with the lifeboat.

Wait—her spoon.

She unzipped her jumpsuit, grabbed the spoon, and used it to slice at the rope. Not a thick rope—just enough to hold the raft in an emergency. Her body wracked with tears as she sawed.

"I'm sorry, Ned, I'm sorry!"

The rope continued to pull.

"No!"

The rope broke from the raft.

"Shae!"

She looked up, and somehow *there he was*. Ned, floating away in the water from the broken line.

"Swim!" She practically launched herself out of the boat, hooking her feet into the straps along the edges. "Swim!"

Ned wore a life jacket and fought the waves. He caught her hand, nearly pulling her down, let go.

She grabbed him. "Hold on!"

He turned his hand, grabbed hers. Then she hauled him toward her, all the way to the edge of the raft.

She fell back, then scrambled to the edge, leaned over, and helped haul him in. He'd grabbed the straps inside, gave a massive scissor kick, and in a moment, had launched himself, breach, into the doorway.

He rolled to the middle, breathing hard. "Zip...the..."

She zipped the door panel shut.

They lay in a good two inches of water, but the life raft bobbed in the waves, fairly waterproof. "Gotcha," she said.

"Funny."

"Maybe a little?"

"I can't feel my hands."

She leaned over him, wishing for light. He still breathed hard. His hands were ice in hers. She rubbed them, blowing on them, then finally opening her thermal suit and pulling them inside.

"What happened?"

He pulled her hard to himself. His chest rose and fell, and she scrambled to open his thermal, get her body, although fully clothed, against his to warm it. She lay on his chest, listening to his heart, and thought it might leave his chest.

"The door...I couldn't...get it open." He swallowed. Took another couple of breaths. "And then I went under, and I thought—this is it. I had nothing, and for a long second I thought...it's over. And weirdly, I didn't panic. I floated there, freezing, my heartbeat slowing, my breath caught, and then...and then I realized—the door wouldn't open before because the water pressure outside was greater than inside. But once we were submerged, the pressure equalized. I pushed the door and it opened. Just like that."

Just like that. "I thought you'd drowned."

"We both would have if you hadn't cut the rope. How did you—"

"A spoon."

Silence. Then, "A spoon?"

"Yeah. Just a little trick being in the joint taught me."

"The joint."

"The slammer. The big house. The clink."

He pulled her down by her hood and kissed her. Cold lips, and he'd started to shiver, but she stretched out beside him and kissed him back. Then she threw a warm leg over him and pulled him into her arms. "Stay alive, big guy. We're not out of this yet. You're not alone. And you're still safe."

He held onto her, shivering as the sea tossed them. But the cocoon of their raft held, even as the sea calmed and the morning sun began to burn the outside of the tent.

He'd stopped shivering sometime in the night, and for a while, she feared he'd succumbed to hypothermia, but she kept waking him, and he kept grunting, so...

She watched as the sun swept over them, turning their cubicle to fire. Such a handsome man. Dark whiskers covered his chin, his eyelashes long on his face and determination etched into the lines around his eyes.

"Want some breakfast?"

He opened those beautiful eyes and frowned at her.

"I stole a couple candy bars and a hydration pack."

She'd relieved her thermal suit of her loot earlier and now retrieved them from a netted pocket and opened the hydration pack.

He took a sip, offered it back to her. "We need to save this in case—"

"We spend five days at sea?"

But he pushed himself up. Looked at her. "Do you hear that?"

She stilled, even tried to quiet her heartbeat. The faraway thump of— "Is that a helicopter?"

Crawling over to the door, she unzipped it and peered out.

A gorgeous red-and-white helicopter flew above the water, the words Air One written on the back behind a massive sliding door.

She waved, and the chopper came closer, the water whipping up with its blades. Around her, the giant swells still rolled, but less violently now, and overhead, the sun spilled gold into the sea.

Then, as she watched, a man came over the edge of the chopper on a line. He was lowered down, and she caught his foot and helped pull him in.

He landed on the floor of the raft. Dressed in a full dry suit, he wore goggles and gloves and carried a rescue halo.

"Hey there. My name is Axel. Let's get you off this raft."

She gestured to Ned. "Him first. He's in rough shape."

"Nope. She goes first," Ned said.

"Sorry, ma'am. I have orders from his brother to do anything he says." Then he tucked the rescue halo around her and clipped her to himself.

"I promise I'll be right back," he said to Ned.

Shae looked at him. "You'd better be right behind me this time."

Axel took her out of the raft, and she was hoisted up to the deck of the chopper. There, another man unhooked her and then secured her to a seat. Handed her a blanket. "Hey," he said. "You haven't met me yet, but I work for your uncle Ian. Name's Harry."

"My uncle Ian is here?"

"On a rescue ship about a hundred miles from here. We've been looking for you all night." He turned to the hoist. "Ready?"

Axel nodded.

"Swimmer's out the door," Harry said over the radio.

She watched as the rescue swimmer went down. Five minutes later, Harry was working the hoist to pull him back up.

Ned's arms were clutched close to his body, and he'd started shivering again. But that was a good thing, his body fighting to stay warm. Harry and Axel brought him on deck, and Harry set him next to her, wrapped a blanket around him.

"We need some warm fluids," he said to Axel, who'd unlatched and closed the door.

"How'd you find us?" Ned said, fighting chattering teeth.

"Your EPRIB. It started beeping about four hours ago."

Ned closed his eyes, smiled. "I forgot I was wearing that."

Then, as the sun broke the plane of the eastern horizon, rising over the water, the chopper followed the golden trail home.

TWELVE

"You okay? You've been pretty quiet since you got home."

The voice came from her uncle Ian, and Shae glanced over as he joined her at the window.

With a new layer of snow, the Montana landscape appeared forgiving, grace layered upon the rolling hills and inspiring peaks in the distance. Glacier National Park. Brutal. Breathtaking.

"I like the remodel," Shae said of the great room, and of course, what wasn't there to like? With the soaring two-story shale-rock fireplace, and wood flooring, overstuffed leather furniture, and a massive hanging chandelier, the inside almost matched the grandeur of the outside.

Ian and his wife Sierra had practically gutted the old ranch house. Of course, when they bought it, Ian had been nearly broke. But the ranch had been on the edge of bankruptcy, sat on the meandering Mercy River and faced the mountains, and Sierra wanted to raise her children on land instead of in the cute bungalow she and Ian had built in town, so Ian had sold his last stocks, bought the house, and rolled up his sleeves.

She didn't know how her uncle had bounced back financially so quickly, but he was a keen businessman, so whatever he'd done, well, it'd worked.

He now owned fifty acres of cattle pasture, a beautiful log home completely remodeled inside. And sure, it was about half the size of his million-dollar estate he'd sold to country music star Ben King, but this was filled with the sound of their toddler daughter, a beautiful baby boy, and Ian and Sierra building a life together.

They'd given her a room, of course, because Ian had told her she'd always have a home with him.

"I'm fine."

"I saw Ned outside earlier."

"He went for a run."

"Surviving in the Bering Sea isn't enough of a workout?"

"He got a call from his Master Chief, and I think he wanted to take it outside."

She blew on her coffee. She'd taken a total of five showers and one very long bath and still didn't feel like she had all the grime of the prison ship off her.

Maybe she never would. Maybe the memories would always be with her.

Not all of them traumatic.

It means that in the middle of battle, when we're surrounded on all sides, God still provides for us. In fact, He blesses us with more than we even need. We are still His chosen ones.

Judah. Her jaw tightened. What if he never made it off the ship?

The hard fist in her gut said he probably didn't.

Her eyes burned.

"Shae?"

"I just..." She looked up at her uncle. Handsome, with dark reddish-brown hair, now in need of cutting, and the slightest reddish beard. Such a good man, he'd had his own losses—like his first wife and baby. "Thank you, Uncle Ian."

He put his arm around her, pulled her to his side. "I told you long ago, Shae, that you were safe with me. You're my family, and I'll always be there for you."

227

"Chartering a coast guard ship—"

"Ex-coast guard ship. I think maybe Fraser's friend Moose might be in need of a ship."

"You're going to buy him a ship?"

"No...well, he runs a SAR outfit out of Alaska, so it's tax-deductible..."

She laughed. "Well...we weren't going to last out there much longer, so...thank you." She looked up at him. "But what I really meant was thank you for coming to get me all those years ago. And for keeping your promises. And for showing me that God does...choose me."

He blinked down at her. Then nodded. "After my wife died, I thought God had abandoned me. Even betrayed me. I'd worked so hard, done all the right things...I thought I was in this life alone and it was up to me to save myself."

She made a face. "I get that."

"I know you do. And funny enough, it took me being thrown overboard and lost at sea to realize that God *hadn't* abandoned me. He, in fact, saved me. And He keeps saving me. Especially when I think I can go it alone."

"So it's in the genes."

He raised an eyebrow.

"This independent streak."

He made a noise of agreement. "I guess it is. I'm hoping that surrender and faith might also be in the genes then, too."

"I think, maybe, God sent an angel to me while I was in prison."

"Really?"

"His name was Judah. Lion. He said he was a spy, but...I don't know. But he protected me and even blew up the ship so we could escape."

"I still can't believe you were on a Russian prison ship."

"Me either. I'm afraid to think what's next." She took a sip of coffee.

Ian just stared at her. "I want to say *probably nothing*, but knowing you, Shae...all I can say is, if anyone can survive, it's you." He smiled at her. "By the way, Ned asked me for my blessing to marry you. He said you already said yes."

"I did. But nice of him to ask you."

"The answer is yes. But my question is, what took you two so long?"

He probably meant it as a joke, but she turned back to the window, sighed. "I don't know his reasons—I mean, a lot of them have to do with his career as a SEAL. But I didn't push either. As much as I wanted to get married, I think I was afraid of it. I loved Dante. And I love Ned. And I think I was afraid of turning into my mother and needing them so much...and then having them betray me." She shook her head. "You'd think after what Ned and I went through with Blackburn I would trust him. And I do—I so do. But he had his career, and sometimes it felt like being a SEAL was more important than being with me." She looked at Uncle Ian. "And I'm not trying to get in the way. Really. But it made me...independent."

"You decided to only need yourself."

She nodded. "Until I went to gulag."

"That's a statement."

She laughed. "I was number twenty-three. And there was a door code written in my container—twenty-three-oh-four. It's also the verse in the twenty-third psalm about walking through darkness without fear because God is with me. I guess I started to believe it."

From down the hall, a baby's cry lifted.

"I gotta go. But for the record, Shae, you aren't your mom. Not because you're stronger or you're marrying the right man, but because you keep fighting for joy. For hope. For faith. That, right there, is your superpower."

He pulled her close and kissed the top of her head. "I'm so proud of you." He let her go and walked down the hallway to his newborn son and wife.

She turned back to the view of the mountains, the glorious sky above.

Her ring sparkled in the light. How she'd managed to keep it on in the ruckus of their escape from the sinking lifeboat, she didn't know.

But it was never coming off again.

Behind her, the mudroom door opened and Ned came in, dressed in boots, cargo pants, a parka, and hat. So, maybe not running. But he did have his ear buds in. He stomped off his boots, then pulled them off and shucked off his jacket. Took off his hat and ran his hand through his damp hair.

He wore a thick beard, his hair curly and wild, and a thermal shirt he'd borrowed from Ian. Filled it out well. The pants, too, were probably borrowed. Maybe from Fraser, who'd met them on the boat, having contacted Moose and then her uncle Ian.

Who had never gotten a call from Lukka Petrov, so there was that.

Fraser had flown straight home from Anchorage after Ned and Shae were admitted to the hospital and cleared.

They'd flown to Montana the next day with Ian. Ned had slept for nearly twenty-four hours straight.

Now showered, the fresh wind and scent of outdoors on his skin, Ned came into the room and joined her at the window.

She stepped back, leaned against him, his hands around her shoulders. He pressed a kiss to her neck. His heart was thundering.

"You okay?"

He sighed. She stepped away, set the coffee mug on a table, then came over and put her arms up around his neck. "What's going on, sailor?"

"Well, this is all top secret, but the part that I can tell you is that we had partial mission failure of our last op."

"Our?"

"The team went after the caesium I gave to the Russians."

She met his eyes. "Are you in trouble?"

"No...not if we can find it. And we might be able to—I left a tracking device in the case. It's just...the team got delayed going in country. And now the package is trapped in Russia."

"In the hands of the Petrov Bratva."

"Maybe. Yes." His mouth pinched. "That was Master Chief Trini asking me if I wanted back on the mission."

Oh.

"I told him I still have two weeks of medical leave, and I'd like to get married." Then he smiled. "What do you think?"

She wanted to be smiling, to say yes, but... "Ned. You need to get that caesium back. Otherwise you could be arrested for treason, get a dishonorable discharge—your life destroyed."

His smile vanished. "What are you saying?"

"I don't want to visit you in jail."

"Why not? I visited you."

"That's not funny."

One side of his mouth tweaked up. "It was a little funny."

She touched her forehead to his chest. "Just...listen to me." She met his eyes. "Go with your team. Find the caesium. I will be right here when you get back. I'm not going anywhere."

His mouth opened. Closed. "I—"

"Call Master Chief back. Tell him you're on a plane for—where? Russia?"

"Classified."

She made to push him away, but he caught her, pulled her in.

"No." He wrapped his arms around her waist. "I'm not leaving. I know my name is on the line, and I know my freedom is at stake. But I told Trini no not only because I want to stay and marry you but because I have to let go. I've spent my entire life afraid of being helpless, but I'm not here to help God. Or even for Him to help me. I'm here to surrender and obey. And God has this. So..." He lowered his mouth to just above hers. "I'm sticking around, babe. At least for right now."

And then he kissed her. Sweetly, but without a hint of

hesitation. Just a full-on kiss, slow, solid, and leaving no room in her mind about his intentions.

He tasted of her future, and the home she'd always wanted.

Wherever it was.

You are not alone, Shae. And you are still safe.

Yes.

He finally let her go, and she reached up and wove her fingers into his beard. "I'm hoping you keep this."

"We'll see."

His phone in his knee pocket buzzed, and he let her go to pull it out. "Fraser." He answered and turned the phone on speaker. "Bro. 'Sup?"

"Have you heard from Iris?"

Ned looked at Shae and she shook her head.

"Not since we left her in Paris."

Silence, and Ned heard Fraser relay this information to someone on the other end.

"What's going on?"

"Mom talked to her about five days ago, but she hasn't heard from her since, and she's not answering her phone. She's worried. I called Roy, and he got ahold of Ziggy. Am I on speaker?"

"Yes, but it's just Shae here."

"Okay." He cut his voice low. "Just me and Jonas here, but Ziggy told me that there's a hit out on Iris."

A beat, and Shae tried to assimilate the words.

"A hit? Like a contract? On her *life? Why?*"

"Mm-hmm. And she's not sure. She has some theories, but biggest issue is that they left for Santorini a couple days ago and she hasn't heard from them. They didn't check in at the resort Hudson had booked."

"They're together?"

Who's Hudson? Shae mouthed. Ned held up his hand.

"Apparently, he took to heart my words to keep her safe. So they're probably fine, but...Mom's worried, and that's without knowing about the contract. So I think...we need to track her down."

Ned looked at Shae.

She just nodded.

"Okay, I'm on a flight home."

"Thanks. I'm sorry to cut short...whatever you're doing out there in Montana."

"See you soon, Fraser," Shae said, just before Ned ended the call.

He looked at her.

"You don't seriously think that I'd let you go without me?"

His expression morphed into a sigh, then a smile. "I guess it's one way to keep you out of trouble."

She stepped up to him, wrapped her arms around his neck and met his gaze. "You wish, sailor. You wish." And then she kissed him. Because their happily-ever-after was just beginning.

What Happens Next

"I could stay here forever." Iris sat on the back of a beautiful two-cabin, forty-six-foot single-hull Beneteau sailboat, her feet up on the bench, holding herself up on her outstretched arms. Her face lifted to the warm wind skimming off the glorious blue Aegean Sea.

Hudson sat behind her at one of the twin helms of the big boat, one hand on the wheel, his gaze behind his Ray-Bans on the tall sail, the scattering of islands around them. He wore a linen shirt, a pair of white shorts, and over the past two days had developed a milky brown tan. The sun also managed to lift all the highlights from his dark-blond hair, and it only deepened the blue of his eyes.

What was she doing here? With Adonis?

Hiding. She probably shouldn't forget that part.

"Me too," Hudson said, and when she looked over, his gaze was on her. "I don't think I've slept so well as I have the last two days."

"Right? There's something about the gentle list of the boat, the waves and the sound of the ocean... How's the headache?"

"Gone."

"Still upset about losing your rental?"

"Not even a little." He grinned at her, his teeth shiny, the wind pressing the shirt against his toned body. "Best idea ever—renting the boat. Good call."

"I just said it looked like fun. I didn't expect you to decide to cancel your reservation and sail away into the blue."

"Seemed like exactly the right move if we really mean to hide."

"You could have chef's prepared fresh catch of the day. Whatever that is."

"I liked the plantain and rice dish you made last night. You're a great cook."

She didn't know why that warmed her through. Maybe it was the sunshine, the unwinding of the stress of the past, well, three years, really.

And she'd definitely never been this relaxed around a man—especially a football player. But maybe it had to do with Hudson's lack of innuendo or even expectation. He hadn't even held her hand since the hospital, so maybe the girlfriend thing hadn't stuck.

Probably not. A guy like Hudson needed a supermodel. Someone who watched his games, didn't ref them.

Besides, the league probably had rules about a player dating a ref, so there was that.

No, they were just friends. But he was easy to be around.

"Feel like snorkeling?"

"Sure." She wore a swimsuit under her sun dress, something she'd picked up at a little shop in a tiny seaside town call Korissia the first day.

He'd made her use cash, which she'd withdrawn from an ATM in Athens. Smart.

"I didn't know you had your captain's license."

Hudson was steering them into shallower water. "My grandparents owned property on King Island, in Tasmania. They had a classic Van de Stadt 40 and would take us out on day trips when we went to visit for Christmas. I got my captain's license the year I turned eighteen."

She turned, put her feet down, spread her arms along the sides of the boat. "I feel a little guilty asking Yannick to find a replacement for me, but—"

"You didn't tell him where you were, right?" He steered them into the wind, and the sails luffed.

"No, of course not. I said I had something coming up. We only had one more commitment on the schedule—a practice then an exhibition game with the Barcelona Dragons. Against the Vikings."

"Yeah, I know. I called Coach Max, our wideout coach as well as my agent, said I needed a few days. Since it's an exhibition game, they gave me the game. Nothing on my radar until the event in Lauchtenland, right before Thanksgiving."

"I'm slotted for that game too," she said. "Vienna Vikings are playing the Minnesota Vikings—that's a fun twist."

"The ELF and the NFL are trying to drum up support for both teams. And it's for charity."

He climbed forward on the boat to throw down the anchor, and she stood up and pulled off her cover-up. He'd parked them in a beautiful private bay with cliffs rising from the sea and a brilliant reef teeming with fish.

"Where are we?"

"That's Santorini to the east." He pointed behind him, and she looked over, cupping her hands over her eyes.

Creamy white buildings climbed up the side of a mountain, one on top of another, with beautiful blue- or gold-domed buildings rising into the horizon.

"That's Thira. We can go there for dinner, but I heard that the sunsets on the north side of the island, near Oia, are gorgeous."

"How do you expect me to return to my life when you show me places like this?"

He grinned at her. "Who says we're returning?"

She laughed and picked up her goggles and snorkel, as well as fins sitting in a webbed bag on the seat. She handed him his fins and mask as he came back.

A few motorboats and other sailboats floated by in the distance, their glorious sails white against the pale blue sky.

It felt like...maybe a honeymoon. Without the romance.

So maybe not a honeymoon, but definitely not a hideout from lethal assassins on her tail.

"I'm still trying to wrap my mind around the idea that someone wants to kill me." She put on her mask. "It doesn't feel real."

He pulled off his shirt, leaving only his swim trunks, the baggy kind. So American.

Phew.

But she also averted her eyes. No need to stare. It was strange enough sharing a boat with him. Like sharing a hotel suite, in a way.

"I know," he said. "We're having too much fun."

Then he ran and cannonballed into the ocean. Water splashed over her, and she screamed. But nothing serious, and in a second, she'd followed him over the side.

The water slicked the heat from her body, cool and perfect as she sat in the water and pulled on her fins. Then she cleared her mask and snorkel and dipped her head in the water.

He was already on the bottom, maybe fifteen feet down, gesturing to her.

She took a breath, then kicked hard and followed him down. He floated near a ledge and pointed.

A giant octopus sat, fat and bulbous, floating in the shadows. It blinked at them, then danced away. A thousand tiny orange fish scooted by, as one. The reef was thick with orange and pink coral, ferns, and what she referred to as blue brains.

She kicked to the surface. Took a breath.

Hudson followed her up. "Did you see the turtle?"

"No—where?"

"I'll show you." He took a breath again and headed back down. She did the same, following him.

He had stopped next to the reef outcropping again and now gestured to her. She kicked close and he reached out, grabbed her hand, pulled her in to him.

Right against him. He put his arm around her waist to hold her, and pointed.

There, in the blue-green shadows, a massive sea turtle lay on the sand, just hanging out, a few fish attached to his shell. His flipper feet dug into the sand.

So close she could touch him.

Hud looked at her, gave her a thumbs-up.

Not. A honeymoon. Not even a date—

A thrum thundered through the water, muffled but violent, and it shifted the sand beneath them. The turtle woke, kicked away. Around them, fish lifted from the reef, scattering.

She looked at Hud, but he was already headed to the surface.

Kicking hard, she followed him.

Gasped for air at the top. "What was—"

Hudson grabbed her arm, turned her.

The beautiful Beneteau burned, a funeral pyre on the sea. "What? Was the stove on?"

Then shots pinged the water, ricocheting near them.

She looked at Hud.

"I think someone's shooting at us!" His eyes widened as another shot pinged the water. "Dive!"

She gulped a deep breath, one filled with fear and shock and terror, took hold of Hud's hand, and dove.

THANK YOU FOR READING NED.

I hope you loved revisiting Shae and Ned's love story, and getting to know more about Iris and Hud.

Find out what happens after they are plunged into the waters of the Mediterranean!

Get Iris at your favorite retailer.

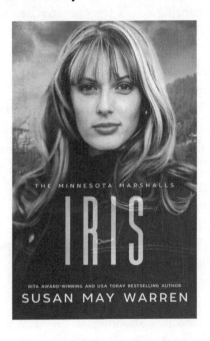

Iris Marshall, a football league official, finds herself on the run from a killer after agreeing to be a courier for the CIA. The last person she expects to protect her is football player Hudson Bly, a man whose career she almost destroyed. More, she never expected to develop feelings for him. Outwitting a dangerous assassin is one thing—figuring how to navigate the treacherous terrain of their hearts might be harder than they think. Turn the page for a sneak peek into the next thrilling romantic adventure of the Minnesota Marshall saga!

IRIS

The Minnesota Marshalls || Book Four

CHAPTER 1

She simply couldn't ignore the bullets.

Or the bombing.

Or even the last twenty-four hours hiding in a damp and dark cave under some cliffside in the Aegean Sea.

Regardless of how much Iris wanted to live in denial.

"You okay, ma'am?"

She looked up from where she sat, shivering on the bench of the fishing trawler, the sun from the cloudless Greek sky warming the towel she draped around her shoulders.

"Yes. Just...tired."

The man, mid-sixties, cast his shadow over her, cutting off the glare of the sun. His skin was the shade and texture of deep leather, with white whiskers, perhaps a couple days old, on his face. He wore a fisherman's hat that shaded his blue eyes, and a navy-and-white striped tank top, a pair of rubber pants, and connected boots held up with suspenders.

But it was his kind eyes that drew her, and now he gave her a small compassionate frown. "How long were you at sea?" His English was choppy, thick with accent.

She glanced at fellow castaway, Hudson Bly, who was now climbing aboard the trawler, being hauled up by a couple younger fishermen, perhaps the sons of the elder. He was pretty scraped up, given his heroics in the cave, his shoulders and back bearing the claw marks of the rocks. But under the sun, with his blond hair, that hard-athlete body, square jaw, dark-blue eyes, he still looked every inch a sort of Australian Adonis.

Who'd nearly lost his life because of her.

"Overnight," she whispered.

The fisherman handed Hudson a towel now also, and he slipped over to sit beside her on the bench, his body warm against hers.

Nope, she wouldn't think about the cave.

Or how they'd nearly died...again.

"Our boat blew up," Hudson said, wiping his face, then shaking his head like he might when he emerged from a shower after one of his Vienna Vikings football games.

"Engine trouble?" This from one of the younger fishermen, same blue eyes, dark-brown hair. He wore a T-shirt, the arms ripped off, and identical rubber coveralls.

"Something like that," Hudson said, and glanced at her.

Oh, she could barely look at him, because the man was so lying, and the truth of it just burned through her.

No, she wanted to say. Not engine trouble. Because someone bombed our boat.

Hudson might have read her mind, because he frowned, then gave the slightest shake of his head.

"Lucky to be alive," said the older man. "We will get you back to port." He nodded toward his son, the one at the helm, and the boat engaged. "We already have our catch."

He gestured to a pile of sopping nets in the front of the boat, writhing with small red lobster-type critters, hundreds of pale silver- or red-patched fish, and a few massive striped blackfish. The net seemed alive, the fish thrashing for air as the younger fisherman threw water from the sea onto the mess.

"We will take them to port and separate them," said the man. "Name is Xaris. That is Theo, my nephew, and my son Nico in front." He hung on to the canopy over the bridge as the boat churned up the water. "Nearly didn't see you. Could have run right over you." He raised an eyebrow.

Yes, it might not have been the best idea for them to swim out of the cave, shouting and yelling for rescue—and not only because the blue-and-orange trawler happened to be motoring by, picking up nets, possibly hooks hanging out. But because of other reasons.

People-hired-to-kill-her reasons.

The boat bounced over the waves as they headed out to the open sea between the island they'd hidden on and bigger Santorini. She'd stared at the lights for the better part of the night, tempted—well, at least until the tide had come in.

But now, as the boat skimmed across the water, cutting through the waves, frothy-tipped out here in the open, Hud had been right.

Better to hide, to take their chances in the dark maw of the cave than at sea.

But it hadn't been without cost.

"Funny that no one picked up your boat fire," said Xaris. "Or found you two floating in the wreckage."

Hudson nodded, his mouth a tight line.

She looked away but felt his hand move to hers, squeeze it.

So, clearly he didn't want her to tell anyone about their desperate underwater swim as bullets pelleted the water, the way they'd surfaced near shore, behind a bevy of rocks, watching as their boat burned black, then sank into the sea as another circled it before setting off down the shore, searching for them.

"Where'd you spend the night?"

Hudson looked at the man and drew in a breath. And just like that, she heard the voice, slightly accented, of a woman named Ziggy, occupation sketchy, who'd just happened to show up a step before trouble found them. *I found out who put the hit on Iris.*

A hit. As in someone wanting her *dead*.

Why, they still hadn't figured out. In fact, Hudson hadn't wanted to stick around to sort out the answers either.

Poor guy. He actually thought he'd been the one to get her into trouble. She could still hear his desperation in the hotel room in Athens nearly five days ago. *Listen. I'm sorry I got you into this. I'm not James Bond. I'm not even Tom Cruise. I'm just a lousy wide receiver with a leaky brain and need to get off this roller coaster ride. And I think you should come with me.*

"We spent the night in a cave," Hudson said.

Xaris's eyes widened. "Not Cave Aspro?"

Hudson lifted a shoulder.

"It's an all-white cave. They say it is covered in the tears of nuns," said Nico, climbing along the deck of the boat and jumping down beside them. "A pirate ship caught them and left them to die there. It's filled with stalactites and dead, jagged coral. At night, the tide completely fills it."

"We know," Hudson said.

Nico raised a dark eyebrow, his gaze going to Hudson's shoulders, the loosened blood that stained the towel.

"Are you on your honeymoon?" This from Xaris. Behind him, the shore grew, along with the port of Santorini with its fishing boats and houses built on the craggy hillside. Along the top of the ridge, like so many hats, sat the whitewashed buildings, one on top of another, many with domed roofs, all nestled together.

Magical. And the perfect place for a honeymoon.

Iris looked at Hudson. She'd used the lie only a few days ago when he'd been hospitalized, but—

"Yes." Hudson lifted their clasped hands. "We're staying in Santorini—just took a rental out for the day. I don't think we're getting our deposit back." He grinned, and wow, she'd seen his charm up close and personal, but now it had the power to loosen the aura of suspicion she hadn't noticed until that moment.

Then, he leaned over and kissed her on the cheek. "I'll bet you can't wait for a warm shower and a gourmet dinner, right, honey?"

She'd be happy for dry clothes and a vending machine sandwich, but she nodded.

"You look familiar," Nico said, frowning. "I don't know where."

Hudson lifted a shoulder. "I get that a lot. I sort of look like an actor."

"Hmm," said Nico, but the boat was turning into the harbor, and he left to pick up a line.

Iris glanced at him. Raised an eyebrow. "An actor?"

"Yeah. Didn't you see the new *Reacher* on Netflix? It's a series—Coach says I look like that actor."

She hadn't seen it, and frankly, Nico probably hadn't either, but, "Right." Because if the man was a fan of American football in Europe, then they both knew exactly why Nico recognized the six-foot-four, blindingly handsome, fit and sturdy wide receiver from the Vienna Vikings.

"Let's hope he's not interested in a selfie," she said.

They pulled up alongside other fishing boats coming into dock. The place smelled of fresh catch, salt, and oil, and dockhands tied up boats as fishermen sat on deck, sorting their fish from the nets. A road switchbacked up from the harbor to the pristine town. Horses snorted nearby, tied up, waiting to pull carts filled with today's catch to market.

Or at least, that's what Iris supposed. She also wanted to suppose that the nightmare was over—that whoever had shot at them yesterday, blown up their boat, and sent them to spend the most terrifying night of her life in a cave made of jagged shells might have decided to give up, and was most definitely not waiting for her in some nearby bistro, drinking coffee and eating baklava.

Her stomach growled as she got up.

"You can't walk around town like that, ma'am," Nico said.

She still clung to her towel, but under that she wore only her swimsuit.

Thank the Lord it wasn't a bikini. But still.

"Here," said Nico and reached for a grimy denim button-up shirt wadded into a cubby near the helm.

"Thanks." She managed a smile, then dropped the towel and pulled on the shirt. It hung about three sizes too big, the cuffs wagging, the tail of the shirt to her knees. "Who owned this? Andre the Giant?"

"My brother, Atlas," Nico said, laughing.

She glanced at Hudson, who appraised her, nodding.

"Thank you." First stop was a store.

Well, no. They might need money, given that her cash was currently swimming with the fish in the depths of the Aegean.

Hudson climbed out first, then held out his hand. "Thanks again for saving us."

Xaris shook his hand. "You know where you're going?"

Not a clue, but Hudson grinned, nodded. "We're staying at resort nearby."

They were?

Hudson took her hand, and she climbed off the boat and onto the dock. Managed not to drop to her knees and kiss the cement jetty.

Nico stood in the boat, hands on his hips. "Really familiar. You sure we haven't met?"

"Really? You run into a lot of shipwrecked Americans?" Hudson reached down to shake his hand.

Nico laughed. "That's it. *In the Heart of the Sea*."

Iris just stared at him.

"You're Chris Hemsworth."

A beat, and then Hudson laughed. Something loud and full, and even Iris had to smile.

"I wish, mate," Hud said, sounding decidedly Australian. "But I'll take it."

Iris rolled her eyes.

Hud took her hand. "C'mon, darlin'. Before more of my fans find me."

"Please." But she held on, because she was hungry and tired, and maybe he did, just a little, resemble a superhero.

Stop. She wasn't looking for a man in her life.

They were barely friends.

In fact, as soon as she could, she needed to ditch him.

Because, despite his words, this was all her fault, and she knew it.

But his hand warmed hers as he led her across the long boardwalk, away from the harbor and toward a row of cafés.

"I could really use a or a dress or—anything."

He glanced down at her. "Not a fan of denim?"

"It smells like fish."

"The dogs like it." He gestured to a stray hunting her down behind them. "Shoo," he said, and the dog loped off.

The air swept off the sea, carrying with it the briny smell, and the sun shone down upon massive trees of bougainvillea that spilled over rooftops and walls, brightening the cliffside with vibrant pink flowers.

So maybe it wasn't a terrible place to be shipwrecked.

"Just take the shirt off."

"Not a chance."

"You don't like walking around town in your swimsuit?"

"Oh sure. It's my favorite. I'd wear one to work, but it could get breezy."

"Not to mention no one would ever catch a pass again." He grinned at her, then pulled her into a nearby shop.

A fishing shop, filled with net supplies and lures and buoys and all manner of seafaring goods. But he spotted something and pulled her over to a display of rain jackets. Picked one up. "This should fit."

"And what are you going to buy it with, Hemsworth?"

"I'm going to barter, like the Greeks do."

He walked up to the counter. A teenager—maybe sixteen, a

hundred pounds soaking wet, dark hair, and big brown eyes—looked at him.

"Would you trade for the jacket?"

The boy looked at him, then at her. "Trade what?"

And then Iris had nothing as Hud pulled off a ring he wore on his right hand. Gold, with a stone set in the middle. "What are you doing?"

He ignored her.

The boy picked it up. Looked it over. Shrugged.

Hud took the jacket and slipped it off the hanger. Then he handed it to her.

She stared at him. "What was that ring?"

"Just something I picked up in Vienna. Not important. Trade you."

"You wear the jacket."

"For one, it's too small. For two, I saw the way you were eying Nico and all his fisherman manliness—"

"Oh, for the love." She pulled off the shirt and handed it over. He gave her the jacket. She put it on, zipped it up. Lightweight, it still fell down to her thighs.

He, in the meantime, completely filled out the shirt.

"How about these shoes too?" He addressed the kid at the counter, holding up two pairs of short rubber boots—one pair for him, the other for her.

The kid nodded, and she slipped on the rubber booties. "I look ridiculous."

"I look like Chris Hemsworth." He too wore the boots.

"Don't let that go to your head."

"Way too late for that."

She followed him out into the sunshine. "Now what, Skipper?"

"We go to the resort."

"What resort?"

He turned to her. "The one we were supposed to stay at five days ago. It's actually not far from here." He pointed up the hill, the one with the switchbacks that led to the sprawling white village on the hill. "Except for the little hike there."

"Now I understand the need for my special shoes."

He smiled at her. "Hope you don't mind the honeymoon suite."

"You did not."

"At the time, you were my girlfriend. Thought it was time to take the next step." He started up the sidewalk.

Hudson. "Okay, stop."

He turned, squinting at her in the sunlight.

"This is...I don't know what's happening here, but this isn't a game, Hud. We...we nearly died. I thought—I've never been so scared in my life. And that was after the bullets and the fire. And you—you're hurt. You might even need medical attention. But more—people are trying kill us!"

He held up his hand, glancing around. "Ixnay on the illkay."

She put her hands over her face. "Please, listen to me—"

"No, you listen to me." And then he was right there, invading her space, so close to her that when she opened her eyes, she had to put a hand to his chest—his very Chris Hemsworth chest—to steady herself.

"I know this is not a game, Iris. But I was there last night too, and I remember how unraveled you were—"

"I wasn't—"

"For Pete's sake, Iris!"

"Just—whatever, okay? I don't want to think about it!"

"Me either. In fact, right now, I just want a bed, and breakfast, and maybe not in that order, but the more I think about the last twenty-four hours, and even the last week, the more I'm back in that cave trying not to drown, so yeah, if I have to make jokes and pretend that we're on a honeymoon, and laugh at your attire and the way you flirted with Nico—"

"I didn't—"

"Kidding. See? You mad at me is better than you scared, right?"

She blew out a breath. "Yeah, I guess so."

"Okay then. Let's get to the hotel, and then if you want to fall apart, that's fine. I'll be on the phone to Ziggy trying to figure out our next step. Okay?"

"I'm not going to fall apart."

He met her eyes, held her gaze. "Right. Okay. Good." He stepped back. Took her hand. "Let's try to not die between here and the hotel, okay?"

She smiled. "You do look a little like Chris Hemsworth."

"I know." He smiled. "Let's hope the front desk clerk thinks so too." Then he winked.

And she followed him. Because maybe denial was exactly where she wanted to be.

Get Iris at your favorite retailer.

Want More Like This?

Meet the Montana Marshalls—cousins to the Minnesota Marshalls—a family with Big Dreams, and Big Trouble, under the Big Sky.

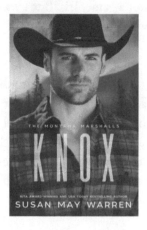

A cowboy protector. A woman in hiding. Forced proximity

might turn friends to sweethearts if a stalker doesn't find them first...

Montana rancher Knox Marshall's danger years are behind him. A former bull-rider, he now runs the Marshall family ranch, raising champion bucking bulls for the National Professional Bullrider's Expo (NBR-X). Wealth and success are his, and he's not looking for trouble.

But trouble is looking for county music star Kelsey Jones. Onstage, the beautiful rising star of the Yankee Belles becomes the person she longs to be - vivacious and confident - burying the brokenness she carries from a violent assault. But her attacker just might be on the loose...

Knox and Kelsey's paths collide when an explosion at an NBR-X event traps them in the rubble, igniting Knox's obsession to find the bomber and protect Kelsey...no matter the cost.

Available now at your favorite retailer.

Thank you for
Reading

Thank you again for reading *Ned*. I hope you enjoyed the story.

If you did enjoy *Ned*, would you be willing to do me a favor? Head over to the **product page** and leave a review. It doesn't have to be long—just a few words to help other readers know what they're getting. (But no spoilers! We don't want to wreck the fun!)

I'd love to hear from you—not only about this story, but about any characters or stories you'd like to read in the future. Write to me at: susan@susanmaywarren.com. And if you'd like to see what's ahead, stop by www.susanmaywarren.com .

And don't forget to sign up to my newsletter at www. susanmaywarren.com.

Susie May

About Susan May Warren

With nearly 2 million books sold, critically acclaimed novelist Susan May Warren is the Christy, RITA, and Carol award-winning author of over ninety novels with Tyndale, Barbour, Steeple Hill, and Summerside Press. Known for her compelling plots and unforgettable characters, Susan has written contemporary and historical romances, romantic-suspense, thrillers, rom-com, and Christmas novellas.

With books translated into eight languages, many of her novels have been ECPA and CBA bestsellers, were chosen as Top Picks by *Romantic Times*, and have won the RWA's Inspirational Reader's Choice contest and the American Christian Fiction Writers Book of the Year award. She's a three-time RITA finalist and an eight-time Christy finalist.

Publishers Weekly has written of her books, "Warren lays bare her characters' human frailties, including fear, grief, and resentment, as openly as she details their virtues of love, devotion, and resiliency. She has crafted an engaging tale of romance, rivalry, and the power of forgiveness."

Library Journal adds, "Warren's characters are well-developed and she knows how to create a first rate contemporary romance..."

Susan is also a nationally acclaimed writing coach, teaching at conferences around the nation, and winner of the 2009 American Christian Fiction Writers Mentor of the Year award. She loves to help people launch their writing careers. She is the founder of www.MyBookTherapy.com and www.learnhow-towriteanovel.com, a writing website that helps authors get published and stay published. She is also the author of the popular writing method *The Story Equation*.

Find excerpts, reviews, and a printable list of her novels at www.susanmaywarren.com and connect with her on social media.

f facebook.com/susanmaywarrenfiction

O instagram.com/susanmaywarren

y twitter.com/susanmaywarren

BB bookbub.com/authors/susan-may-warren

g goodreads.com/susanmaywarren

a amazon.com/Susan-May-Warren

The Marshall Family Saga

THE MINNESOTA MARSHALLS

Fraser

Jonas

Ned

Iris

Creed

THE EPIC STORY OF RJ AND YORK

Out of the Night

I Will Find You

No Matter the Cost

THE MONTANA MARSHALLS

Knox

Tate

Ford

Wyatt

Ruby Jane

Also by Susan May Warren

SKY KING RANCH

Sunrise

Sunburst

Sundown

GLOBAL SEARCH AND RESCUE

The Way of the Brave

The Heart of a Hero

The Price of Valor

MONTANA FIRE

Where There's Smoke (Summer of Fire)

Playing with Fire (Summer of Fire)

Burnin' For You (Summer of Fire)

Oh, The Weather Outside is Frightful (Christmas novella)

I'll be There (Montana Fire/Deep Haven crossover)

Light My Fire (Summer of the Burning Sky)

The Heat is On (Summer of the Burning Sky)

Some Like it Hot (Summer of the Burning Sky)

You Don't Have to Be a Star (Montana Fire spin-off)

MONTANA RESCUE

If Ever I Would Leave You (novella prequel)

Wild Montana Skies

Rescue Me

A Matter of Trust

Crossfire (novella)

Troubled Waters

Storm Front

Wait for Me

MISSIONS OF MERCY SERIES

Point of No Return

Mission: Out of Control

Undercover Pursuit

TEAM HOPE: (Search and Rescue series)

Waiting for Dawn (novella prequel)

Flee the Night

Escape to Morning

Expect the Sunrise

NOBLE LEGACY (Montana Ranch Trilogy)

Reclaiming Nick

Taming Rafe

Finding Stefanie

THE CHRISTIANSEN FAMILY

I Really Do Miss your Smile (novella prequel)

Take a Chance on Me

It Had to Be You

When I Fall in Love

Evergreen (Christmas novella)

Always on My Mind

The Wonder of Your

You're the One that I Want

THE DEEP HAVEN COLLECTION

Happily Ever After

Tying the Knot

The Perfect Match

My Foolish Heart

The Shadow of your Smile

You Don't Know Me

**A complete list of Susan's novels can be found at susanmaywarren.
com/novels/bibliography/.**

Made in United States
Troutdale, OR
06/19/2024

20683371R00163